I0824627

A Siege of Owls

ALSO BY UCHENNA AWOKE

The Liquid Eye of a Moon

A Siege of Owls

A Novel

Uchenna Awoke

CATAPULT
NEW YORK

A SIEGE OF OWLS

This is a work of fiction. All the characters, organizations, and events portrayed in this novel are either products of the author's imagination or used fictitiously.

First Catapult edition: 2026

ISBN: 978-1-64622-333-6

Library of Congress Control Number: 2026931353

Jacket design by Emily Mahon
Jacket image: Private Collection © Osinachi;
All Rights Reserved 2025 / Bridgeman Images
Book design by tracy danes

Catapult
New York, NY
books.catapult.co

Printed in the United States of America

1 3 5 7 9 10 8 6 4 2

Book One

The Great Horned Owl

HIS SKIN PRICKLED.

At first Ekwe did not see the owl, which had alighted from a fig tree as he made his last turn, a raptor with dappled brown feathers and fuzzy ear tufts melding with the colours of drought. Papa Ekwe had described the bird: *Silently cruising around the woodlands, the owl hunts for a delicious meal amidst the darkest of weathers as the raptor listens for the footsteps of its prey.* As Papa Ekwe's whispering voice morphed into uncanny winds, Ekwe turned and saw the bird watching him with large, spooky eyes. He raised his legs to catch up with his family. The path was narrow, and they walked in a single file, Mama Ekwe in the front followed by Azuka, Ekwe's cousin, and his sister, Oyibo. Ekwe led the rear, in a sullen mood after he was dragged out of his early-morning sleep and hustled off to the farm.

They cleared the area where the houses ended, a few clumps of bushes at its margins, and then the village splayed its arms over a wide area of open country. The land unfolded like Ekwe's raffia mat, revealing itself in a seamless and organic way, reminding him of the times he peed in his sleep and woke up the next morning wet and stinking. His mother would swear at him for still wetting himself at the age of eight. She would take the mat outside and unroll it in the sun to dry it of the soggy black patch of his urine. His sister and his cousin would ridicule him, "O nyu mammiri n' elu akwa." But he had finally stopped pissing himself since passing it like an inheritance to his twin younger brothers.

Ekwe thought of his village Enu-Ozara as his mother's oil lamp globe. The wick of Mama Ekwe's old oil lamp was erratic and often spewed black smoke. Mama Ekwe would ask him to clean the globe every time it got stained for better illumination. One day, after he had grudgingly wiped it with a dry cloth, he lost his grip on the globe and it fell and broke. He thought of the fragments of glass as Enu-Ozara splintered into old tin houses around village squares. A dusty road tracked through the village to the local market—Eke Enu-Ozara. Once, during the week of the forefathers, women gathered in unwalled tin sheds with wooden pillars to sell groceries and other little things; hair braiders rendered their services; palm wine tapers sold their drinks in gourds; and local artisans displayed their baskets, brooms, flutes, and all. A chemist and a barbershop fronted a motor park, and a few workshops lined the dusty road: one motorcycle mechanic, one carpenter, one welder, and one vulcanizer.

At the next bifurcation, Mama Ekwe and Azuka continued across the broad sweep of country to their farmland, and Ekwe and Oyibo turned towards a grove at the foot of a hill. The grove enclosed a natural rock formation—Ogele—from which water spurted, formed a pool at the base, and followed a sinuous trail through the valley. But the spring merely dribbled now in the height of a long, hard drought. The pool drained out in wet spongy land in some areas, looking dark and opaque, and the morning sunlight floated on rainbow swamps.

"Hoo-h'HOO-hoo-hoo."

The low eerie sound startled Ekwe and led his eyes to the great horned owl he had seen earlier. The bird was watching them now with grim and forbidding eyes from the tangle of bush behind the rocky outcrops as they approached. Something tingled Ekwe's spine. He did not know if the raptor had followed their movements. As the bird fluttered away silently, he rested his eyes on her perch flourishing with ekwukwonju. He stared at the bright green leaves as if hypnotized. Papa Ekwe had warned them, his children, against touching this mystical leaf. "You will be consumed by wanderlust if you touch ekwukwonju. You will lose your sense of direction, and you will be lucky to find your way back home."

Ekwe would stare at the leaf with wonder every time his eyes met it after Papa Ekwe's warning. And now it needled him again, a strong feeling of doubt, provoking a curiosity to touch the leaf. He withdrew to allow his sister to go ahead of him into the water as Oyibo squelched across the swamp, where sunlight illuminated the area in a dramatic glow, dipped her metal bucket into a pool, lifted the bucketful of water to her head, and waded out.

"What are you staring at?" She turned to frown at Ekwe. "Fetch water, and let's go. Mother and Azuka are waiting to water the plants."

He dallied.

She hissed and walked away, realizing they were meant to go several rounds and would not stop until Mama Ekwe and Azuka had finished watering the tomato and habanero farm.

Ekwe stared at her sister as she walked away swinging her small hips. Yesterday, another suitor came to ask Papa Ekwe for his sister's hand in marriage. More than four suitors had shown up in their house in just the space of a few weeks. Ekwe was happy that she had rejected all her suitors. He did not want to lose his sister to any man.

When Oyibo was out of sight, he took a few steps towards the thicket, his eyes fixed on ekwukwonju. He could hear Oyibo's feet rustling through fallen dry leaves, growing faint in the heavily canopied grove. He stopped to listen to his heart beating loudly. At close range, ekwekwonju looked like any other leaf in the grove, with a cylindrical shape and a thin blade. Papa Ekwe's voice drummed a loud warning into his ears again, but Ekwe's sense of adventure fed off curiosity, his being all alone.

He tensed and held his breath as he stretched a hand to touch the leaf.

ııııı

At the end of the day's work, Ekwe climbed to the top of the hill range that enfolded Enu-Ozara into its womb like a fetus. He did this sometimes, dodging his family as they filed home with tired steps and sneaking to the top of the hill to watch the sunset. And now he stood at the pinnacle and watched the world below him: the curving-and-sloping, rising-and-falling pattern of the land—valley after valley, ridge beyond ridge. He gazed with wonder at wavering cornfields midwived by grasslands where they met the sky, at the peak of the mountain far off to the west above the cloud lines, and at mangroves that loomed over towns like gods and goddesses.

Enu-Ozara was tucked away in Adada River basin, in the belly of larger communities sitting on a green table, beneath a mountainous region. In the distance the towns of Nrobo, Abbi, Ugbene-Ajima, and Nimbo were embosomed in a mountain chain—Mother Nature with her big warm arms wrapped around her offspring. He glimpsed the river. It snaked along in a delicate arc around mangrove valleys as Earth Mother breastfed her children. The emerald-green tableland, the most breathtaking of the views, stretched forever towards the northeast like a poisoned apple.

Farming was the main occupation in Enu-Ozara. The population had thinned, though, after families started moving to Ozara-Agu, a new settlement prospering on the southern borders. The families had resettled near Adada River for ease of labour, because even with source in Enu-Ozara, Ogele, a tributary of Adada River, dried up in the peak of dry season and made manual irrigation difficult. Ekwe's family had not joined the exodus to Ozara-Agu. Papa Ekwe had worked here almost all his life like a good number of other men, although, season after season, he was rewarded with a harvest too scant for his large, polygamous family.

Daylight had unclothed Papa Ekwe's lie once again, just as it did his deceit. Mama Ekwe sometimes made soup with a chicken from her flock, and gave the gizzard to Papa Ekwe to eat, and when Ekwe asked why, Papa Ekwe told him that gizzards were meant to be eaten by the head of the family, and if eaten by someone other than the head of the family, the person would grow a gigantic Adam's apple. One day, Ekwe cornered one of the feral chickens that sometimes roosted in Papa Ekwe's barn, abandoned there because they no longer came home to their owners with the rest of the flock. He roasted the bird in the seclusion of the barn and ate the gizzard, but he did not grow a gigantic Adam's apple. Papa Ekwe apparently wanted to enjoy the delicious crunchy taste of a gizzard all to himself. Ekwe remembered his warning about the powers of ekwukwonju. "You will be lost if you touch ekwukwonju. You will be blown away by wild wandering winds." Ekwe did not only touch the leaf, he plucked and smelt it, inhaling the distinctive, lightly menthol scent, but nothing happened. It was all lies.

A thin orange wash had formed in the distant evening sky. It spread and became fused with grey. Sunset was always a magical moment for Ekwe as it transitioned from colour to colour, from blue to orange, and the horizon slowly swallowed a big red sun like a python consuming its prey. Ekwe started to climb down, a chicken summoned to its roost by twilight. A chilled breeze stung him as the day closed its mouth over him, like a lizard putting away an insect. The old moon had long since completed its luminous cycle in the sky and a new moon was very much in anticipation in Enu-Ozara.

Mama Ekwe made dinner. The family ate ayaraya and went to bed tired. Mama Ekwe and the twins slept on the only bed in the room, but it was not a proper bed. Mama Ekwe had packed some bricks in the shape of a bed and stitched a mattress filled with rags. Ekwe lay on a mat on the floor sandwiched by Oyibo and Azuka. His eyes were wide open, but he was far gone, filled with thoughts of faraway places.

The sensation was like his consciousness was departing his body. He felt disconnected, as if the orchestra led by Mama Ekwe had put him in a trance—the altos and sopranos of snoring amplified by the silence of the old framed family photographs adorning the mud walls—a mischief of mice scuttling around and nosing into every corner with the faintest smell of food—and the endless vocals of beetles punctuated by "hoo-h'HOO-hoo-hoo" coming from the eyrie of owls on the tall iroko tree at the village square.

In Transit

NKWA WAS PLAYING HIS UKULELE IN HIS WORN blouse when Ekwe got to the motor park around noon in his threadbare jumper. People threw coins to the talented, blind ukulelist as Ekwe climbed into a crumbling yellow bus, sat by a window, and listened to the tuneful rhythms. The bus took a long time filling up, so beguiled by the serenade, Ekwe dozed off. Nkwa always came to the park to entertain the passengers with his sentimental tunes.

Mama Ekwe had told Ekwe that Nkwa was not born blind. "He lost his sight at the age of sixteen," Mama Ekwe had said. "His mother did everything humanly possible to save her child's eyes. She squeezed all kinds of leaves into them, hoping their herbal juices would heal him. And when this did not work, she took him to Paulinus, the village chemist, who also squeezed different kinds of eye drops into his eyes and gave him big tablets to swallow. But Nkwa's eyes continued to die slowly. Some people blame his mother for not taking him to the eye clinic in the city of Enugu where a white man plucks out people's eyes with his magic, washes off the dirt caked around them, and fixes them back into their hollows. But how could the poor old widow afford that if she couldn't even afford the transport fare to Enugu?" Mama Ekwe had lamented.

Nkwa had learned to play the ukulele from his father early in life and his skills improved even after his eyes died like a flame thrown over with water and darkness pervaded.

The bus was full when Ekwe woke up. The angular driver and his scraggy conductor got the motley of passengers underway. No sooner had the journey begun than the conductor started yelling at the passengers for his fare. His words dispersed in the air like fireworks. Some passengers engaged him in a shouting match. The driver ignored them, one callused hand gripping the steering wheel, smoke curling menacingly from the cigarette between his free fingers, mingling with the dust that rose into the noon air.

Finally, the bus got to Obollo Afor after many stalls. It spilled its passengers coated in browns and reds from the trip. Ekwe climbed out and dusted his brown jumper. He looked around. Hawkers flocked to cars and trucks. A fully loaded gwongworo stood by the grocery-fronted busy road. Ekwe goggled at the bananas, cucumbers, and watermelons peeking at him through the wooden lattice of the lorry's body. He was hungry, but he had no more money. His last note had been spent on the bus fare. He walked round to the front of the gwongworo and paused to peer into the cabin at empty seats. The face of the lorry resembled a man with an ugly grin. A man with a square forehead, a huge nose, round wide-set eyes, and full lips. He could not read the inscription "Mercedes 911" on the lorry's face painted in faded orange.

Hunger needled Ekwe's stomach and put thoughts into his head. The place was lively with people walking and talking, but no one seemed interested in him. He circled back to the rear of the gwongworo and threw glances around. Reassured that no one was watching him, he quickly climbed up the tailboard and snuggled down into a warm hollow in between stacks of groceries. A sweet and fruity smell filled his nose as he fell upon the fruits and wolfed them down.

Suddenly the engine cracked to life and the woodwork shook with motion. Realizing the gwongworo was leaving with him, he tried to scramble out, mashing bananas and oranges and cucumbers. He had a look of wild panic in his eyes as the lorry picked up speed, making it impossible for him to jump out. He peeped through the wooden latticework at the ghosts of Amalla blurring away as the lorry sped northwards. Papa Ekwe had told him that in Amalla, human beings and ethereal entities interacted between both the spiritual and living worlds. "If you bent backwards and looked through your straddled legs you could see a ghost walking on air."

Seized again by his hunger for adventure, Ekwe's fear leaped out of him, morphed into trees, and raced in the opposite direction. He fell back on the fruits and swallowed more bananas until his stomach ached. And then he lay down on a bed of vegetables and fell to a deep sleep. He woke to faint voices in conversation, clambered closer to the rear window, so he could eavesdrop on the crew in the cabin—the driver and his guard. Male adult voices reached him through a broken pane, but he couldn't see their owners.

"A Tiv man will not only offer his guest shelter but will also offer him his pretty wife for sex as kola," a deep voice said as the lorry approached Makurdi metropolis.

His companion laughed as though little bits of him were catching fire, and the salty tang of sea air blew in a string across North Bank, leaving Makurdi warm as toast. The city smelt of fornication.

"Do you know that rat is their best meat?"

"Rat?"

"Yes. Rat is a popular delicacy with Tiv people."

His companion found it unbelievable. "Don't they know that they are eating Lassa fever in the name of meat?"

It was the turn of the other man to laugh in his deep voice.

Adult gossip about eating rats and having sex tickled Ekwe's imagination as the lorry travelled through vast stretches of country dotted with round-hut settlements. He gazed out at the receding savanna, ate and slept and woke again and peered into darkness and brightening clouds and Sahelian landscapes.

ııııı

The gwongworo finally stopped and the driver and his guard climbed out and slammed the doors. Ekwe heard the splash of water as they washed their faces, and he sensed that they had arrived at their destination. He crawled towards the gwongworo's tailboard and peered out into an early morning wearing a thin veil of mist. A few men were moving around in robes and a fusty smell clung to the air, the beginnings of a new day. The driver and his guard were talking. He waited, breathless, and strained his ears but could not hear what they were saying. They stood farther from the tailboard. They might not see him if he climbed out, but the men in robes might see him, and they might assume that he was part of the gwongworo's crew. He took a deep breath and started to climb noiselessly down the tailboard. He crossed himself when his legs finally touched the ground, then stood looking around an open-air grocery market. They had travelled all night, arriving in Maiduguri in daylight. For the first time he saw the lorry's crew, two men leaning against the front bumper, smoking, probably waiting for the owners of the shipment. They had their backs to him, making it easy for him to steal away and melt into treeless expanses.

Danjuma

IT WAS MORNING, THIN MIST HUNG OVER THE VALley, and Danjuma watched as a parliament of owls set upon a lamb with their powerful talons and sharp beaks. The lamb had no chance against the birds that descended in a flurry of grey and brown wings. They went for the eyes and pecked the poor animal blind. The lamb ran this and that way, sightlessly, trying to escape. Danjuma started to hurry towards the scene across the meadow, but before he got there the owls were already feasting on the lamb's protruding eyes. He picked up a stone and threw it at them. Freed but blinded, the lamb went bleating and foundering down the valley towards the swamps as Danjuma turned with a hiss and started to walk back.

Ekwe watched from a distance, unsettled by the grisly scene. Owls were a case study of witchcraft and taboo wildlife. He remembered the nights lying snug on his mat, with the silence absolute around him, until an owl would break the peace with her classic call.

"Away with you, evil bird." Mama Ekwe would throw curses from the window at the owl beyond the darkness. "Why do you hoot around my window? And why is it that when you hoot at night, a child almost always dies mysteriously in the neighbourhood?"

"Owls hoot at night because they are nocturnal birds," Papa Ekwe, smiling, would explain every time Mama Ekwe made a fuss about them.

Now Ekwe sat back in the grass and watched as cattle munched across the grazing field. He watched egrets riding the cattle. The man who threw stones at the carnivorous birds owned the herd, Ekwe could tell. Some four boys with braided hair were watching over the cattle. They sat together over a meal at a distance from where the man smoked under a tree. Ekwe swallowed his spittle each time someone lifted a morsel of food to his mouth. He was hungry and homeless. He was sure he was the hungriest and unhappiest human being in the world. Even the cattle had something to eat. He debated with himself, wondering if he should approach the man to ask for food and shelter. He did not know where he was, but he was sure that this unfamiliar Sahelian grassland that stretched endlessly around him was not anywhere near home. It was quite unlike Enu-Ozara, which was set in a landscape of rolling hills and mangroves. He must be far-far away from home.

He started to move with nervous steps towards the man's hunched back. His heart beat fast, and he thought of turning and retreating, but then the man heard his light footsteps and swung round to face him.

"My name is Ekwe. I can look after your cattle, too, if you employ me," he said, speaking very quickly in Igbo.

The man regarded him with raised eyebrows.

Ekwe thought, He does not understand me. In Enu-Ozara you either spoke Igbo or you chewed your tongue trying to speak English. But he could not speak English.

Ekwe touched his stomach and mouth to show that he was hungry. He then made gestures begging the man to employ him, to let him join the other boys looking after his cattle in exchange for food and a place to lay his head.

The man's countenance suddenly relaxed in a clement smile. His eyes were friendly. He gestured towards the boys to indicate that Ekwe could join them, his sons. His name was Danjuma, he told Ekwe, and he was a cowherd. But Ekwe understood nothing of what he had said.

Danguma drove cattle for rich Higi merchants and politicians. For his wage, one of every four newborn calves belonged to him. In this way, he nurtured a small livestock trade he was hoping would expand with time. He had a large family to care for, with three wives and eight children, not counting three grown-up boys who had left home to become Almajirai. The four younger sons were in the cowherding business with him, his wives traded in maize and millet at the kasuwar gari, and his girls hawked fura da nono around the market.

As Danjuma walked Ekwe over to introduce him to his sons, they noticed that something was not right. Danjuma's sons had abandoned their meal. In the distance, they were bent over a fallen cow. Ekwe and Danjuma hurried to the spot to find Bara, Danjuma's Black Angus and favourite cow, lying flat on her side.

"What happened to her?" Danjuma's voice was gruff as he bent over and stroked the salivating animal.

"She suddenly dropped to her knees," said one of the boys.

Danjuma took some antibiotic capsules from a grey belt bag. He called for a bowl and mixed the contents of the capsules in water. Then he forced the lame cow on her back and asked the boys to hold her while he forced the drink into her. Minutes later, Bara started kicking out in agony.

"La ilaha illallah," Danjuma hissed after the animal stilled. She was dead.

He walked and sat a ways off, lit a joint, and watched as the boys dragged Bara down the valley and buried her in the swamps. They returned to their food, which they now shared with the new boy, Ekwe. Danjuma was moved by his sons' benevolence of accepting the unfamiliar boy even without a proper introduction. He smoked and grieved and gazed absently down a stark swampy valley, nose quivering at the tip with pleasure, perhaps with pain. Smoking hemp was one of Danjuma's pleasures. And he cherished eating tuwo and miyan kuka after a good hemp smoke to broaden his appetite. Born the second child to seminomadic parents, he migrated with his family from Lake Chad when he was a child. He spent most of his boyhood pasturing across the Sahel savanna. He started to live a settled life only after he married Aisha, his second wife who was of Torodbe clan, and made his home in Kasar Aminci, where he had lived over the years. His parents had been dead a long time, shortly before he came to live in Kasar Aminci, and his brothers had continued with their seminomadic life, their paths never crossing again. Life had been peaceful for him and his family in Kasar Aminci until recently when Izghe, the very next community bordering Kasar Aminci to the east, was attacked and razed down. Since then, Danjuma had been left with a fluttering feeling in his stomach.

Foreboding

AT DUSK, AS DANJUMA MADE HIS WAY HOME IN THE company of his sons and cattle, the image came back again to haunt him in gruesome detail: the owls with their large, broad heads and downward-curving beaks, ripping and tearing at the lamb with their talons. A mild dusty wind searched the street, but far from bringing relief from the heat, it seemed to grow warmer. Danjuma unwound his turban to let in the breeze. The shawl he wore over a grey silk garment drew attention to his impressive height and austere look, arms twined around a herding stick as he led the rear, a proud father watching his sons drive the cattle home in a cloud of dust. He was happy that his sons were getting along with Ekwe already. He glanced at the foreigner as Ekwe walked hand in hand with his last son, Balarabe. They were about the same age, but Balarabe was a little taller and thinner. The new boy seemed lost, from a faraway place, and Danjuma had questions to ask, but Ekwe did not understand Hausa or Fula, the two languages Danjuma and his sons spoke.

Bats skimmed over trees and houses in the fading light. As they passed children practicing with toy bows and arrows, Danjuma rebuked them. "Run along home to help your mothers with chores." He shooed them away.

The group broke up and fled to their homes in all directions.

Danjuma waved at a few men sitting outside a shop front. "Assalamu alaikum," he said, surprised at his own dismal voice.

"Alaikum salam," they chorused a reply.

A few lanterns glowed from compounds with a dull phosphorescence as they crossed a cluster of round huts. The fumes of a dung fire reached Ekwe. He heard Danjuma hail another neighbour, Ahmed, who milked a cow over a dwarf brick fence by a fire. The same dung-fuelled fires burned brightly under steel dinner pots outside of huts in neighbouring compounds.

They arrived home to a lively household preparing dinner. Danjuma's sons had driven the cattle to a small valley at the back of the house. Within the lamplit compound, enclosed by a few huts made of water reed and straw, his daughters moved briskly, attending to their dinner chores.

"Sannu, Baba," they greeted him one by one.

Azhaar, the last born, and Aamaal, her half sister who was older by a year, both fetched a stool for Danjuma, and each insisted he sit on her own stool. He smiled at their rivalry and took both stools, set them down in front of his hut, sat on one, and stretched his legs over the other. And then he leaned back against the straw wall. That seemed to settle the dispute, but only for a moment; now they fought over who would take his herding stick into his hut.

"Take the herding stick inside," he said to Aamaal, "while Azhaar fetches a cup of water for me."

His decision seemed a balanced one for the girls, as they ran off to their respective tasks.

Ekwe watched on, amused by the rivalry.

"You look bothered, mairaina," Danjuma's soft-spoken first wife, Zainab, said in an affectionate voice.

Danjuma hissed. After spending the whole day in the fields under the burning sun, the rich brown skin of his skinny face had turned a lustrous burnt umber, the colour of debino. They were close, Danjuma and this woman who had borne him three sons and a daughter and who understood him more than his other wives.

"Don't worry about the dead cow. Kuma Allah zan mayar da kowane iri nasara." Her reassurance that Allah would replenish his loss soothed him just as her atampa wrappa sat well on her dark skin in mint green and lemon yellow.

News of Bara's death had come home ahead of their arrival from the field. Aside from the loss, Danjuma felt a sort of tightness in the pit of his stomach, as if he was going to have diarrhea. He reckoned this feeling had nothing to do with his loss. It had nothing to do with the heat that reflected from the heavy, moist clouds that hung over the village. It was premonition, he thought.

"You have been working too hard. You must take some time off. Allah has blessed you with sons who can do the work in your place," she said.

Danjuma appreciated her concern, but he was certain that work was not the reason for his jumpiness. The last time he had sensations like streaks of lightning in his stomach was when a son of Higi tribe was found dead in the bushes with a slit throat, slaughtered like a cow. The cruelty of it still made Danjuma retch. He took a long, deep breath as he reached for his small old radio and tuned it. The musical flow of Hausa followed a brief rendition of "Sangaya." And then a female voice recapped the bombing of a mosque in the neighbouring town of Mubi and the killing of worshipers. The news had been on air for days; now the broadcaster reported that the killers had declared Mubi a caliphate.

Danjuma sensed the reason for his mood. He had purchased the radio about four years ago to listen to news and music for his relaxation, but the small transistor radio now emitted nothing but war and brutality and filled Danjuma's mind with scenes of violence and bloodletting. He loathed violence. His anxiety stemmed from the possibility that one day, the peace enjoyed in Kasar Aminci would be gone, plucked away like a ripe fruit stolen from its orchard.

He snorted.

Insurgents

WHEN EKWE FOUND HIMSELF ALONE BEFORE HE WAS served dinner by Danjuma's wife, the image snuck back in his mind: the owls gorging themselves on the poor lamb's eyeballs. He shut his own eyes, pictured those birds with their great horns and facial disks, and wondered if, as Papa Ekwe had insisted, owls were merely objects of myth and superstition with their hypnotic, yellow-eyed stare and deep hooting voices. He thought about Danjuma's family, how friendly everyone seemed, and how, like a parliament of owls, they moved about with a sense of purpose.

Danjuma's youngest wife, Rekiya, interrupted his train of thought as she emerged with a supper of tuwo shinkafa with miyan kuka for him. It was Rekiya's turn to cook for the family. They all ate together outdoors. Danjuma usually ate with Azhaar and Aamaal. He wasn't hungry tonight, but he ate a few morsels to please his two favourite girls sitting on a mat from across to him.

"Baba." Azhaar's large eyes were fixed on him. "You are eating as if you don't like the food."

"But I like the food," he said, and peered into the night, sure he saw a movement, just a moment of occluding shadow.

He peered again into nothingness. It was probably only his imagination.

"I know it's because you prefer to eat tuwo shinkafa with miyan tause, but my stepmother will like it with miyan kuka," Aamaal said.

"It's not that." Sometimes he could not help but wonder at their level of reasoning at the ages of five and six. "As a matter of fact, I have started to like miyan kuka. But I am not very hungry tonight."

"I am sorry about Bara, Baba," Azhaar said. "But you must eat so that you will have the strength to forget what happened. The strength for tomorrow's work."

He ate for her sake, this girl of his who inherited his golden-brown skin, her mother's long-lashed eyes, and the wisdom of an old woman.

They cleared the dishes after the meal and returned with a bowl of nono each from their mothers for him, set them down, and watched him as he drank from both bowls in turns.

"Do you like the nono?" Azhaar asked.

"Yes, I like it."

"Is it sweet?" Aamaal asked.

"It is very sweet. Take some to our guest," he said, glancing in Ekwe's direction.

Aamaal moved with quick steps to beat Azhaar to their father's errand. Ekwe took the gift in both hands and took a sip. Face buried in the calabash vessel of nono as he took more delicious sips, Ekwe did not notice a furtive movement in the surrounding darkness.

"My mother says she will teach me how to milk a cow." Azhaar's eyes shone with anticipation.

Just then, Zainab's fruity laughter floated across the compound. Danjuma's wives were enjoying a post-dinner chat as usual. Their laughter opened like flower buds in his heart. They had managed to live in peace, but they too were unaware of the covert movements in the abyss of the night.

"My mother will teach me too." Aamaal mimicked Azhaar as she resettled on the mat.

"That is very good." Danjuma's voice was toneless.

Suddenly a shape emerged from the void of darkness. Danjuma glimpsed the intruder before the lantern flew into the air. In that moment, before the light of the lantern flickered and went dead, plunging the compound into darkness, Danjuma caught sight of a colossus of a gun with a belt of bullets slung sash-style over a great shoulder as the full beam of a powerful torchlight fell on his face and blinded him.

"Who are you? What do you want from us?" Danjuma barked into the light.

"Jama'atu Ahlis-Sunna Lidda'awati Wal-Jihad," a rough voice said gruffly.

The mantra set Danjuma's limbs in motion. He swept Azhaar and Aamaal into his arms and shielded them from danger with his body as the torchlight lunged forwards and threw him out of focus for a split second, just long enough for him to make a dash for safety, seconds before the shots came with the staccato rhythm of a quick bracing rain, and screams filled the air.

"Mutum banza!" Danjuma felt his right arm sag with a dead weight as sticky liquid streaked down. He let go of his daughters and threw himself at the attacker like Shango's wrath. In charging forwards blindly, he provided a lifeline for his family from the raptors. But then his body exploded in pain as he pitched forwards and crashed down, and dark skies suddenly turned orange, and supper notes were drowned in a terrible din.

▲▲▲▲▲

A new day unfolded with carnage. A rust smell clutched the air, forcing Ekwe to throw up the supper he had eaten before the raptors swooped down on their prey. He counted dead lambs as he moved from place to place trailed by a skinny black dog. The mongrel sniffed at the dead and loured at officers of the State Environmental Health Monitoring Unit. Ekwe saw large, bald vultures loitering, surveying the landscape, waiting for a chance to descend upon the carnage from their low perches. Sirens screamed, trucks vomited soldiers, and cops scowled at newsmen amidst a dark looming of owls, circling, staying aloft in high altitudes, peeling off from one thermal and gliding on to the next.

Ghosts

DANJUMA SAT OUTSIDE HIS HUT, THE SAME CUStomary position where he had had dinner with little Azhaar and Aamaal on the night of the attack. He wore a bandage around his left shoulder, where the slugs had left badly torn tissue. The raptors had left him for dead. Azhaar sat on her little mat across from him, her large sympathetic eyes fixed on his injured shoulder.

"Yi hakuri, Baba," she said, soothingly.

He took her hand in his and pressed it softly. "Where have you been?"

"I went to play at filinwasa. But I am here now. Are you hungry?"

"No," he said.

"But you must eat so that your injury will heal faster," she said. "Mother made nono. I will get you some to drink."

She rose and ran towards her mother's hut. His affectionate gaze followed her until she fizzled out into nothingness.

"Haba maigida." Aisha's voice gave Danjuma a start. "You are talking to yourself again."

She had been standing next to him with hands on her hips, unnoticed. Now her voice nudged him back to reality, causing his sight to travel to the garden beyond the courtyard, where it rested on the rectangular mounds—one large and the other small—both fresh. Danjuma had preferred to bury his wife and daughter in the garden facing his hut, so that their graves would be the first things he saw when he woke up every morning and came to the door.

"It's time to let go." Aisha settled next to him on the bench. "Sitting here talking to yourself and staring at their graves will not bring back Zainab and Azhaar from the land of the dead."

He let out a deep groan.

"I have never seen anything like that in my life." Aisha relived the trauma of that night again. "They are cowards swooping down on a helpless man and his family."

Danjuma knew little or nothing about guns. He used bows and arrows when performing his neighbourhood watch duties, but the guns the soldiers carried around in the wake of the attack on Kasar Aminci were mere toys compared to the machines the men who ambushed his family had been shouldering.

"I wasn't able to save my wife and daughter." His lamentation was piercing, a deep sense of loss that left him without a grain of energy.

The loss of two people Danjuma cherished in his life came close to upsetting his complete mental balance. He sat in that customary position outside his hut all day and listened to the voice of his little girl Azhaar, and responded to her many questions.

"You fought like a lion." Aisha consoled him, sitting close to him. "You stopped them from finishing off all of us, the entire family. This should be some consolation."

He hissed. Perhaps she was right. Though he lost a wife and daughter, he had not lost everything. His other wives and children and his guest, Ekwe, all survived the ambush because of his bravery. His closest neighbour, Ahmed, died with his entire family. Danjuma shut his eyes and saw Ahmed again milking a cow behind his dwarf fence on the evening of the attack.

"I have a bad feeling about the future," he said. He knew that the ghosts of his wife and daughter would haunt him for as long as he lived in Kasar Aminci.

"The soldiers are already here to protect us," Aisha said.

"I doubt if the soldiers can do much to help." He shook his head. "If you ask a man to catch a shrew, you should also provide him with water and soap to wash off the bad smell from his hands."

She understood his proverb. "Where shall we run to?" she said.

He considered her question, its slight note of sarcasm. They could travel inland, towards the belt of rolling highlands along the Cameroon borders, or towards the coastal plains of the southeast.

"Maybe south," he said.

"Don't you think we should resettle in Zaria or Suleja?"

"The violence is spreading its tentacles throughout the northern region. That's why we are going south."

"But the violence is not restricted to the North alone," she argued. "You have a radio that daily sings songs of the conflicts between farmers and herders in the South."

Danjuma gave a low grunt. He had a foreboding about more attacks on Kasar Aminci and did not wish to put the lives of his children and wives on the line. Though a curfew was imposed and a state of emergency rule declared, the fear of the raptors swooping down again from their thermal sat tight at the doorstep of every heart. Tension was spreading throughout the district with mosques, churches, villages, army bases, and police stations going up in flames. It was all mayhem and massacre when you listened to the radio or turned the pages of the newspaper.

ııııı

Danjuma was ready to leave Kasar Aminci with his family a few months after the attack. His injuries had healed, but not the wound in his heart, nor the fear of the raptors returning. He summoned Ekwe one morning, happy the boy now understood and spoke more than a smattering of Hausa and even Fula, amazed how quickly children picked up a foreign tongue.

"I am sorry you got involved in all this," he said. "We are going away. I have a premonition of more attacks coming. My family is not safe; my business is not safe, so we are moving southwards. You are from that culture. I am sure you will be of great help to our itinerary if you will come with us."

"I am sorry again for the loss of your wife and daughter," Ekwe said. "I am excited to go with you, and happy to help. Thank you for giving me food and shelter."

Fulani Extremists

THEY LEFT AT SUNRISE, FOLLOWING THE NORTH-south pathway of migratory birds. Ekwe enjoyed bird migrations. In Enu-Ozara he would gaze up at the winged creatures as they flew in echelon with one another. Sometimes they appeared to write the letter V across the sky. Now he wondered about owls and what kind of flight formations they adopted. Papa Ekwe had said that owls were nocturnal birds, that unlike the many birds in that kingdom known for their long migratory journeys, most species of owls dwelt in the same region all year round. "They only move a few hundred miles, but some stay in their breeding territories throughout the year, adapting to the seasons by changing their hunting ways."

With owls on his thoughts, Ekwe set forth on a long pastoral sojourn that stretched for months with Danjuma and his surviving family. They trekked and rested, ate and slept, and continued trekking. They made large fires to drive away dangerous animals—buffaloes, hyenas, and large prowling cats—while they slept or rested. Sometimes they grazed their cattle in lush, tempting pastures for a few days or stopped over on the periphery of large towns to experience urban life. And then they moved on again, pushing steadily southwards, away from the Sahel. The youngest of the family, Aamaal, rode most of the way on the back of the only donkey in the pack.

The sandy wastes of the Sahara and the great rolling plains gradually gave way to chains of hills and mountains rising over river valleys. The journey bore its troubles. They had lost a few cattle to diseases, snakebites, and lightning strikes. There were newborns, though. Ekwe had the novel pleasure of watching a pregnant cow drop a calf. He watched as the calf flopped down on the grass like a dollop of grey dung. While the mother gave the baby a thorough lick, a few other cows came around and nosed at it, then turned away as if the smell of birth was nauseating. Ekwe watched the baby as it flailed its spindly legs in a weary but determined effort to rise to its feet, but it kept falling again with each attempt, and then a second calf began to emerge from the mother's vulva, head and forelegs first, as she pushed. Motivated by the birth of a twin, the first baby staggered to its hind legs and took its first tottering steps towards its sibling.

By now they were completely cut off from the rest of the world, and the signals in Danjuma's shortwave radio had become epileptic. The waves flew in and out again like swallows in and out of a nest, but they managed to catch the news of another attack, a second and more brutal raid on Kasar Aminci.

"Our departure was timely," Aisha said.

Rekiya flung her a look. "I am surprised to hear you talk like that after you tried to talk our husband into not leaving."

"Is finding fault not your area of expertise?" Aisha returned the look with the same intensity.

"What I don't understand is why they picked on Kasar Aminci," Danjuma cut in quickly to avert the hostility fermenting between the women. "Allahu Akbar."

Days turned into weeks, and weeks rolled into months as they moved deeper into the wooded savannas and floodplains of the north-central region. Danjuma was thankful for the fortunate timing of their flight. It was better to brave the elements and the predators than to sit with arms folded and allow one's family to be wiped out. He had done well to hide his worries. He wasn't sure going south was a wonderful idea with news of farmers fighting cowherds, but it was a chance they had to take.

They arrived at a steppe. The landscape had dropped to a belt of level parklike country, and Danjuma whistled with amazement, figuring they were somewhere on the Mambilla Plateau in the Middle Belt region. As a boy, he used to traverse the Bamenda Highlands with his seminomadic family, the stunning scenery and tea plantations, extending towards Cameroon—but now his sense of location was lost to the passage of time.

"Behold the Eden we have been searching for." He sighed.

"Nature is benevolent," Rekiya cried.

"Come on, boys." Danjuma beckoned Ekwe and his sons over. "Get your tools. Let's get the place fixed."

The boys retrieved their construction tools from sacks loaded onto the backs of the cattle and went to work as Danjuma took a walk around the steppe with his radio and a joint. The radio had become a bearer of the ugly news of violence and massacres going on in the country. An announcer reported now, *Killers have infiltrated Gwoza Mountains and*

Sambisa Forest from where they ambush the communities. Numerous deaths have also been attributed to Fulani extremists, while further violent outcomes have characterized conflicts among herdsmen, farmers, and other ethnic groups especially in the south of the country.

Danjuma was startled by the news. Did others see him as a Fulani extremist? A killer? He pondered this even as he walked back to his family hours later. This place offered prospects of peace and lush pastures, too good a gift to be real, but how safe was it for his family to dwell among communities who saw them as enemies? They could settle in the steppe and keep watch, though, in the meantime. The boys had finished the clearing and raised grass shelters. And now his wives and daughters were busy securing their spaces and putting feminine touches to them.

"You have all done a good job," he said as he walked in and contemplated his new home with a nervous smile.

▲▲▲▲▲

"I am nervous," Danjuma's first daughter, Rukaitu, said in a conversation a few days after their arrival. "Not a soul has been glimpsed around here since we came."

"Beat it if you don't like it here," her younger sister Maimuna snapped at her. "After all, your grandfather was a full-blown nomad."

"I wasn't talking to you." Rukaitu pursed her lips with defiance.

They argued hotly.

Ekwe was watching the two sisters, but he was thinking

about his own sister, Oyibo, and how they argued all the time. He wondered about her suitors. Had she agreed to marry any of her suitors?

"Haba. Must you two turn every little conversation into a heated argument?" Aisha said.

Danjuma stared into the middle distance. "I hate to admit it, but I am a bit uncomfortable about this place too. It seems too good to be real."

"You see?" Rukaitu gave Maimuna a withering, self-vindicated look.

She replied with a raspberry.

"The land bears evidence of neglect in areas of crusted farm ridges." Danjuma recalled what he had observed while he was taking a walk. "It looks like a hastily abandoned farmland."

"Abandoned by whom?" Aisha wondered.

"I don't know." Danjuma shrugged. "It's just a hunch."

Danjuma went to explore further and made an interesting find. The steppe was only about ten miles to a cattle market in the heart of Jalingo town. Some of Danjuma's cattle were getting quite old, no longer active in reproductive performance, and he needed to sell them since they had become liabilities. Elijah, one of the cattle traders, a large middle-aged man who wore a pair of footwear hacked out of a rough hide, was eager to buy the cattle.

"We used to take delivery of lorry loads of cattle," explained Elijah in Hausa. His rugged footwear seemed custom made for his extra-large feet with its crooked, protruding toes. "We have been running a serious shortage lately due to the violence up north."

Danjuma and Elijah talked briefly about it while scant

trading went on in the market square. A few cattle loitered about, staring listlessly at humans.

Danjuma told Elijah about the nocturnal attack that triggered their itinerary. "They came for us at supper." He recalled the ambush with a tight jaw. "My wife and daughter had barely eaten their last meals."

"I am sorry." Elijah looked thoughtful. "The government seems helpless. I have wondered what exactly the insurgents' agenda is."

A brown cow raised her head and gave them a languid look.

"I have wondered about it myself," Danjuma said. "The men who shot my wife and daughter said something about the purification of Islam." Danjuma was about to offer more explanation, but Elijah cut in angrily.

"Is that how it is? Does the Koran condone violence and killing? Is the purification of Islam the shedding of so much blood?"

"The Koran tells us, Muslims, *Fight those who believe not in Allah*," Danjuma quoted. "But the widespread violence and killings, I am sure they are not acts of purifying Islam."

"I am Christian. We have similar passages in the scripture about nonbelievers. We are told in Psalm 137, *Blessed is he who seizes your infants and dashes them against the rocks*, and such terrible verses which are recited on a daily basis, yet we have found some peace among ourselves."

Danjuma snorted, thinking about news of clergymen accused of forced sodomy and rape daily violating his radio. On his way back to the steppe, he passed through a yam market, where traders sat behind neat stacks of yams and haggled with customers, and bought a few tubers he took back.

Tribal War

EKWE WAS HAVING A LUNCH OF DOYA DA MIYA WITH Danjuma and his family one afternoon when a bunch of vicious-looking youths materialized with clubs and machetes and descended on their cattle. They fought the attackers off with bows and arrows, but not before six of the cattle had fallen to the enemies' machetes.

"They must be rustlers?" Rekiya gasped with a flushed face.

"They didn't look like rustlers," Aisha said. "I have had a terrible premonition about this place."

"What if they come back?" Rekiya said. "What if they surprise us when we are asleep in the dead of night and kill us all?"

A pulsating silence followed.

Ekwe was rattled by the attack, the suddenness of it, and how quickly and efficiently Danjuma and his sons responded to it with bows and arrows.

Danjuma rose to his feet. "I will be back," he said as if pinched by Rekiya's words. "I am going back to see Elijah about this."

▲▲▲▲▲

"The land has been in dispute between the Tiv and Jukun tribesmen," Elijah said.

"Dispute?" Danjuma stared at him.

"Yes. It's a tribal war that has claimed many lives. It's not safe out there. I'm sorry I didn't mention it until now, but I suggest you leave before the attackers regroup. You don't want to be caught in their cross fire."

Danjuma crossed his arms in despair. "Is there anywhere in the world where it is safe?"

Elijah shrugged. "North is a battlefield, south a combat zone."

"We are headed south." Danjuma shrugged.

"A lot has transpired between cowherds and crop farmers in the South," Elijah said. "They no longer see your people merely as cowherds. They see you as dangerous, armed militia and instruments of ethnic domination."

Danjuma looked thoughtful and bowed his head.

Elijah patted him on the back. "Follow your instincts, my friend."

Danjuma did not return to his family straightaway. He needed time alone to think, to figure out what to do, so he lit hemp and took a stroll around the steppe. Only as the sun was setting with silhouettes of palm trees leaning against the horizon, where the land rose gently towards a rugged skyline, did he start to walk back, and once back among his family, he told them what Elijah had said.

"What are we going to do now?" There was a slight tremble in Aisha's voice.

From a nearby yellowwood came a rhetorical reply: a short, deep, repeated "hoo" followed by a long "hoooooooo" that travelled for miles across the quiet steppe. Ekwe glimpsed an owl as it fluttered away in a slow, silent cruise flight. According to Papa Ekwe, owls have wings that alter air turbulence; their soft, velvety feathers mop up high-frequency sounds and make them silent predators of the night.

"Baba. Why don't we return to home in Kasar Aminci?" Balarabe said.

Danjuma gave the boy an indulgent stroke. "We left because there is too much fighting there."

"But there is fighting here too."

"That's why we are leaving here and going to some other place where we will find peace."

The boy frowned.

"Don't worry." He stroked the boy again. "From now on you and Ekwe will share the donkey with Aamaal. You won't have to trek all the way."

He shook his head. "I don't want to share the donkey with Aamaal. I don't even want to ride a donkey. I am a boy, and Aamaal is a girl, and I am four years older."

Danjuma smiled at the boy's nomadic instincts. He had started to ask for a herd to take charge of like his older brothers. Danjuma laughed as the boy bounced off like a cricket ball, determined to own his own small herd soon.

A Siege of Owls

EKWE FOUND HIMSELF IN A SIEGE OF OWLS, FEROcious birds that flew at him with terrifying talons. He fought them off with wild kicks and punches, but as he fled from the raptors, he came face-to-face with a man clothed in bullets and a machine gun that spewed fire. Sandwiched between the birds of prey and a drumroll of bullets, Ekwe started from a light trance.

This woolgathering, which Ekwe shared with Danjuma and his family, was the push Danjuma needed. The message was clear, communicated through a dream. Their attackers had come in broad daylight that first time but might attack again when it was dark and catch them defenceless. Danjuma did not wait for that to happen; he collected his family and hit the road again with the cattle straggling into the distance, driven by his stick-wielding sons, and behind them his chattering wives and daughters, and Ekwe, who glanced back one last time and caught sight of a large grey bird sitting on the branch of the yellowwood, shooing them away with eyes like fireballs.

▲▲▲▲▲

They arrived at the savanna belt north of Adada River after weeks of exploring the rainforests, a landscape marked by hills and vast areas of open grassland dotted with oil palm trees. They set up a dwelling with bamboo and grass in a mangrove valley. Over the course of their long journey, Allah had blessed them with twenty-four newborn calves, but they had lost several others. The days following their arrival were peaceful, and they set about familiarizing themselves with their new surroundings. The mangrove forests canopied hamlets that looked frighteningly familiar to Ekwe. The geometric pattern of farmlands and pastures filled him with a sense of déjà vu as he wandered over hill and dale with Balarabe.

But Danjuma was worried. This new place looked like the perfect Garden of Eden, with open grasslands stretching forever, but there were no grazing routes that he could see. It had the look of a potential source of conflict, because to get to meadow pasture, his children had to walk the cattle through farmlands. It worried him slightly, but he waved it away. He insisted that Ekwe accompany him everywhere he went for easy interaction with the locals. Ekwe was more beneficial to him as an interpreter than a cowherd. They were together the morning the call of the minaret led Danjuma to a mosque squatting in the most unlikely nook of the community. They walked into the cold, almost empty mosque with only the muezzin and the imam seated for prayer.

"I see you are new in this neighbourhood," Ali Mustapha, the thickset imam, said to Danjuma after the prayer. He spoke fluent Hausa.

"I only just arrived with my family." Danjuma pointed towards the heights in the distant north.

"That must be Nrobo," the imam said. "Hostility between cowherds and the locals started in the South and is slowly spreading across the region. But Nrobo and its environs are relatively safe. In any case, I know of an influential king in one of those upland communities. I can speak to him about a lease on your behalf."

As he pondered the imam's offer, Danjuma realized that a lease would give his occupation legality in the absence of grazing reserves. The king's approval would save him from a bunch of rascals turning up suddenly to embarrass his family.

"He must be your son," Ali Mustapha patted Ekwe's back.

"He is my little friend," Danjuma said.

▲▲▲▲▲

Days later, Danjuma and Ekwe were ushered into the presence of His Royal Highness Igwe Okosisi Idoko, king of Enu-Ozara, by Ali Mustapha, in the thatched assembly hall of his palace on a warm Tuesday morning that smelt of nutmeg. The king listened as the dark, pudgy man in white garb and turban introduced himself.

"I am the imam of a small Muslim community in the neighbourhood." He made the introduction speaking the local language with a seamless fluency that surprised the king. "I am from Ugbene-Ajima," he added to explain his dual identities as Igbo and Muslim—a rarity in a community dominated by the white man's religion. Even the religion of the ancestors had been displaced. "My grandfather was one of the earliest Igbo Muslim clerics. My father was himself an imam."

"Gbaga," the king said, welcoming the guests once more to his palace.

Ekwe watched as goats and fowls loitered in the courtyard in friendly forage. A plumed guinea fowl trailed behind a flock of chickens, clucking and scratching in the dirt in her beautifully dotted feathers. A rooster did his seductive, lopsided dance towards a hen, then chased her down.

"Your Highness, I have come to you on behalf of my friend." Ali gave Danjuma a friendly slap on the thigh. "He is a cowherd seeking space in your community to graze his cattle. He is a northerner and doesn't understand our tongue."

King Okosisi gave Ali Mustapha and Danjuma a sharp look, alarm mirrored in his long face, his lower lip thick like brick.

"Cowherd," he said as if the mere mention of that word was abominable, combustible. "Did you say you were from Ugbene-Ajima?"

"Yes, Your Highness," Ali said.

A woman came to the door of the large family house and threw handfuls of grains into the space from a blue plastic bowl. The birds raced for the grains in great competition; over and above their squawking came the familiar smell of breakfast to Ekwe's nose—as well as the clatter of dishes and the chatter of the king's wives and many children.

"If you are from Ugbene-Ajima, then you should know about the conflicts between cowherds and farmers."

"Unfortunately, yes, Your Highness," Ali said.

"Herdsmen are troublesome, and I don't want trouble in my community." King Okosisi's voice was firm.

Ekwe moved his gaze from the birds to a mongrel that strolled into the palace with a bunch of flies. The dog contemplated the guests, brushed her long, scraggy body against the king's feet, and strolled out again in the company of her winged companions as though merely checking for the king's safety.

"It's actually just this man and his family." Ali gestured towards Danjuma. "He will not give the community any trouble. He is a good Muslim who holds Allah in great awe. I have only known him for a short time, but I feel like I have known him for ages. He comes to the mosque under my care for Ṣalāt al-Jumuʿah. We are talking of a responsible man here, a man with a beautiful family. He fled from violence in his hometown in the North. He managed to bring his family and cattle down south for a new beginning. This time, he wants to obtain legitimate permission to use a portion of the backcountry expanses for grazing until it is time for him to get moving again."

The king gazed outside the palace in silent contemplation. Dark clouds of doubt hung over his heavy, droopy-lipped face.

"He will pay for the space, of course," Ali said.

Ekwe noted a slight shift in the dark clouds.

"Your Highness," Ali continued, "may I advise you not to allow such natural endowment as your kingdom is blessed with to go to waste when it can be financially rewarding? What happened in Nimbo could have been avoided if the herders and leaders of the community had properly managed the situation. The country belongs to all of us, and we have equal rights to freedom of movement. A southerner has the right to live anywhere in the North as much as a northerner who chooses to migrate to the South."

The king raised himself to his full height and started to pace. Ekwe liked how the crunch-crunch rhythm of the king's feet against the palace's palm kernel–husk floor punctuated the stiff silence.

"He will help you raise your own livestock and then look after the cattle for you," Ali said. "It's a flourishing trade many in this part of the country have not discovered."

A small-boned woman in a tall head gear and brown lace blouse tied into a pink George wrappa around her waist caught Ekwe's attention as she emerged from the family house. Ekwe watched her hobble to the assembly hall on high heels. She greeted the guests, bent before the king, and waited for him to place a large hand on her back. And then she straightened, told the king she was going to the women's meeting, and started to walk towards the old rusty gate with ungainly steps. Ekwe was sure that her heavy, cumbersome dressing was meant to simulate the look that set a lolo, a king's wife, apart from other village women.

"I do not want to make a hasty decision." King Okosisi resettled on the throne. He sat for a long time again in ponderous silence.

Ekwe turned his gaze to a big redheaded agama lizard that slithered down a bamboo post, stopped, and nodded as if in agreement with the king's decision not to act in a mad rush. Ekwe's eyes shifted to Danjuma, who was busy with his prayer beads, his mouth moving furtively.

King Okosisi broke the silence. "I will need to make consultations with my people. I cannot make a unilateral decision on such an important matter. So, you will have to wait to know what we decide."

"That's fine with us, Your Highness." Ali rose to his thick tubby height with a big grin and bowed. "We will stretch our legs outside while we wait. I could show the visitor a bit of the village."

Danjuma rose and bowed too, then headed out with Ekwe and Ali Mustapha as the king lapsed into another awkward silence, hands resting on the arms of the throne, head cresting the palmette, eyes thoughtfully raised to the conical roof. His kingdom was blessed with a landmass disproportionate to its small population; unploughed and fallowing land running into hundreds of hectares lay covered in lush meadows. Aside from serving the farming needs of his subjects, the large expanse of green was of no other use to the kingdom other than its decorative value.

The Lease

BECAUSE OF THE URGENT TONE OF HIS VOICE ON the phone, the men the king had summoned came hurrying to the palace in no time. The first to arrive was the town's president general, a sturdy, shrewd-eyed, middle-aged man with a toothbrush moustache. He was closely followed by a scruffy elderly man, who had forgotten to button his frayed old shirt properly in his hurry, a member of the palace council of chiefs. The ward councillor drove into the palace on a red Yamaha RX 100 motorcycle, a soft-faced young man whose stomach was beginning to show the earliest hints of a paunch. He was accompanied by the town union's youth arm leader, who had the wild, combative look of a prizefighter. Once they were all seated, the king introduced the guests who had returned from their tour of the village. He recounted Ali Mustapha's proposal. They listened with changing expressions, now an impatient scowl, now throwing Danjuma a suspicious look. When the king passed that Danjuma would pay for the space, all four men sat up with ears cocked.

Ekwe thought that they looked like saucer-eyed bush babies.

The king had picked the four men based on their political clout or social leverage in the community. The elderly man was the most radical of his council of chiefs; the town's president general was next in hierarchy to the king. Eche, the youth leader, had earned his position through brute force. His belief in violence meant the youths feared him and the elders were wary of his badly keloided face. He had been in a famous fight at the motor park in Nsukka, where he used to work as a tout, with a fellow tout who was equally tough and violent. It was easily the bloodiest fight ever witnessed at the motor park, fought freely with bottles and knives. Eche had come out of it with two long ugly scars: one running across his forehead and the other across his left cheek. His opponent had sustained worse injuries; he probably lost an eye.

Ubaka, the soft-talking, soft-smiling ward councillor, had no less an influence on the youths, having been returned to office for a second term. He had sponsored the community's Christmas football competition and awarded two hundred thousand naira to the team that had emerged champions. Gestures like that endeared him to the youths.

"I invited the four of you to decide if we should grant the cowherd his request. If yes, how much shall we ask him to pay? Are we going to make the transaction public to the villagers? You know about the conflicts between cowherds and farmers. If we allow them into this community, will they not attack us one day?"

Silence settled on the room like cinders.

"I think we should allow him to graze his animals," the president general broke the silence. "He has asked us nicely to allow him the use of the pasture rather than encroach on our land as most cowherds do. Besides, what is the use of all that expanse of land if it won't fetch money into our pockets?"

Ali Mustapha gave Danjuma and Ekwe a look full of prospects.

"We definitely shall grant him his request." Eche's gruff voice marched his thick, soupy face. "How can we even think of saying no to such a good business proposal for fear of being attacked? We won't allow that to happen in our kingdom. And this idea of making the proposal public is not a good one. We let him use the pasture and keep the money to ourselves as compensation for our leadership duties to the community. What else do we stand to gain for our services besides little favours of this nature?"

"I completely agree with those who have spoken." Ubaka smiled his approval of Eche's opinion, as always. "There is no sense in rejecting the stranger's request. How can we spit out the honey he has fed to us? Our village is not that weak and divided. We have always been known for our sense of communal living and the ability to fight back."

The look Ali Mustapha gave Danjuma and Ekwe now was promising.

The king looked at the oldest man with curious eyes. Clearly his opinion was of great essence.

"I am a human being with needs that money can take care of like every one of you," the elderly man said, "but we must tread with caution. If we say no to him, the land will remain unused, but if we grant his request, then we have a duty to protect our people from any dangerous incursion. I am an old man. Gone are the days when I hastened fights meant for tomorrow and encouraged them to begin at once." He gestured towards Eche and Ubaka. "I like your energy. We rely on your strength. The truth is, the cynics we have in our midst will oppose the lease considering the recent hostilities around us, so the sensible thing to do would be to keep them in the dark and protect our little secret if we can."

"Women are the ones with balls if men like us cannot keep a little secret," Eche said, and everyone laughed. "I'd suggest a lease of four and a half million naira. We get one million each and the king gets one and a half million naira."

They agreed it was a good bargain.

Ali Mustapha interpreted the bargain to Danjuma in Hausa, but instead of four and a half million naira, he told Danjuma that the king and his men had asked for five million naira. Danjuma seemed happy to sacrifice such a huge sum for the peace and well-being of his family and business, but Ekwe was outraged. He knew enough of Hausa language to understand Ali Mustapha's treachery. Danjuma would never know about the inflated bargain because he would receive no written agreement from the palace, a cunning plan to leave him with no evidence of this treachery. Ekwe itched to expose Ali Mustapha, but he waited to be alone with Danjuma. However, Ali Mustapha read his body language.

"I know what you are thinking," he growled in Igbo when he finally cornered Ekwe. He pointed to the long hunting barrel bound to his motorcycle. "I will kill you with that gun if you betray me."

The woman who had gone to the women's meeting earlier, the king's lolo, showed up at the gate and interrupted them. Her powdered face was now streaked with sweat. She walked barefoot, hands encumbered with her troublesome footwear and the rebellious George wrappa.

Hypocrisy

EKWE FINALLY FOUND THE OWL'S PERCH HIGH UP on a sycamore. The bird had been calling from the tree towering over their new settlement—a cluster of grass huts in a clearing around the forest wall—worsening the pulsing pain at the back of his skull. He had woken up with a headache. Danjuma had insisted he stay home and just eat, rest, and get better. Ekwe was happy with how Danjuma made choices for his surviving family, always thinking of how to protect them. His wives and children seemed happy to acquaint themselves with the villagers, especially Rekiya and Rukaitu, after the king's approval for Danjuma to pasture his cattle in the kingdom. They were working hard to pick up the local tongue, though still struggling to memorize words of greeting. "Gbaga," they'd say to people they met on the village path with a friendly smile. "Efim atagi ihegi." Their diction and syntax amused and delighted Ekwe more than their gratuitous reassurance that their cattle would not graze in the villagers' farmlands.

"Who cooks for you, who cooks for you all?" inquired the owl.

The bird's odd question drew Ekwe's attention to two pillars of smoke that rose from the cluster of huts. He found it uncanny that the bird could say those words, and even more unsettling because it chose the moment Rekiya was cooking to say them. He remembered Papa Ekwe saying, "Owls have reversible toes that can point forwards or backwards," and he thought how eerie it sounded. He picked up a stone and threw it at the bird and watched it flutter away silently through the trees.

The sudden vroom of a motorcycle scared a bat that hung upside down from a fecund walnut tree into flight, sending it rowing through the air as Ali Mustapha loomed into sight on a brand-new red Carter motorcycle. The last time he showed up at the settlement, he had driven his old smoking Suzuki double-pipe motorcycle. Ekwe was dazzled by the glare of new steel in the noon sun as Ali now bumped his way to the settlement on a rocky hillside track and forest path protruding with roots. He was sure the new motorcycle was purchased with the money Ali had stolen from Danjuma. He thought of how well the man inhabited his contradictory identities—an Igbo imam as well as a cheat and a liar—in much the same way as that flying mammal on a walnut tree.

"Allah Hafiz," Ali greeted the household as he alighted from the motorcycle and stretched himself in his rich brown lace and a native black cap.

"Salam," they chorused. Aisha sat astride Maimuna and braided her hair.

"Rabbaitul bait," he addressed Rekiya, then commended her beauty as she tended her fire in a rainbow-striped singlet.

"You are welcome, mallam." Rekiya smiled at him warmly, her thin body covered with henna drawings.

Danjuma rose to receive the guest. His tall, skinny, grey-garbed figure dwarfed Ali as he led him to the mat under a banyan tree, where his prayer beads lay. He picked up the beads as they settled down. He called for nono. The drink arrived shortly, served by his daughter Aamaal. They drank and talked as Aamaal settled at her father's feet.

"The king summoned me." Ali's voice was urgent.

"Why?" Danjuma gave him a worried little frown.

"Your cattle broke into their farmland and ate up their crops."

"Allahu Akbar."

"I was equally shocked. Mallam, how can this be happening after our agreement with the king? I feel very embarrassed."

"I am very sorry." Danjuma ran a hand over his coarse hair. "I had no idea."

"The king is livid. He insists the farmers must be paid some kind of restitution for the damage to their crops."

Ekwe knew that the herd had gone wild and grabbed mouthfuls from the farmland the day before, but Musa, Danjuma's first son and the chief cowherd, had asked them not to report it to Danjuma.

Rukaitu emerged from one of the huts fully dressed and ready to go to the market. "Sannu." She genuflected before her father's guest in greeting.

"Kyakkyawa nyarinya." Ali extolled her beauty.

She sidled away, shyly. "Zo, mu tafi, Aamaal," she called out to the girl, interrupting the flow of Danjuma's thoughts.

Aamaal left her father's feet and raced to meet Rukaitu, who was leaving for her afternoon sales and enjoyed her younger sister's company whenever she was going out to sell. Two calabash vessels of nono and fura sat high on the older girl's head, one on top of the other, and her wrappa was tied short and firm around her slim waist.

"Baba zan tafi." She took Aamaal by her hand and started down the tree-lined exit.

"Rukaitu," Danjuma called after her. "It is not proper to walk away while our guest is still around."

Rukaitu returned, eased the vessels down, and apologized to her father.

"You are blessed." Ali grinned at Danjuma. "Such lovely children."

"Allahu Akbar."

"Please let her go to the market and make her sales," Ali pleaded on behalf of Rukaitu.

"There's still time to make enough sales," Rukaitu said in obedience to her father.

This must be another opportunity for the cheat to rake in more money for himself, Ekwe pondered. He was angry that Danjuma saw Ali as Allah's disciple who had devoted his time to helping him, and Ekwe was even angrier with himself that he could do nothing about it. He glanced at the long hunting gun always tied to Ali's motorcycle.

"How much are they asking for?" Danjuma said.

"Countless crops were ruined." Ali rose to his feet, ready to leave. "The farmers are asking for half a million naira."

Danjuma took a deep breath as he walked his guest to his motorcycle. After he lost the small herd he had inherited from his family and poverty ate deep, he approached a few Higi merchants and offered to drive their cattle on the understanding that one out of every four births would be his. Two of the merchants had accepted his proposal and raised capital. They were big politicians in Maiduguri. They had given him their trust and support when he came up with the idea of moving the large herd south. He hoped they would not frown at these unforeseen expenses.

"You may want to go out there and look at the destruction yourself." Ali mounted his motorcycle and pushed the start button.

"Beautiful motorcycle," Danjuma said.

Ali wrung the throttle, hitting a rumbling note, and when he relaxed his grip, the sound dropped off to a deep-throated, almost silent vibration. "Well," he said with pride in his eyes. "When will you have the money?"

"Soon."

"Excellent. I don't want the locals bringing a fight here." He revved the motorcycle again and roared off.

Hands on her hips, Aisha sneered at Ali's disappearing form as the thrumpy exhaust notes of a new engine sang into the afternoon.

"He's too smooth for my liking," she said, and continued working on Maimuna's braids.

"But he seems a very sincere man," Danjuma said. "Remember he is Allah's disciple."

Ekwe choked on a calabash of nono.

"Yankuri." Danjuma said to him soothingly.

"That doesn't make him any less Nyamiri." Aisha spoke in Arabic out of respect for Ekwe, who did not understand Arabic. Her voice was edged with scorn. She had regained her old flesh, lost to the lengthy and rough travels. "They are too greedy for my liking; that's why I am not interested in their dirty language."

"I am learning the language, but that's only because it helps me sell my nono." Rekiya leaned out to stir her gruel.

Curls of smoke from the open-air cooking searched the wood.

"I think I like it here." Rukaitu played with her braids. She had a coy look. "There is so much to admire, from the rivulet to the hills to the valleys to the trees to the birds. The weather is amazingly clement. Nyamiri are not what you think they are. Those you meet at the market and along the village paths will treat you to generous smiles. The ones I have come across are gentle and nice. And the boys are good-looking."

Maimuna raised her head to give Rukaitu a long, narrow look, forcing Aisha to pause her braiding momentarily.

Rukaitu picked up and balanced her calabash vessel on her head, took Aamaal's hand once more, and walked away, giggling.

"Be careful." Danjuma's eyes shone. "There's tension between those people and our people. The good thing is our people always have the upper hand."

Aisha looked pleased. "We are descended from Usman dan Fodio, down a long line of warriors."

Danjuma gave a little conceited smile as he resettled on his haunches on the mat where he performed his dhuhr.

"I still think paying a whooping five million naira on lease to the palace is inconsiderate of the king," Aisha said. "And now the palace is asking for restitution for the farmers because of an unfounded allegation that the cattle ate a few crops."

"The problem with you, Maigida, is you are too quick to trust people," Rekiya said.

Danjuma scratched his head, feeling sandwiched between his overprotective women and the wild harmattan winds that scotched the pasture and forced his cattle to trespass into farmlands.

Reprisal

SHEHU RUSHED BACK TO THE SETTLEMENT, PANTING and looking ruffled, on a windy afternoon, his short and kinky hair peppered with particles of dust and dry grass, his clothes torn and caked with dirt. Ekwe came hot on his heels.

"Twenty heads of cattle have been slain by the villagers," Shehu announced as he burst in.

Danjuma was taking the day off to rest. He sat up on his mat, eyes wide with alarm. "Why? Where?"

"The cattle ate their crops," Ekwe said.

Danjuma ran his panicked eyes over Shehu's ruffled clothes and wild, frightened look. "Was anyone hurt, your brothers?" he asked.

Shehu shook his head.

Danjuma sighed with relief. "What happened to the rest of the herd?" he asked.

"We managed to drive them safely to the valley."

"Go back to your brothers and make sure you are all safe," Danjuma said. He lit a big wrap of hemp and smoked in silence after Shehu and Ekwe sprinted off.

"Are you going to sit there and smoke?" Aisha demanded in a grating voice. "Are you going to do nothing about the slain cattle?"

"I need time to think," he said.

"You paid a large sum of money to be allowed to pasture your cattle in this kingdom. You paid restitution because the cattle strayed into their farmland, now they slaughter twenty heads of cattle, and you sit there thinking instead of acting."

He ignored her and started to walk away.

"They must pay for it." Her voice followed him. "I always knew that they are a wicked and selfish tribe. They are all over the place doing business in the North unmolested, but they won't let us stay here in this small place in peace."

Danjuma strolled to the valley, his face wrung tight with anger. He stood at the edge of the grazing land and watched his cattle fraternizing with egrets. Birds enjoyed a high ride on the backs of cattle. He envied them for their mismatched friendship as Shehu's voice echoed through the clouded valley of his mind . . . *twenty heads of cattle* . . . He mentally tabulated the cost. It was a huge loss. Added to the money spent on the lease and the one paid on restitution, it came to a sum that gave him a dull ache at the back of the head, as he wandered aimlessly around the parched pasture.

He began to feel better and think more clearly only after he had smoked two joints and lit a third one. He bent over and pulled at a tuft of dry grass. The harmattan had been very strong. Severe winds were battering the country and weeds lay limp and rusty for miles. The whole place looked bruised and bare. Even the villagers agreed the harmattan had not been this wild and severe in recent times. The sight and smell of greenery in the irrigated farms must tempt the cattle.

Ekwe and Balarabe came bounding over to meet him.

"I saw so many dead cattle." Balarabe's curious eyes were raised to meet his father's steady gaze. "Did you also see them, Baba?"

"I know," Danjuma said for lack of something better to say to the boy.

Danjuma could not bring himself to go to the scene. He didn't think he could bear the sight of the fallen cattle littering the field. Soon their decomposing carcasses would become meat for the vultures.

Balarabe's eyebrows pulled together to the centre of his forehead with worry. "Are they going to kill all our cattle?"

Danjuma drew in smoke with spluttering sounds. "They will not kill any more cattle, and I haven't forgotten my promise to you."

Relief brought a smile to Balarabe's lips over his father's reassurance that he would soon control a small herd.

"Run along to your brothers, you two," Danjuma said to the boys. "Ask Shehu to meet me here."

He watched them as they bounded off again, Balarabe's loose kente dress flapping in the harmattan wind blowing across the valley. The colourful motif interwoven into the kente became suddenly animated as the image of a tribal mask filled Danjuma's vision, its intimidating square-eyed stare waking in him a sense of foreboding. He finally summoned the courage to make the phone call he had dreaded. His employers needed to know about the slain cattle. He dreaded their reaction. Losing twenty heads of cattle didn't sound like competence to him.

He was on the phone for half an hour with Alhaji Garba Shehu, listening patiently to the grating voice. "They dare to touch my cattle, those Nyamiri. They will pay with their blood. Na rantse da Allah," Alhaji Garba Shehu swore. "Tell me your exact location. I will get in touch with the branch of the Miyetti Allah Cattle Breeders Association in that region and have logistics sent for a bloody revenge."

When Danjuma spoke with the other man, Alhaji Babangida Tukur, he sounded no less infuriated. He too wanted revenge and was ready to spend much more than the cost of twenty heads of cattle to get it done. "I will get the president involved in this if I have to," Alhaji Babangida Tukur fumed. "Those people need to be taught a lesson. The country is ours and you have the right to drive the cattle to any part of it without molestation."

Danjuma ended the phone call and lit another joint. He had not expected the conversation with Alhaji Garba Shehu, a top politician in the country with influence and power, and Alhaji Babangida Tukur, a cattle merchant with strong political connections and countless herds of cattle and cowherds under his employ, to be any less intense.

"Baba. You sent for me."

Danjuma turned and contemplated Shehu as though noticing the tuft of hair on the boy's face for the first time, as if he was just realizing how much Shehu looked like him on his ascension to manhood. Under normal circumstances, Shehu would have left home by now in search of Islamic knowledge like his older brothers.

"What do you think we should do to the people who slew twenty heads of our cattle?" Danjuma felt anger warm his face like a whiff of hot air.

The weight of his baba's question seemed too heavy for Shehu, and he lowered his head.

Danjuma waited for an answer.

"Since they killed our cattle in revenge, we should also serve vengeance back to them hot as porridge yam," Shehu said.

"Kai dan ubanka ne." Danjuma's voice shook with emotion, eyes full of pride for a son who had the pluck of his father.

Shehu waited for instructions.

"Unleash the cattle on their farmland," Danjuma snarled. "Let them eat up everything, even swallow the farmland if they can. Take Ekwe and your brothers with you, harvest the crops with your own hands, and feed them to the cattle."

Shehu ran back to the valley with his father's instruction.

Murder

EKWE DID NOT LIKE THE BRUTALITY OF THE FARMers, who slew twenty heads of Danjuma's cattle, but he also felt for the farmers when he thought of the wild way the cattle had set on the farmlands and devoured yams, cassava, and greens. He had equal sympathy for Danjuma for his loss, but vengeance would only make things worse. He had an awful premonition of minor clashes escalating into full-blown violence. Danjuma was always wandering about in search of network service on his mobile. He talked on the phone with people Ekwe did not know but whose anger Ekwe could see forming deep furrows in Danjuma's brow. Danjuma moved around with his sons as hostilities deepened, not letting them out of his sight, always armed with weapons and charms. He made sure the boys wore their amulets at all times to keep them invincible. He could afford to lose his cattle, but not another member of his family. He would give his life to protect them.

Ekwe's sense of foreboding grew when Balarabe went missing. No one knew his whereabouts. Not even Ekwe, Balarabe's closest companion, could explain his movements. Ekwe sensed that Balarabe's sudden disappearance was connected to the hostilities growing between Danjuma and the villagers like a big red boil. The family waited all afternoon without Balarabe showing up. And when news filtered in that a boy's body was lying by the waterside, it threw the family into a panic. Balarabe's mother, Rekiya, went out of her mind with anxiety. Her hysterics sent Danjuma out in a frantic search for the boy. He headed towards the rivulet, walking with raised legs on a track protruding with mangrove stumps, a forest filled with birdsong and a choir of cicadas. Ghosts taunted his vision as leadwoods and sycamores fused into dancing figures with limbs and a face. He felt haunted by Zainab and Azhaar, by the long malicious echoes of their accusations—his inability to protect them. He stopped for one dark, ponderous moment to shake them from his mind. He smelt the river, a faint antiseptic tang. He did not feel like going forwards again. His injured heart might not survive another shock after the deaths of Azhaar and Zainab. If the body by the rivulet turned out to be his son's, and he prayed not, then the locals had taken this conflict to a whole new level. This would then be a full-scale war. He leaned against a mopane tree and listened to the loud pitter-patter of his heartbeat. Silence had fallen on the avian choristers and sunset filtered through in weak and reluctant rays, the silence momentary, broken by the strains of a hummingbird. As he drew closer to the rivulet, the dark, broody water reared up with a strong whiff, a metallic smell that banished the pure spring aura of the wood. A cold shiver of familiarity washed over him as he glimpsed a body. He started to tremble. Beads of sweat broke out on his forehead as he recognized the kente dress Balarabe had worn. He grabbed hold of a tree to stop himself from falling, and slowly, very slowly, he lowered himself to the ground.

▲▲▲▲▲

The ghosts of Zainab and Azhaar mocked Danjuma in the days following Balarabe's murder. They sat across from him on the prayer mat and laughed at him with eyes dripping blood. Their laughter reminded him of his weaknesses as a father and a husband, his not being able to protect his own family. It grew hysterical and filled his head. He got up and fled inside, but it followed him, filled every hollow in the bamboo walls, all the arches and curves in the grass roof. He fled to the valley, but the hills echoed their laughter until he thought he was losing his mind. He spent the days moping, mostly in the company of Aamaal. He found great comfort with the little girl who grew sulky with the absence of her brother.

"When is Balarabe coming back from the errand?" The poor little girl kept pestering him with questions.

Her mother had lied to her about Balarabe. "Baba sent him on an errand to a distant place," Rekiya had said.

"It will take a very long time," Danjuma said.

She sulked.

"Can you stop sulking about him?" he said. "He is happy where he is. You will upset him if you keep calling his name. Do you want to upset him?"

She shook her head.

"Then stop talking about him."

She never mentioned his name again.

The days were drawing in with longer nights. Ramadan was only weeks away. It was early spring already. The first rain had fallen. And then it rained again and again in between intervals of sunshine and nourished the pasture.

"I can't imagine Ramadan without Balarabe." Rekiya blinked a tear away.

Danjuma sucked hard on a joint with thin, chapped lips. The voice of combustion sputtered down the valley and the hills sent back a faint echo of a ghost's haunting laughter.

Book Two

Jafari's Interception

OVERPOWERED BY MISERY AND GRIEF, EKWE strolled towards the valley as a blinding platinum sunshine exploded and lit the hills, where a massive bird with striking golden-brown plumage was suspended in air over the valley—its thermal—long, graceful legs hidden in soft, downy fluff. Ekwe had never seen such a monstrous raptorial bird. The thermal seemed to have suddenly lost its lift as the gigantic bird circled and circled above. From that height Ekwe was no more than a pika rummaging far below.

Suddenly the enormous creature swooped down, grabbed Ekwe by his arms, and fluttered away with her human prey trapped in strong talons. The valley echoed her "tu-whit tu-whoo" in varied pitch, nuance, and modulation as the bird flew into clouds that looked like a great mass of feathers, plumes extending into the skies in multistorey layers. The higher they flew, the larger and more dramatic the clouds. As if angry at being disturbed in his repose, Amadioha grumbled and bared his teeth and flicked his fiery tongue voraciously. The bird pitched downwards, intimidated by thunderheads, buffeted by superstorms over oceans and rivers. Mountains and hills started to outline below as the colossal avian flew over changing landscapes, now alpine, now a rolling plateau.

She circled and circled over a widespread Sahelian acacia savanna with a few trees dotting thatched colonies.

Finally, as the immense bird alighted on a mahogany, a stone whizzed past and narrowly missed the raptor's great head. Rattled by the force of the projectile, the bird lost her grip on her prey and fluttered away with a great roar of her wings. Ekwe plunged, a long dangerous fall from the mahogany, but he managed to catch a branch and dangled.

"Let go," a voice shouted to him from below, offering its arms. "I will give you a soft landing."

Ekwe peered down. The voice belonged to a dwarf from that distance, with hands and feet too spindly for his large head. A slingshot dangled around the dwarf's neck. He spoke in a strange tongue, but his gestures were expressive. Ekwe admired his pluck. He would be the senseless one not to take the chance, after the dwarf offered to put his own fragile body on the line to break Ekwe's fall.

"Come on."

Ekwe closed his eyes and jumped, dropping into strong, lean arms. As he opened his eyes, he found himself staring into the face of a full-grown man, who eased him down as though a baby. The man was dressed for bird hunting, in worn singlet and khaki shorts.

"My name is Jafari," the man said.

His curious brown eyes were all over Ekwe, asking questions: Who are you? Where are you from? Did that just happen, a bird preying on a human being? Was that a species of monster bird?

Ekwe made gestures to explain that he did not understand him.

Jafari switched to Hausa, his face lighting up upon realizing that Ekwe understood him now. During the months with Danjuma and his nomadic family, Ekwe had learned to speak a great deal of Hausa and Fulani languages. He told Jafari his name and narrated his incredible aeronautic story from Igboland.

"Do you know where you are right now?"

Ekwe shook his head.

"You are in Central Africa," Jafari said.

Ekwe stared wide-eyed at him. He had never heard of a place called Central Africa.

"You are very far away from home if you are from Igboland. Fortunately, your tribesman lives in this village. I am sure he will be happy to see you."

Ekwe was silent.

"I had to do something to save you when I saw you in the deathly grips of that monster bird," Jafari said as he walked Ekwe back towards the village. "Was that a crowned hawk-eagle?"

"I think it was an owl," Ekwe said.

Wattle and Daub

JAFARI THREW HIS WIFE, MARIYA, A TEPID EYE FROM where he sat on a stool in his compound and grumpily ate cassava and soup with thin fingers. He was bare down to a pair of worn-out shorts, a small-boned man with a pointed jaw and a nose that curved like a sickle on his face. The shorts, made of wool, hung loose around his thin, bony waist and left him looking scrawny as a scarecrow. But they had sentimental value, coming all the way from a used clothes shop in faraway Monrovia. He missed Monrovia, though that city awakened sick images, a memory that reeked of violence. "You should see Monrovia" were his words to Mariya accompanying a smug smile when he returned from the war. "Bangui is pigpen compared to Monrovia."

"The only valuable you came back with is a cheap phone," she had sneered.

Mariya was right. He had come home with nothing but the Nokia 3310 mobile that drowned after everything. He cursed Charles Taylor again under his breath as he stretched a bony leg that could pass for firewood. Charles Taylor was the reason his wardrobe was down to one grey threadbare kaftan and a pair of shorts greying with dirt and age. He hissed at the end of his meal, licked his fingers with a loud smack, and snuck Mariya another eye—his wife who bore him five children. His listless eyes moved from his wife to his children. They were crowded around lunch—a big bowl of cassava and soup—in a corner of the hut: two girls and three boys who followed each other nose to tail like swarmer termites, with barely one-year gap in between parturition. Samora and Bonga even looked like twins. Bonga was only five months older, born prematurely. "Immature lungs," said the mountain matron who midwifed his birth. Jafari's first, a son, took after his mother in size, a big and indolent boy with a bottomless pit for a stomach. He ate like a pit-digging coal miner but worked like a koala, setting a bad example for his siblings by turning eating into a domestic contest of sorts in Jafari's house. Jafari often amused himself with the thought that, if ever eating became an Olympic game, one of his sons would sure win gold. He chuckled to himself now and focused his attention on Ekwe. Since his arrival, the boy had been going on and on about fufu not being his favourite even though his father swallowed child-head sizes of it, but that was only in theory, looking at the way he took Jafari's kids on in every single meal. Jafari liked him, though. Ekwe was funny, so settled on his preoccupations. He was mad that his family wasn't better and that he ate only fufu and slept in a house so old it brought nightmares. As for Jafari and his family, they lived off the fat of the land as far as food was concerned, though he was often out of cash.

"The Séléka Christians used to say, 'Man shall not live off bread alone,' he mumbled.

"Did you say something?" Mariya's sleepy voice sauntered across the semicircle of the compound to him.

"Just thinking aloud," he said.

"Find something to do instead of sitting idly and talking to yourself like Gia Huy," she hissed at him.

He stood up and went into the house away from her searing, reproachful eyes. How could Mariya compare him to Gia Huy, the famous village madman? He must irritate her extremely, like a live coal to her skin. He ought to get away for a while, take his old drought self away and come back as refreshed as new rain. Sometimes he felt like a kangaroo in a thick forest, cut out from civilization. He was bored out of his mind and wanted a little action. He supposed a few weeks away from the mountain would cleanse Mariya's heart of the toxins and hate lurking inside it. But there was nowhere to go to. Everything went quiet after the Liberia job. His Nokia 3310 got drowned in the river and severed his connections with Yacine. He had worked for Yacine before when he was hired to fight for the National Patriotic Front of Liberia in the Liberian Civil War. But when he became president, Charles Taylor forgot the mercenaries who helped him win the war. Jafari had returned penniless to his family in this mountain home of red mud and grass roof; to hunting, pasturing, and growing crops.

The sitting room was barren, almost empty of furniture, but rich in trash. A single tattered-looking cushion sat among a bumper supply of garbage. An old, wheelless bicycle leaned against the bare wall and motorcycle tyres littered the floor. Abdelmonin and his brothers rolled the tyres around the village. That boy had no shame naming tyres after choice cars. At his age and size, this was something he was supposed to have outgrown long ago. They collected beer corks too and stored them in empty beverage tins and cans. Every morning, they rushed off and gleaned Joe's Grocery & Bush Bar hoping to win cars under crown corks. "You better tell that boy to stop his dreaming and use the corks to improve his mathematics," Jafari had said to Mariya. Abdelmonin had repeated Primary 2 twice, coming bottom of his class each time.

The family cushion had been in bad condition since Bonga was two. The journey of its ruin started after the little rascal slashed it with a sharp blade. Somehow, he had found himself alone with a blade at his beck and call, so he had set to work on the cushion, which was the first fruit of Jafari's prime. But the boy had paid the price for his rascality, accidentally gashing himself in the palm. After that he stayed clear of blades. Jafari didn't even want to think about the battered table where all the wood lice in Central African Republic made their home. The bedroom was full of useless articles. An unclothed mattress lay flattened to the floor, blackened with urine and shimmering with bedbugs. The mattress had seen hell carrying the weight of an entire family for years. It was long due for a change, but he had no money.

"Even a steamroller could not do a better job of flattening," he had teased Mariya.

"It's your fault, so deal with it," she had snapped. "You don't expect us to trim down when cassava and chikwangue are all you feed my children and me in your house?"

The room was thick with dirt. Grout hung everywhere from the ceiling-less roof like entrails. The place stank, but Jafari reckoned it was better to have a house of one's own even if it was a wattle and daub, even if it was the last house in the village before a sprawling mass of mountain. He started to search around the room. He began under the mattress, searched in a pile of dirty clothes, in a small crude cupboard. He frantically searched through Mariya's untidiness. At last, he found a note among her ragtag belongings. He quickly squeezed it into the pocket of his shorts. Mariya had green fingers. She could weave a fine washcloth she sold to some woman, a clothier, who came all the way from Bangui to buy up Mariya's needlework.

"Leave me be, you plague." Mariya was shooing off Bonga, who was pestering her for more food, when Jafari emerged from the room through the front door. He had wanted to steal away through the back door, but Mariya would still see him from where she sat knitting in front of the thatched kitchen.

Bonga's siblings and Ekwe waited in a tight knot around the empty food bowl in front of the raffia palm goat pen, bellies round and shiny, oily fingers suspended midair in anticipation, and shrewd eyes fixed on Bonga, who had been sent to coax more food out of their mother.

"I am going to get myself a smoke down at Joe's," Jafari announced, and invited Ekwe to accompany him.

"You don't dare touch my money," Mariya threw at him, eyes narrowed.

He ignored her and started to walk away.

"Don't just get a smoke from that Joe," Mariya said, "let him teach you his Igboman's sense of scrounging wealth from nothing."

When it became clear that Mariya wasn't going to oblige them another morsel of food, Ekwe struggled into a shirt he quickly grabbed at Jafari's invitation to go on a stroll. They headed for Joe's Grocery & Bush Bar located in the central area of the village. Joe had materialized from nowhere, said to have come all the way from Nigeria to set up his flourishing business, married a local Banda woman, and now ran a shop that had grown overnight like a mushroom. Most people in the village were envious of his success. Wives like Mariya used him to spite their ne'er-do-well husbands.

EKWE LIKED JAFARI'S COMPANY BECAUSE JAFARI told him stories of his guerrilla exploits and how Jean-Bédel Bokassa wasted a quarter of his empire's annual budget on his coronation, and because Jafari took his wife's coins and spent them on himself and Ekwe at Joe's grocery shop. Joe was Ekwe's countryman. Ekwe enjoyed speaking Igbo with him, and Joe always had a gift for Ekwe, thrilled about finding a brother in the Diaspora, in this remote rural mountain village in a faraway land. Ekwe sometimes felt like a lost soul. He sometimes thought of Papa Ekwe and Mama Ekwe and Azuka and Oyibo and the twins and his stepmothers and half-siblings and habaneros. He sometimes thought of Danjuma and his family. The weight of the sadness in Danjuma's household had become too much on the man after Balarabe's murder. Danjuma had started to see the ghosts of his dead wife and children in broad daylight. His head was filled with vengeance and he spent hours on the phone plotting revenge.

"I want smoke and batteries." Jafari cowered before Joe's mahogany counter.

The bush bar stood away from the regular grocery shop, a hut of veldt grass roof supported by many oak pillars. It was empty at this time.

"Money." Joe, a sturdy man with a few days' old stubble scattered on his face, extended a thick palm. Joe didn't care about his looks. People said he spent the time he could have used to take care of himself chasing money. He turned and smiled at Ekwe, "Nwannem."

Ekwe returned the greeting in Igbo.

Jafari's eyes lingered on a sign on the door of the shop that glared at him in red letters: NO CREDIT TODAY COME TOMORROW. He grinned at Joe and passed him the stolen note.

"This money is only enough for a pair of batteries." Joe took the money and gave him the batteries, his face set.

Jafari's eyes went to the sign again as guilt stabbed him in the chest. It wasn't there a few days ago. Joe probably put up the sign for him, to remind him of his debt, his unpaid-for cigarettes and beers.

Ekwe smelt food spiced with ogiri, a Nigerian homemade seasoning, and swallowed his spittle.

"Give a poor fellow a smoke." Jafari grinned at Joe again. "I will pay off my debt soon."

"No more credit." Joe returned the grin, his voice firm, his shrewd little eyes darting towards the sign.

Jafari lingered, not sure how to coax a cigarette stick out of Joe. Joe with his square forehead, quick little eyes, and unsmiling face would likely not fall for any of his tricks again.

"I can't remember the last time I listened to a radio," Jafari said for lack of anything else to say. He was anxious to get the conversation going.

As an answer, Joe tuned a small foxhole radio sitting among his wares on the counter. As soukous music gave off good vibes, he went back to speaking to Ekwe and touching things distractedly on the shelves, the self-conscious grin still on his wide face. He had come to this village almost empty-handed. How he had found his way to this mountain region said so much about the resourcefulness and enterprising spirit of Igbo migrants. He started with little things: cheap cigarettes, sweets, chewing gum. In no time groceries and confectioneries started to fight for space on the floor-to-ceiling shelves of his shop. The man had created something out of nothing. But he hadn't achieved all that without making policies and sacrifices, without self-denials, and one of them was to only extend credit to people he knew could pay.

"When was the last time you visited Igboland?" Jafari tried another stunt.

Joe scowled. When he scowled, he erected a thick wall between him and Jafari, and Jafari wondered how to scale over the wall.

"I have not been there for fifteen years." Joe's voice was flat.

Jafari changed tactics. He went and sat on a bench outside the bush bar, hoping someone would come along who would be willing to share his cigarette. Ekwe joined him.

"Don't you miss your people?" Jafari said chattily.

Joe laughed dryly. "I can't help it. It's a long journey."

"Yeah." Jafari frowned and peered down the long, dry road leading up to the bar. "Buddy," he whispered to Ekwe in Hausa. "See if you can get me a smoke with language from that damned brother of yours."

Ekwe tried but failed. Joe told him not to stick his nose into his business with Jafari.

Finally, Jafari gave up all hope of anyone strolling up to share a cigarette, and they left. He was bankrupt and had been for too long.

"Not even money for batteries or cigarettes," he moaned on their way home. "The world is sunset yellow."

He did not like this reign of peace among people living in civilization. It meant suffering and boredom and no smoke for people like him who lived off wars and violence. He cast another look back at Joe's Bush Bar. If ever another war broke out, he promised himself, Joe would be his first choice of prey.

ıııııı

Back home, Jafari dusted the radio, an old utility radio, and fed it batteries. He took a mat to the flame tree outside, away from Mariya's reproving eyes, and lay down to listen to world news. For the first time, he heard about the Arab Spring revolution. The whole of the Arab world was on fire: Egypt, Yemen, Syria, Tunisia, and Libya. *It was triggered by the first protests that occurred in Tunisia on December 18, 2010, in Sidi Bouzid, following Mohamed Bouazizi's self-immolation in protest of police corruption and ill treatment.* The radio also talked about the violence of Fulani militants and Boko Haram insurgents in Nigeria, Al-Shabaab in East Africa, and the Taliban in Afghanistan. His eyes widened as he listened to stories of violence in the region of Tigray.

"The world is a theatre of war," Jafari said to Ekwe.

Before going to Liberia as a mercenary, Jafari had been

involved in local guerrilla warfare. He hadn't earned much from it, but enough to pay Mariya's bride price and buy a radio and the now-battered cushion in the house. Yacine had disappeared completely after the mission in Liberia. Yacine was his contact with civilization, his eyes into the world beyond the mountains. Jafari's stomach knotted with fear. What if the man was dead? It could be a good explanation for his silence. He hissed, sat up against the tree, and peered into the distance at the bleak outline of the mountain.

"Who stole my note?"

He looked up at Mariya's massive, incensed frame. "You said something?"

"Someone stole my note."

He scratched his thin jaw. "I didn't steal it. I took it."

She put her hands on her hips for his audacity. "What's the difference between stealing it and taking it without my say-so?"

"I didn't buy a smoke with it, if that's what you think." His tone was conciliatory. "I needed to get the radio working again. As I am talking to you, the whole world is going up in flames."

"I don't care if the whole world burns to ashes," she snapped. "What I will not accept is your taking money meant for more important things and spending it on frivolities."

"News is important, isn't it?" He raised his brows at Ekwe.

She cut her eyes after him and stalked off.

"Women!" he said, his rueful gaze following her into the house, as he suddenly realized that he had never bought his wife a gift since they got married, that in place of gifts, he had taken from her. He lowered his eyes with shame and guilt.

"Buddy. What would be the best gift to give a woman, a wife?" he said.

Ekwe looked lost. He had never been married. "Rice," he said after a thoughtful silence.

Jafari laughed. "Buddy! Are you on oath to rice or something?"

Land Flowing with Milk and Honey

THINKING OF YACINE EVERY NOW AND AGAIN FINALLY summoned him in his full height and an unapologetic air, a towering figure that loomed up like a spectre among the tulipwood trees bordering the long approach to Jafari's compound. Jafari shaded his eyes with a curved palm for a better view in the intense afternoon sun as Yacine walked towards the hut with that familiar slowness of gait. He couldn't believe his eyes. It was Yacine all right, with the same rough features, the clumsy arm swing.

"Long time no see," Jafari cried in Sangho. He rose from the raffia mat where he sat with Ekwe and pumped Yacine's hand and felt the coolness of the long-pointed fingers wrapped around his small hand. "I thought you had forgotten me."

Yacine unstrapped his rucksack and joined them on the mat. His eyes fell on Ekwe as Jafari introduced them to one another.

"I tried reaching you on your phone, but I couldn't," Yacine said.

"My phone got drowned."

They lit cigarettes from a brand-new pack Yacine fished out of his green kaftan pocket. Jafari took a long-starved draw, happy that Yacine came with a whole packet of his favourite Gold Leaf. He hadn't smoked in a long time. Yacine searched in the bag and came out with an apple for Ekwe.

"What about my sister?" Yacine's eyes travelled to the wattle-and-daub hut.

"Mariya and the children are off to see her old man in the alp. The children enjoy shepherding their sick grandfather's miserable herd."

Yacine relaxed against the flame tree with a soft sigh.

"Your presence was strong in my mind," Jafari said.

"So much has happened, but I don't want to go into all that." Yacine's tone was businesslike. "I am here now, and I have a job for you, that's what's important."

Jafari's eyes narrowed with curiosity. "What job and where?"

Yacine threw Ekwe a glance.

Jafari patted Ekwe's back. "Ekwe is my buddy, my good luck charm. He is not at all a threat to whatever you want to say."

"The job is in Nigeria." Yacine huffed through a broken nose.

Jafari sat up. If there was a land flowing with milk and honey, it was that country called Nigeria. "I hear that oceans of oil flow everywhere in that country," he said. "Even fish swim in oil."

"Nigeria is an oil-rich country, yes." Yacine's brown eyes were moist with excitement. "The job is this: Nigeria is going to elect a new president. A region of the country feels cheated out of power and wants to grab it back at all costs. The opposition party is fielding a candidate from that marginalized region. The president is no longer popular because of a high level of corruption in his government, but he is still very formidable, and there is speculation that the elections will be rigged. In the eventuality that this happens, the opposition candidate, who happens to be an ex-general, will make the country ungovernable for the cheating president. This is why you are being hired. My contact is recruiting mercenaries for this purpose, to make that country ungovernable, so I recommended you."

Jafari smoked in quiet contemplation. "What's in it for me?"

"I do not know what's in it for you, but I know it's a juicy job. You are leaving in a few days along with other mercenaries. Your transportation has been arranged. You will be taken to a base near the Mandara Mountains. The opposition candidate, Baba, who happens to be an ex-general, will be there to address the mercenaries by himself, and you know what that means. You will find out what's in it for you then. The mercenaries will spend weeks training in the mountains, after which they are expected to go into the cities, familiarize themselves to the environment to make their jobs easier pending when they are required to strike, but that will only be after the election if Baba loses."

They smoked in silence. Was he to trust Yacine? Yacine was like a monitor lizard. Jafari had never really profited from his connections, but somehow Yacine had made himself indispensable in his life.

"Are you going to accept the job?"

He considered the question. "Tell me, Yacine, what's the best gift to give a woman?"

Yacine thought for a moment. "A white woman will value

the gift of a rose, perfume, or even sweets, but with an African woman you won't make any impression with those kinds of gifts. Take her away from this dump to a house in Bangui and give her a better life, if you are thinking of a gift for your wife."

"Then to ask me if I am going to accept the job is asking a dog if it will eat bones."

They laughed.

"You don't know what I have seen in this village these past years," Jafari said. "I hadn't smoked in many days."

Yacine fished out another packet of cigarettes and another apple for Ekwe. He counted off some CFA franc notes and passed them to Jafari. "Use the money for your preparations and family upkeep."

"Singila mingi." Jafari bowed his thanks.

Yacine reached into his khaki rucksack and came out with a Motorola mobile. "Here is a phone with a SIM card for you."

Jafari took the phone in both palms as if he was receiving the Military Cross.

"Let's keep in touch," Yacine said. "There's so much going on out there." He went on to talk about the Kivu and Ituri conflicts and the war in Darfur. But it was the insurgency in Khyber Pakhtunkhwa that held prospects for him beyond the Nigerian job.

"What started the fighting in Khyber Pakhtunkhwa?" Jafari said.

"The conflict started in 2004," he said. "Tensions arising from the Pakistan Army's search for Al-Qaeda fighters in Pakistan's mountainous Waziristan area spiralled into armed resistance."

Jafari gazed at him with shrinking pupils.

"I have always dreamed of working for Al-Qaeda." Yacine's eyes were liquid. "Finally, I have contact with the group, something I have worked very hard to achieve. I may be heading to Waziristan right after the Nigerian job."

"I hope you take me along," Jafari said.

Yacine smiled at Ekwe and patted Jafari on the back as he rose to leave. "Let's see how it turns out."

They saw him off to the wide road that connected the nearest town of Bahamo and watched him board a minibus.

"Please take me with you to Nigeria," Ekwe pleaded with Jafari as they turned and headed in the direction of Joe's shop.

"Of course, you are welcome to come along," Jafari said. "You will find your way to Mama Ekwe and Papa Ekwe once we are in Nigeria, won't you?"

Ekwe was very excited at the prospect of going home. He had missed his family.

At Joe's shop Jafari bought canned rice for Ekwe and a few beers for himself and paid off his debt.

▲▲▲▲▲

"I am going to Nigeria."

"What was that?"

"Yacine has found me a job in Nigeria."

Mariya looked away. Yacine was a distant cousin of hers from her mother's side, a paradox who kept disappearing and appearing. But gone were the times when she looked on him as family. That ended when he got himself entangled with rebels and started to involve Jafari in guerrilla warfare, before vanishing for a long, long time, only to reappear now like a plague.

"That woyendawopusa was here?" she said, chastising Yacine for his wanderings in Chichewa, her mother tongue.

Jafari flaunted his new phone. "He gave me this."

Her surprise registered on her face for a fleeting moment. "I am not stopping you from going," she said, "but make sure the vehicle that will convey you is roomy enough to accommodate the kids and me, because you aren't leaving us behind."

"Please allow me to go. You don't need me here like this. I feel I am the worst kind of father and husband. I am just a liability to you, right?"

"What kind of job is taking you to Nigeria? Are you going there to stick your neck out only to come back with nothing, as always?"

"Don't use Liberia as a benchmark. Nigeria is a land flowing with milk and honey."

"And how are you sure that wanderer is not using you to enrich himself?"

"You are prejudiced," Jafari said curtly. "Anyway, we are going there to make sure the president of that country doesn't cheat in their election."

She looked him over and burst into laughter. "You think a million of your size can stop the president?"

"It is not about size," he said with a knowing look.

"Are you being sarcastic?"

"I am saying it is the brain, not the size, that matters." If only she knew how fast and deadly this half-a-pint husband of hers could be in war situations, pondered Jafari.

Mariya relaxed her antagonism and even became conversational. "Tell me one African leader who doesn't cheat in elections, who doesn't want to die in office and be succeeded by a son he has spent time grooming into a ruthless, thieving, sardonic leader?"

"You talk sensible sometimes," he said as he fetched the mint notes Yacine had given him. "Yacine said to give you and the kids these for your upkeep while I am away."

She took the money and counted it. "What is in it for you, anyway?"

"The general will make the pronouncement when we meet him at the Mandara Mountains."

"How many times is he taking you for a ride?" She tucked the money into her bra. "He made you similar promises when you went with him to Liberia."

"I know," he said. "But I am giving him another chance."

"You will have to swear by the god of thunder to come back to me and the kids before I can let you out of my sight."

Jafari mulled over Mariya's reaction. He was ready to swear by anything for an opportunity to change their lives.

African Warlords

KANO WAS SULTRY BUT FINE, EKWE MUSED, AS HE walked the wide busy streets with Jafari, stopping now and again to admire the tectonic beauty of the ancient city. A mix of old and modern architecture shepherded crowds of people, cars, rickshaws, motorcycles, and bicycles to their destinations. Kano was the first large city Ekwe had seen, unlike Jafari, who had been to Monrovia but never had time to take in the sights because of the war. Jafari had seen Bangui briefly as part of a local militia in the face-off between Séléka and General Bozizé's anti-Balaka. Truth was he was not a city man. He preferred his rural mountain life: hunting and pasturing spiced with occasional guerrilla exploits. He loved birds. At sunset he watched them rise and dip in their colourful plumage. His favourite time was during bird migration season when flocks of them winged at terrific speed and made hairpin turns down the valley.

The sun blazed. Throngs of pedestrians streamed past Ekwe and Jafari either way in kaftans, turbans, and veils. Dressed in a grey kaftan and red taqiyah, and with a little boy in his company, Jafari easily passed as any civilian hustling against the crowd, going about their business. He had spent weeks in a base around the Mandara chain in the company of men from different climes: Chad, Cameroon, Niger, Mali, Sudan, Eritrea, and so on. For weeks, the men had camped together, eating, sleeping, drinking, and sharing smoke while he hid Ekwe in his condo and smuggled in food to him. "Bonding" was what Yacine had called the gathering of mercenaries. Baba had been there to address the mercenaries. He hadn't said anything much different from what Jafari had heard from Yacine already. The austere general had made big promises if he came to power. "You will be part and parcel of my government," he had said in Hausa, the language understood by all the mercenaries. "You will enjoy access into government house for as long as I will be president."

A loud cheering had erupted from the army of mercenaries.

"You will reassemble here immediately after the election for deployment."

Chants of "Baba" had rented the air.

Ekwe could tell that Baba had Jafari's sympathy. Jafari knew nearly nothing about continental politics, but he had heard enough to know that sub-Saharan Africa was volatile with political uprisings and military coups. He told Ekwe that the violence was mostly caused by warlords trying to chase out sit-tight presidents and heads of state only to turn around and become dictators themselves. He had accepted the invitation to fight with the Séléka not because some people believed the conflict was about the control of diamond, and not because to others it was about religious identity between Muslim Séléka and Christian anti-Balaka, but because of François Bozizé's oppressive position after the Bush War. Ekwe had noticed how much Jafari abhorred oppression. He liked Jafari even more for that and desired to stay by his side. The Nigerian general had touched a soft spot in Jafari when he said that the incumbent president was oppressing the opposition and the rest of the country. Jafari had become so moved he suddenly didn't care about what the job paid.

They boarded a taxi going to Sabon Gari as rickshaws scudded around like excited ants. Two little boys drove a donkey loaded with a heavy hessian sack. Ekwe caught a glimpse of fine golden grains as the cab swept past the donkey.

"Are you a visitor to Kano?" The girl who spoke had a blue-eyed smile and a soft conversational tone. She sat next to Ekwe in the cab, but she was addressing Jafari.

"We're a few days old in this city." Jafari didn't realize his naivety had been so obvious. Instead of telling her, "You are beautiful," he said, "Have you always lived here?"

"I was born here." She wore a blue hijab. The scarf framed her lovely face and complemented her eyes.

They chatted in free-flowing Hausa. He told her he was a Central African. She told him her mother was Kanuri and her father a Shuwa Arab. He didn't know it was not considered haram when hijab-wearing Muslim women shared cab seats with men and chatted freely with them in big cities.

"You know, as they say, no man ever stays alone with a woman, but Satan becomes their third companion," he said.

She laughed unrestrainedly.

Ekwe continued to see the lady's face, its flushed walnut freshness, long after they had dropped out of the cab. The more he mused over her, the more he thought of blossoms in flamboyant reds. They stopped around a textile market. There was too much human traffic here, too much hassle.

The market was full and bubbling. Stalls and warehouses were stacked with bales of textile from floor to ceiling. Ekwe imagined how rich the textile merchants who owned those stalls and warehouses must be. He sometimes dreamed of himself as a rich cattle merchant dressed in fancy clothes with pretty wives and a flock of beggars besieging his mansion for food and charity. Jafari would laugh at his innocent fantasizing. He wasn't really moved by riches. Jafari valued his freedom. He loathed the restrictions riches brought, like not being free to walk into a kantinsayar da giya for a swig and good gossip because he was afraid of enemies. A fly must mingle with excrement.

The sun smouldered down on the crowds, which swallowed them. A turbaned horse rider cantered through a thick human traffic made up of schoolgirls dressed in white hijab outfits. The crowd parted like stage curtains to let the horseman through. Jafari allowed himself to get lost in the transhumance while he imagined the havoc one tiny little explosive could do to the multitude. He had handled bombs before, in Monrovia, he told Ekwe. He once threw an explosive at a congregation in a church in Bangui.

They emerged again in a street and walked into a ramshackle tea shop. Four men were seated on crooked benches around a table crowded with used tins of Bournvita and Coast Milk. The owner of the tea shop, simply called Mai Shai, a slender man with narrow features, was spooning powdered milk into a plastic cup. A kettle sang on a stove fire. He lifted the kettle and poured hot water into the plastic cup. Ekwe watched him as he sent the hot tea into alternate cups to cool it with a precision that amazed Ekwe as he settled down next to Jafari on the bench and waited for the breakfast Jafari had ordered.

"The only way Baba will lose the election is by being rigged out," Mai Shai said in Hausa as he set about making them their cups of tea, speaking to one of his customers.

"This country will go up in flames if that southern infidel attempts to rig Baba out of the election." The man who spoke looked thick and cast his words like granite.

"We will burn their shops and houses and kill all their brothers in this city if the president attempts to do anything stupid," the man sitting next to Ekwe said. A nameless odour issued from him.

Ekwe sniffed himself furtively. He must smell the same way, if not worse, after many days of not bathing or changing clothes. The mercenaries were allowanced before being unleashed from the camp. But lodging in a hotel was no matter for consideration as far as Jafari was concerned. He would rather they live in the street and spend his allowance on beer and cigarettes.

"No one need remind them of what to expect," Mai Shai said.

"There may be reprisals in the South," another man cautioned.

Ekwe looked on as Jafari spent time chatting with unfamiliar people at the tea shop. In a few days, the country would be going to the polls. Ekwe wished for Baba to lose in the elections. Jafari's job as a mercenary would die a stillborn should Baba win. He could tell Jafari had started to like it here. In a rich and turbulent country like Nigeria, survival seemed a matter of instinct, a matter of choice, Jafari kept singing. The tension was tangible. Everyone was talking about the presidential election, how desperately Baba wanted power, deserved it. His posters dominated the city. He flashed his gap-toothed smile from billboards. But Jafari wasn't deceived by the softness of the smile. He saw steel beneath the simper. Everywhere they went, there were the same feelings, the same emotions, and the same intensity. He enjoyed going round and hearing those things. He wondered what people were saying down south. The southern minority seemed very quiet here. He understood why. The big motor spare parts businesses belonged to southerners. So, their silence was a kind of shield. Defensive mechanism. From his conjectures, instances of past violence had made a big impression on the southerners. He reckoned this time they were being cautious, waiting for Election Day to make their choice through the secret ballot system.

Travesty

ELECTION DAY DAWNED CALMLY, WITH AN EARLY sunrise and a mild breeze. The mosque where Ekwe and Jafari slept stood off Independence Road. Most of the shops were closed when they came out, streets deserted, a police Hilux parked down Independence Road. A policeman sat on the bonnet in his black-and-periwinkle-blue uniform. They docked into a back street off Independence Road, found a small café, and sat down to eat breakfast. Jafari kept avoiding the police.

"Aren't you going to vote?" Jafari said to Mai Shai, a hatchet-faced little man, as he stirred their cups of tea.

The man flaunted his index finger stained cobalt with ink. "I already did. I was the second person to vote. What about you? Have you voted?"

"Will do that right after the meal," Jafari said.

The man's questioning gaze fell on Ekwe.

"He is underage," Jafari explained. "He is just around ten."

"But he can vote for Baba," Mai Shai said. "Even those who are younger will all vote for Baba. He must get this victory."

"Anyone who fails to vote for Baba should be considered

an infidel and stoned to death," Hatchet Face said, his brown hooded eyes narrowing.

Jafari agreed completely with him, and because he agreed completely with him, Hatchet Face was moved.

"Don't bother about paying for your tea and that of your son," he said. "Today is a special day, and I am giving out free breakfast. It's my little way of supporting Baba."

Jafari thanked him for the tea and bread, but he thought the man was foolish giving out free breakfast to everyone in support of Baba. A pot half full giving water to a full one, he mused. Jafari had never voted in any elections in his country. If he could not stop the politicians/thieves from stealing the diamond, he wasn't going to help them do it with his vote. He considered politicians thieves. They were after oil, not diamonds, here in Nigeria.

After they finished breakfast, Ekwe followed Jafari to a polling booth, where they mixed up with the crowd and watched long queues of voters. Their eagerness shone on their foreheads and those of the voters. Ekwe observed that half the voters were children and that Hatchet Face had joined the queue again. He wasn't the only voter who returned to cast his vote a second time. Most of the voters voted multiple times.

They left the polling booth. Shops were opening for a lively and sunny afternoon. Jafari drank a few beers and bought Ekwe fried rice. He wondered what Mariya was doing now. She was probably sitting in front of the door working on a washcloth. Bonga was most likely squatting naked across from her, weeping because he wanted more food. He pictured Bonga, stomach ballooning around him like an outsized tube, tears and snot flowing into his mouth. He reckoned Abdelmonin would be chasing, roasting, and eating grasshoppers.

Sirens wailed across the city. Jafari hated deceit, whether it came in the image of Charles Taylor or François Bozizé or a multiple voter or his uncle Ousmane. His uncle Ousmane and his father inherited a strip of land each from their father, one in Bambari city centre and the other in the province. Being the older one and the person to choose first, Jafari's father had chosen the land in the city centre and left the one in the province for Jafari's uncle. But his uncle had persuaded his father to relinquish the city land to him in exchange for his portion in the province. His father had agreed for the love of a brother. His uncle was going to start a small-scale block industry on the strip of land in Bambari and try to grow it, but it turned out to be a trick Ousmane used to get his father to agree to relinquish the city land. After his father had given up ownership of the land to him, his uncle leased it to a telecommunications company to erect their mast for millions of CFA francs. His action had caused bad blood between Jafari's father and his uncle, and Ousmane had cursed his father, causing him to fall sick and die with juju. The man was diabolical. He was evil by Jafari's calculation. After the death of his father, Jafari paid his uncle a little visit in his farmstead. The two had a chat about his father in the lonely farmstead in the middle of the night. It led to an argument, and Jafari shot his uncle, but the bullet didn't penetrate the old man's voodooed body. Jafari became furious. He stripped his uncle of his clothes and talismans, tied him down and wrenched his bony legs apart. He placed the old man's testicles on a large stone. Among the weapons he took to the farmstead he picked a sledgehammer, raised the sledgehammer to the skies, brought it down with all his strength and smashed the man's testicles.

Sai Baba

EKWE AND JAFARI RODE AROUND TOWN IN A TAXI. They weren't going anywhere in particular, only checking the temperature of the city after voting in a country where tension loomed like a giant ukwa tree with large heads of ripened breadfruit. Papa Ekwe had warned him never to stand under an ukwa tree because it was a bad death getting crushed by a falling head of breadfruit. A jovial radio voice wafted through a symphony swinging happily from the cab stereo. *The elections went peacefully across the country. In Kano, the turnout was nothing anyone had witnessed in the history of elections in the country. Men, women, children, and even cattle were given equal opportunities to exercise their civic duties. Several heads of cattle were sighted at polling booths exercising their franchise. That is how popular Baba has grown among man and beast. Baba also had the support of Lagos voters. They covered the polling booths like grains of sand on a beach. Even the paranoid and tribalised Onitsha voters cast their votes for Baba.*

The voice chuckled.

Ekwe closed his eyes. He savoured the lilting melody. He didn't know how to describe how he felt. He seemed afloat—borne on a gentle current downstream. He thought of the blue-eyed Shuwa Arab queen and settings in flamboyant reds. He opened his eyes again and glanced through the car window—the sky had never been bluer. *Having fulfilled your civic rights, we urge you, the good citizens of our beloved country, to remain calm as we await the final results. Do not take laws into your hands, we entreat you, countrymen and women, even if the results do not announce the candidate of your choice as the winner. Do not resort to violence. Be a patriotic citizen and accept the results in the spirit of sportsmanship.*

The radio voice gave way to a reign of symphony. They got down somewhere on France Road. Ekwe would have loved to keep riding and listening to music. He had never enjoyed music before the way he enjoyed that song back in the taxi, but Jafari had emptied his pocket.

"That song outclassed soukous or rumba," Jafari said. "Even cha-cha or merengue is no match. There are good bands in Central Africa, you know. Real good bands: Musiki, Makembe, Cannon Stars, and so on."

No band in the world could compete with Oriental Brothers, Ekwe thought, as they took a slow and aimless stroll. He cherished hearing the highlife band's golden vocals. Somewhere down the road they caught a glimpse of Baba in a long black robe on a street TV outside a bar. He was looking emaciated, almost painfully thin, but warlike. A small crowd had gathered in front of the bar to watch him. The crowd was chanting his support. "Sai Baba. Sai Baba. Sai Baba."

"Have they started announcing the results?" Jafari asked a triangular-faced man in the small crowd in Hausa.

"I heard he is maintaining a clear lead," Triangular Face said in a loud and excited voice. "He most certainly will emerge the winner in a landslide."

"Sai Baba. Sai Baba. Sai Baba," the crowd chanted.

They waited a little and moved on. Ekwe didn't like the news. The Beethoven symphony lingered in his head like light wine. He saw Jafari fish out his mobile and check for text messages or missed calls. There were none. Jafari called Yacine's phone repeatedly, but it was still switched off. The phone had been switched off since they parted ways with Yacine at the camping ground. And Jafari had run out of cash. They would starve in the next few days if the signal to return to Mandara Mountains did not come in.

A thought suddenly pricked Ekwe to attention. If Baba was maintaining a clear lead as Triangular Face had claimed, then the signal might never come. If he won the election, Baba could decide to abandon the mercenaries because he had no more use for them. Ekwe tried to push the thought out of his mind, focusing instead on the worms clamouring in his stomach. Jafari squeezed out the last note in his pocket and stopped to buy akara from a roadside food vendor, a woman with enormous hips that spilled over her short stool. Dark as coal tar, her round face was a network of fierce tribal marks. Her kose scented the air as she cupped bean paste from a squat mortar into a sputtering frying pan.

Ekwe watched with greedy eyes as the kose browned. He liked his kose brownie-brown, he said to the woman.

"I will let your balls linger a little longer in the frying pan," the woman said cheerfully as she spooned the rest of the kose into a bowl.

Ekwe chuckled at the allusion to his balls, at the woman's innocent remark.

The kose remained in the fire until they were almost the

colour of Mariya's skin. It was what drew Jafari to her, Mariya's chocolate skin, the only thing about her that had not changed, the corpse of her once-upon-a-time-audacious beauty. The woman wrapped the balls in an old newspaper. They moved on, eating greedily, Jafari feeling stupid and surprised at the turn of events. He was no stranger to surprises. He remembered the song, the Beethoven symphony, and how it had made him feel like Jean-Bédel Bokassa. But Jean-Bédel Bokassa was not a man to allow hunger to poke needles into his stomach. He was not a man to be fooled twice.

Baba was coasting home to victory. Everywhere in the city crowds gathered to watch the verdict on street TVs, working themselves to frenzy. But the southerners went about their business with a look of stoic resignation. A look that screamed, You have politics, we have commerce. Their renunciation walled across their foreheads, thick as Joe's brow. They seemed to see with Joe's shrewd little eyes and laugh with his unbending voice.

When at last Baba was declared winner, the crowds went mad. They broke up and poured into the streets in wild jubilation. Cars, buses, rickshaws, and motorcycles took to the road in a driving hysteria, horns hooting, human beings hanging dangerously from windows and doors of fast-moving vehicles. Kronenbourg and Bergedorf were drunk freely; bottles, cans, and cigarette butts littered the city. The celebration spilled over to the next day.

It is a victory for all. Cattle broke out of ranches and emptied into the streets in their hundreds in celebration of Baba's victory. You won't believe it: cows drank Kronenbourg, smoked Target, and chanted "Sai Baba, sai Baba" with their human masters. They are excited, apparently sick and tired of ranch life—tired of being imprisoned in barbed wire and fed with straw and chaff. Baba's administration promises to legalize open grazing. It promises to dig out the gazette of the First Republic and vigorously pursue the recovery of grazing routes in states across the country. Cows like good food too. In open grazing, there will be varieties of food for their gastronomic delight: cassava, okra, corn, yam, and so on. They also desire a change of scene. In open grazing, they will live their normal open-air life instead of being imprisoned by some barbed-wire fence. They will enjoy good healthy walks and plenty of oriental air, away from the remorseless Sahara desert sun.

Fugitives

THE JOVIAL VOICE OF THE BROADCASTER WOKE Ekwe up outside a bar on France Road among fallen chairs and tumbled tables. He stared sleepily at the portable radio whose owner lay completely knocked out across from Ekwe and Jafari. The man's kaftan was soiled with vomit. Ekwe peered into a grey and exhausted morning down the broad vista of the road. Other bars had also set up tables outside during the frenzy of the night activity. Ekwe swayed to his feet and smelt his own soured breath. He was forced down on his buttocks again by a throbbing headache. He felt slightly damp with dew. Jafari was sprawled next to him. He was awake. There were others like them all around.

The waiter arrived for the day's business, a thin young man who had locked up in the early hours of the morning, gone home to catch a little sleep, returned refreshed.

"Ina kwana?" he said with a bright smile as he unlocked the door.

"Lafia," Jafari drawled.

"What do I get you? They have been paid for, all the drinks in our supply, and not half of it was consumed last night."

Ekwe grimaced. The idea of drinking another beer was revolting. He belched. His breath reeked.

Jafari yawned and said to the waiter, "Give me Bergedorf."

The waiter laughed. "There is no better cure for hangover than more beer." He returned with a bottle of Bergedorf. "Care for a cigarette? It's all paid for."

"Yeah. Gold Leaf."

The waiter raised his brow at Ekwe.

Hangover drummed a dull ache at the back of Ekwe's head.

Other shops were also opening, mostly bars and restaurants. The city was overcoming its hangover and waking up to a new political dawn. After many decades of the South clinging to power, Baba had finally recaptured it for the northerners. He had wrested it from the South's iron fist like a banana from a monkey's grip.

The beer tasted like poison when Ekwe took a sip.

Jafari smacked his lips as the waiter flicked the TV on and Baba loomed into view like a pine tree, robed in the same satin black. His dressing accentuated his ascetic constitution as he addressed a cross section of journalists. They had chased him down to his hometown for an interview. His kinsmen crowded in the background and cheered him as he spit his feelings out in his thickly accented English, his hard military nuance tempered by intervening gap-toothed smiles.

"Sai Baba. Sai Baba."

A pang of hunger stabbed Ekwe in the stomach. The taste of the beer had changed after he managed to swallow a few mouthfuls. He was now on the second bottle, feeling light, and warm, and starving. The waiter overheard him professing his hunger to Jafari.

"But you can walk into any restaurant and ask for any food of your choice. It's all paid for," the waiter said.

Jafari scanned the road. All they had to do was walk into one of the restaurants, make their choices of food, eat to their satisfaction, and then walk back to the bar for more beers and cigarettes. Wasn't this what life was supposed to be?

"Life has never been so good," he said to the waiter as he finished his drink. "Thank you for giving us the cure to a hangover. My buddy and I are going over there to that restaurant to have ourselves a good breakfast."

▴▴▴▴▴

The celebration lasted the whole week. Ekwe and Jafari enjoyed free drinks, free food, and free cigarettes. But by the second week, excitement began to whittle down. The free gifts started to trickle off. Hunger stole back like a mouse and gnawed at their innards. They had still not heard from Yacine. Jafari had been dialling his number, but as many times as he called, a sensuous and annoying female voice kept asking him to try again later because the number was switched off. Reality was starting to dawn on him. He reckoned he had been taken for a ride. Mariya had warned him. Was Yacine part of the plot? He liked to think otherwise. The truth was Baba had no more use for the mercenaries. Why should he care about a few distractions in place of concentrating on over one hundred and fifty million Nigerians he had just been elected to lead? Still, why had Yacine not at least reached out to explain the situation?

Calm and sanity returned to the streets. Business picked

up again. Bars and restaurants hunched their backs against Jafari and his penniless likes. They wandered around broke. Jafari had never stolen anything. Of course, he didn't consider taking from Mariya stealing, but to continue surviving here, he would need to bend his rules. Going back to Mariya and the kids empty-handed was not an option. The first victim of his hunger, anger, and frustration was a lady he cornered on a lonely back road. He pulled a dagger from under his grey kaftan, tore her handbag off her shoulder, ripped the bag open with the dagger, found nothing but a few useless items of makeup in it, and, angered, charged at the lady with the dagger. Ekwe stood by and gazed at the spectacle as she fled to safety on high heels. For days they roamed the streets and robbed people of their money and possessions. One day, Jafari ambushed a trader around a motor park, and realizing that Ekwe was an accomplice, the man grabbed the boy and raised the alarm, but Jafari quickly stabbed the man to free Ekwe and escape the crowd starting to gather around him like swarmer termites. Now fugitives, they fled Kano with their loot and got on a train to Maiduguri.

A Broken Truce

THEY ARRIVED IN THE CITY OF MAIDUGURI AT night, almost in total darkness, streets half lit by headlamps that fell on the debris of beggars littering culverts and pavements. Ekwe and Jafari easily passed for beggars themselves, having worn one dress each since coming into the country, unwashed, hair uncombed and knotted. With that look of destitution, and reeking of a nameless smell, they checked into a small motel somewhere in Old Maiduguri. They had a bath for the first time in a long time and washed their thick-with-dirt clothes. While Ekwe slept, Jafari sat by the window and smoked and watched the view in its hush and darkness. In the distance, car headlamps swept the night, their light falling on the tower of the great Indimi Mosque.

Ekwe and Jafari were eating breakfast in a local café around a motor park one morning when a small man in a milk-white kanzu entered, sat next to Jafari on a bench, and ordered breakfast in a shrill, tiny voice. He seemed a regular. He looked to be in his twenties and had the dark curly hair and fine thin features of an Afro-Asiatic Fulani. Jafari observed all this as he removed his embroidered cap. The café owner, a large man dressed in a yellow apron, set about making the small man a breakfast. He broke an egg into a dish. He broke a second, a third, and a fourth. Jafari continued sipping his tea in silence. Growing up, he did not have the luxury of eating eggs.

"Hello," the shrill, aggressive voice said in Hausa.

Jafari turned.

"My name is Radaminho, but I am not a Brazilian." The pointed face smiled at him. "You know, Brazilians must have 'inho' suffixed to their names. For instance, a man who is Rashidi is Rashidinho in Brazil. If you are Danlami, you are Danlaminho, and if you are Danladi, you are Danladinho in that football-crazy nation. Now if you tell me your name, I will tell you its Brazilian collocation."

Jafari squinted at him. He didn't miss the cruelty in the dirty white eyes. "I am Jafari."

Radaminho extended his hand and beamed. "It is my pleasure to meet you, Jafarinho."

Jafari laughed heartily and grabbed the small, manicured hand. "This is my buddy Ekwe."

"Then permit me to call your buddy Ekwedinho."

The café owner laughed, and the frying pan hissed loudly, sending out a delicious smell as he sliced onions into it.

Jafari stopped sipping his tea and followed the dirty white eyes to a soldier crossing in front of the café. Radaminho's scowl trailed the camouflaged soldier shouldering an INSAS rifle. He stared at the soldier with a glare as intense as a shooting star until he disappeared behind a screen of commuter buses.

"Dan iska, soja." The shrill voice dropped to a fierce whisper.

The food arrived: an omelette and a large cup of tea.

The small man took a big bite and sipped his tea. A small man who ate big, thought Ekwe, as Radaminho settled on the meal like a fruit fly. The café was getting crowded. Two more customers had strolled in and ordered breakfast, one had a wide face, the other a black patch on his left forehead. Another man entered, looking as flustered as a hen before a hawk. The café owner called him Yerima as he settled on the bench.

"Kosho fell yesterday." Yerima spoke in a ruffled voice. "More than one hundred villagers massacred at the rice fields. Their throats slit."

The café owner lost grip of an onion. It hit the bare floor and rolled outside into a small puddle of dirt.

As Yerima was narrating his story, Ekwe remembered the last Omabe Festival in Enu-Ozara and how Papa Ekwe had tied up a sow and cut her throat and made kebabs for the festival.

The café owner ignored the errant bulb, picked up a new one, and began slicing it into the frying pan in practiced motions. The shrill voice of the frying pan chastised the silence as each man communed with his thoughts.

Radaminho ate in suspicious silence. He was really stuffing his face. It was obvious he didn't combine eating with talking, however grave the subject, so engrossed in his food he missed the camouflaged soldier as he returned.

Jafari was half watching the soldier and half thinking of his son Bonga. He wondered what Bonga had eaten for breakfast.

"Soldiers everywhere, but they are doing nothing to stop

the violence," Wide Face said as the café owner delivered a plate of omelette to him and returned quietly to his warm, sputtering corner.

Ekwe listened as the men ate and routinely discussed prey and predators. Radaminho had finished his large breakfast. He was cleaning his hands and mouth with a serviette. Ekwe had expected him to put in a word or two into the conversation. But he grinned smugly at Jafari.

"I am going to have a smoke. Mind joining me? Your buddy can come along."

Jafari didn't mind.

"*The Tricky Jester, you leave your shame at the door. The new places, you have to comb your hair and put on perfume just to get a drink. Times change, you know. World going one way, people another.*" Radaminho's voice rang with enthusiasm as he recited the quote. "I read and write English," he said. "I read those lines from Kevin Jared Hosein's story. He is a writer who writes in Trinidadian and Tobagonian English, awfully talented." He tapped his forehead to remember the title of the award-winning short story. "The story is named 'Passage.' I am not sure I could ever forget the title of such a powerful story anyway. The Tricky Jester is where I am taking you two."

He took them to an underground bar, one of the few surviving bars in the old city, obviously owned by a politician with powerful connections. The state had banned the sale of alcohol and smoke outside of military barracks and Mammy Markets, their idea of fighting insurgency in the city, so Maiduguri had no nightlife. The bar was quiet and poorly lit. Customers walked in, sat in dingy corners, and called for a drink. A few lovers swayed to African pop tracks rumbling in the hall.

They sat down and called for drinks and cigarettes.

A few teeth peeked at Jafari in the suspicion of a smile as Radaminho said, "Pardon my asking. You are new in town, aren't you?"

"Yeah," Jafari said. "We have been around for a few days."

"I thought as much."

"The name sounds Chadian," Jafari said.

"I am a Chadian/Nigerian. What about you?"

"A Central African. My buddy is Nigerian."

"Oh. Tell me about the Bush War."

Jafari started to explain that Séléka, which was a coalition of five separate rebel groups, had launched its insurgency accusing Bozizé of reneging on a 2007 peace deal meant to provide jobs and money to insurgents who had laid down their weapons.

"Renege." Radaminho scowled. "That's one word drives me crazy."

Jafari took a sip of beer and smacked his lips.

"I have watched you with interest these past few days," Radaminho said.

Jafari said he hadn't realized someone was watching him.

"I think I like you."

Jafari chuckled. He felt himself reddening in the face.

"I am not gay, though." Radaminho grinned at him. "The universe is yet to see the worst from the Western world. Today a man marries a man, and a woman weds another woman, and I will not be shocked if tomorrow they legalize marriage between human beings and animals, considering how they are romancing dogs!"

Jafari laughed.

"I have a proposal for you, but first I would like to know you more. Who are you?"

Jafari narrowed his eyes.

"It's fine if you don't feel like talking about yourself."

Jafari shrugged. "It's not a narrative that would interest just anyone." He told him anyway.

"Why should people renege on their word?" Radaminho mumbled as if talking to himself. "That's something I can't seem to comprehend, people making promises and breaking those promises without any scruples."

"We seem to have something in common," Jafari said.

"Yeah." He paused to take a draw at his cigarette. "My grandfather migrated up from Chad. He came into the country as a mercenary, hired to fight in the Nigerian Civil War on the side of Nigeria."

Jafari shifted in his seat, eyes kindling with interest.

"At the end of the war, the government failed to keep to the terms of the contract. My grandfather—who, along with many other mercenaries, had been hired from neighbouring countries to help the Nigerian government poised to lose the war against the determined and resourceful combatant Biafra—found himself stranded and impoverished. The mercenaries went through hell trying to survive in a foreign country fresh from a civil war, which lasted up to three years. Many of those who survived the war among the mercenaries later died of hardship and neglect. Others like my grandfather managed to survive the storm." He paused and drank down his Kronenbourg. He also lit another stick of Gold Leaf and blew smoke into the fuzzy room.

Jafari listened closely. Ekwe sat away from them, engrossed in the music, nodding to the groovy percussion of Fela's *Zombie* wafting from woofer speakers and thinking about his sister, wondering if she had married any of her peasant suitors.

"They are a team of embittered veterans who are nursing a grievance against the Nigerian government. Some of them were able to break into the economy and the corridors of power. They came together and vowed to avenge the injustice perpetrated against them by the Nigerian government. They want to make things a bit uncomfortable for the country. My grandfather is among this vengeance-seeking gang of powerful old men. Somehow, he had found his way into the military after the war. His opportunity came during the military interregnum in the eighties. He got involved in the succession of coups d'état symbolizing that period in history and ushering in the nineties. He rose up in the military hierarchy."

Jafari was now so entranced in the story he accidentally let his cigarette burn out.

"My father is a general. He was born five years before the war. My grandfather had gone back to Chad to bring his family soon after he resettled in the foreign country. His proximity to the successive governments had influenced my father's success in the military. I am a lieutenant in the army. I was commissioned two years ago after passing out of the Nigerian Defence Academy. I went AWOL at the request of my grandfather and his allies. They wanted me to work for them. I accepted because I hate deceit, and because the blood of the mercenaries who died of hunger and starvation cries out for vengeance." He paused to finish his beer and ordered another one.

Jafari was already on his fifth, Ekwe still on his first, now trying out a cigarette and struggling to smother a fit of coughing.

"I am recruiting men for this mission—men like you who are themselves victims of man's inhumanity to man. Up to twenty-five hundred men are being mobilized for the mission. We are looking for men who bear bitter grudges against this godforsaken, treacherous country. The man who was declared winner of the election was part of the deception. Our mission is to make his fraudulent government accountable for his atrocities."

When the beer arrived, he broke off, tore the cork off with his teeth, and took a large swig from the bottle.

"Let me know what you think of the proposal. You will be handsomely rewarded. Already we have several men out there in various disguises, some as cowherds and others as plain bandits, but with one purpose, which is to make the country generally ungovernable."

Jafari gave his beer a swig. It was not yet noon and he had downed five bottles of beer. He was surprised he was still clearheaded.

"Did I tell you I have a family, a wife and children?" Jafari said slowly, and tapped ash into a heart-shaped tray. "I was becoming one big liability to Mariya. I needed to get away for a break. I knew I would return to her despite her grossness. She doesn't give me trouble, and she doesn't snore." He laughs. "My boys are big eaters. I had hoped to make some money so they could have varieties to eat and not stuff themselves on cassava. I accepted the job that brought me to this country because I had hoped that when I get paid, I would have something to take home to my family. I had hoped to give Mariya a fat and graceful meaning to life. I wanted to be a better father to my children and a better man to Mariya, but my hopes were dashed. Yacine brought me out to this wilderness and abandoned me in the cold. So, tell me, what would you do if you were me with a proposal like this on the table in front of you?"

The Goddess Lamashtu

THEY DROVE ALL THE WAY TO BAGA, A TOWN IN THE peninsula extending into Lake Chad, in Radaminho's Pontiac. They arrived in the afternoon. The sun burned as Radaminho slowed down near a road market and pulled in under a large banyan tree in front of a mosque. Some traders were chatting away a sweaty afternoon on mats unfurled under the tree whose dense foliage cast a wide shadow and served as a parking lot for cars. They hailed Radaminho as he climbed out of the car. He seemed quite popular here, Ekwe thought, as he looked around the market that spilled to the other side of the road at piles of sugarcanes, plastic buckets, pillows, mattresses, and other wares on display in shop fronts. Young slender girls who wore hijab and ostentatious makeup moved around hawking fura da nono. Upon sighting Radaminho as he alighted, a band of Almajirai invaded his car. He waved a food vendor over and paid for everything she was selling. Ekwe watched the Almajirai as they pounced on the food like cats.

They walked through a dirt track beside the mosque, Ekwe closely following Radaminho and Jafari. A sprawling complex loomed into view. The steel roll-up door of the complex told Ekwe it was a warehouse. A youth dressed in an off-white yukata materialized. He prostrated himself before Radaminho and Jafari and scowled at Ekwe. Following Radaminho's instructions, the youth led them to the heavy-duty steel door. He unlocked the door and pulled it open. Dunlop mattresses were neatly stacked from floor to ceiling. He led them through a dark aisle, lighting the way with his torchlight. The path was so narrow they had to walk single file between a stockpile of mattresses. About fifty metres into the warehouse, they came to another steel door. The youth had to move mattresses aside to reveal this second door. He unlocked and pulled the door up. And then he flashed his torchlight.

Jafari staggered back.

He had been wondering why Radaminho brought them there, but now as the youth opened this steel door, in place of Dunlop latex mattresses, a dark mountain of weaponry and ammunition confronted them. Before bringing them to the cache, Radaminho had driven Jafari and Ekwe to his residence—a sprawling estate sitting on a five-acre land on the north bank of Ngadda River, with an Olympic-size swimming pool, a landscaped garden, and cascading fountains. They had followed him into an exquisite interior with marble floors, high-tech furniture, and walls with a mirror finish. They had entered a room, brightly lit to reveal a fierce female figure kneeling on an ass and holding a double-headed serpent in each hand. Had they not been led to it, Jafari would never have guessed that a spine-chilling altar of that nature existed in this age and time. Of all the places the shrine could have found a home, it was in a mansion of that class. Radaminho took them there and made them swear an oath of loyalty to the goddess Lamashtu.

▲▲▲▲▲

"Grab something to protect yourselves with." Radaminho's voice brought Jafari back to the present as he waved them to the array of weaponry.

Ekwe was frightened. He didn't want a gun, but Jafari grabbed a fully loaded handgun, a .500 Smith & Wesson Magnum, from the piles of arms and ammunition. He lifted his kaftan and shoved the revolver into his pocket.

"That cache contains over fifty tons of explosives," Radaminho said as they left the warehouse and walked back to the car.

Jafari whistled. "Are you planning to start another world war?"

Radaminho chuckled. "If ever there will be another world war, it is going to originate from the Persian Gulf," he said. "But with the biological agents in existence today, and with nuclear enrichment programs, there's potential for absolute destruction of the human race."

Jafari didn't have any reason to doubt him.

"Let's go see the ranch."

They climbed back into the car. Jafari felt in his pocket for the handgun as he got in beside Radaminho. Ekwe sat behind while they drove about nine miles inland to a ranch that stretched towards a small hill.

"My grandfather owns it," Radaminho said. "He owns ranches everywhere in this region."

They drove through the wrought iron gates. Ekwe scanned the ranch as they alighted from the car. It was extensive, the cattle seemingly numberless. A well-water faucet stretched its long neck like a crested grebe outside a small ranch house in the distance. Beyond the barbed-wire fence the wind kicked up dust devils in the middle of barren plains. The workers prostrated themselves in greeting as Radaminho took them around.

"You should select any twenty heads of cattle of your choice," Radaminho said. "It's your start-off payment. The cows are a safe way to convey the arms and ammunition that will be allocated to you. Two herders are also allocated to you. We have an endless reservoir of teenagers, Almajirai who are eager for adventure. You can have more than the two allocated to you, but at no extra cost to us; the extras are your responsibility. Go to any place of your choice, create tensions, burn down government installations, and bring down whole communities if you can. Call for reinforcements, if necessary, but always remember you are on oath to be loyal to your employers. You will lose your life the day you go against that oath. Lamashtu is an unforgiving Mesopotamian goddess and the most terrible of all female demons. She slays children and drinks the blood of men and eats their flesh."

Jafari lit a cigarette and tried to look at the bigger picture. Some people in the corridors of power who bore a grudge against the government were spending hundreds of millions, probably billions, in arms and logistics, just so they could settle an old score. How logical was this? Who was Radaminho? What was the content of the truth in all that he had said? Jafari suddenly had a funny feeling. The story of Radaminho's Chadian grandfather could be falsified. Who was he working for, and what was their goal?

He shrugged. It made no difference if Radaminho was working for a team of vindictive, disgruntled elements who set out to sabotage the government or a powerful cartel whose agenda was a total coup. What mattered was that he had been deceived, and working for Radaminho would not only enrich him but also satisfy his lust for revenge. Jafari was five years old when his father left the mountain region for Sudan with his second and favourite riverine wife. Jafari had turned fifteen and was living with his Isungu mother in their mountain home where he was raised without eating omelettes when news came of his father's passing. He hoped to return to his homeland richer and more responsible to his family than his father had ever been to his mother and him.

The King of Trees

EKWE AND JAFARI SET FORTH A WEEK LATER WITH A herd of twenty cattle and two youths, Garba and Mandla. They kept to the expressway, which was the most direct route to the eastern bank of the Niger River. Boko Haram was already dominating the northern region, so Radaminho was pushing more mercenaries down south. Garba was seventeen and Mandla eighteen, but they both looked dangerous and could handle guns. They watched over the cattle and cooked for the team. Jafari handled the arms and ammunition tied to the backs of the cattle in burlap sacks. And he took hostages. Ekwe helped with little things. When a new hostage arrived and Garba and Mandla were busy tending to the cattle and Jafari was indulging in a nap, Ekwe watched the hostage tied to a stake.

Wushishi was their first stopover, where they spent weeks in a forest bordering the town, where the raptor snatched prey and flayed them for their beautiful wool. In Koton-Karfe, their next stop, the raptor preyed on lambs along Abaji-Koton-Karfe Road, dragged them into the eyrie of owls, copulated with their females, and generally fed on their mutton.

"Welcome to our humble abode," Jafari said as he walked

a lad of not more than sixteen years old into their middle-of-nowhere shelter in Koton-Karfe—a hut of bamboo sticks and dry jaragua grass—one afternoon.

The boy cowered in fear.

"The good thing is that he understands Hausa, so language is not going to be a problem," Jafari said to Ekwe, Garba, and Mandla, who were stretched out on mats. "These are my friends," he said to the boy. "Feel at home. You can sit anywhere."

Jafari went and settled next to Ekwe in the beautiful shade of a marula tree. The boy chose to sit on bare ground. He looked to Ekwe like a rich lad with his shining coffee-brown skin and an overgrown constitution.

"Oh, you didn't tell me your name." Jafari placed a gun by his side.

"Ezuhio," the lad said in a trembling voice.

"No one is going to hurt you if you follow instructions, Ezuhio." Jafari lit a cigarette. "I need you to answer a few questions." He hissed in smoke. "Tell me. Who is your father?"

The boy said his father was Agabaidu, a local Egbira chief. He was his father's youngest son.

"You have been abducted, but you don't have to worry," Jafari said. "You are in safe hands. Let me have your phone. I want to speak to your father. I will let you go if he gives me what I want. Everyone is happy, right?"

The boy gave him his smartphone.

Jafari studied the phone and showed it to Ekwe. "Big fine phone," he said. "I am sure your father will be able to give me what I want. We will give him a call. I will let you go back to your family so long as he gives me what I want, but that will be later; for now, I am going to get some rest. You have something to eat and get some rest too."

He finished his weed, crushed it out, stretched out on the mat, turned his back, and was soon snoring. He woke up hours later, went to an enamel pot sitting on huge stones, and spooned sorghum onto two plates. He took one plate and passed the other to Ezuhio, who declined the food.

"I am sorry if you don't like the food," Jafari said. "Unfortunately, that's what we can afford."

He ate in silence. When he finished, he lit a cigarette and passed the phone to the boy.

"Call your father," he said. "Put the phone on speaker. Tell him what has happened to you. Tell him we are in the middle of nowhere. Tell him we gave you sorghum to eat, but you rejected it because you don't like sorghum. Of course, he knows you don't like sorghum, right, but it's the only food we can afford in this bush. Tell him you don't want to starve. And then give back the phone."

The boy did as he was told. His father's thick voice almost tore the phone's speaker as he spoke in frantic Egbira. The boy's mother whimpered in the background.

"Your son is my guest." Jafari broke into the dew-eyed telephone reunion in Hausa. "I need you to give me five million naira if you want to see him again. He doesn't like sorghum, and it happens to be the only food we have in this middle of nowhere, so the earlier you give me what I want, the better for everyone, so he won't starve. Don't try to look for him, because you will never find him. And don't bother calling this phone again, because I am going to turn it off right after this conversation. I will call to let you know how you will get the money to me." He ended the call, lay back on the mat, and hissed in smoke fiercely.

The wood was bathed in the weak rays of a falling sun. A mile from their hideout or so stood a large tree in the middle of a champaign; that was the nearest another tree grew next to this tree. The singularity of the tree had struck Ekwe with wonder the first time he saw it standing in isolation in the thick surrounding bush. He was sure the tree was anunuebe.

"Anunuebe is the king of trees, and it's a no-perch for any bird," Papa Ekwe had said. "It's the most powerful and feared tree in the world, a natural oracle, and, when the spirit residing in it is out wandering, that's the only time any human can get close to it. Its bark and root are widely used in the preparation of potent charms. They can cure leprosy and even worse diseases, but it takes blood sacrifices and incantations by a strong dibia to approach the tree for their powerful herbs."

Ekwe tried to warn Jafari about this mysterious tree when he chose to collect Ezuhio's ransom there, but Jafari insisted it was the best place for the handoff. The tree stood in a wide-open area, in the middle of the forest, offering no hiding place for the cops. Besides, the distance between the anunuebe and the far tree line made it impossible for an arrow to travel that stretch to hit a target. And it would take a sniper from Hollywood to pick Jafari from that distance using a high-precision rifle and not the dane gun policemen used in this country.

Jafari approached the tree with caution, not out of the fear of its mysticism, which to him was mere superstition, but out of the wariness of a man committing a crime. The bag stood temptingly at the foot of the tree. He saw it clearly as he approached. He stopped, his heart lurching, his eyes sweeping around the llano down the far tree line. He knew that Ekwe and Mandla were watching the tree from a distance. Earlier they had seen a man drop the bag and hurry away. The man was unaccompanied, so it seemed safe for Jafari to pick up the money.

A few quick steps brought Jafari to the bag. He paused to think about Mariya and the children. When all this was over, he would go home and take them on holiday trips to Quirimbas Archipelago in Mozambique, and to Bom Bom Island in São Tomé and Principe. He did not know those places. He only heard about them in Joe's Bush Bar gossip. But with money, all things were possible.

Jafari leaned forwards to grab the bag, but as he straightened, pain—hot and searing—tore through his left shoulder.

A Raging Wildfire

EKWE DISAGREED WITH GARBA'S THEORY THAT WHO-ever shot Jafari with a bow had hidden in the canopy of the anunuebe and watched him walk up and try to grab the bag with Ezuhio's ransom. Ekwe had watched the tree with Mandla. The only man who came anywhere close to the tree, the man who dropped the ransom, had left at once. So where did it come from, the arrow that sank into Jafari's left shoulder as though into soft banana stem, narrowly missing his head? Ekwe was sure it was the hands of karma that drew the bow, because anunuebe was a sacred tree.

Jafari suffered a hemorrhage. The wound got bad because he did not have the balls to show his face in a hospital. It festered. He became delirious and called Ekwe Bonga, and said that Mariya was a bad, greedy wife. He was going to die. But Garba and Mandla bundled his half-conscious body to a hospital at the last minute. They got Radaminho involved with a phone call, and he invoked his powers and connection to get rid of the infected arm without the police nosing in.

Thinking about it now, the buildup to the loss of his arm and how careless he had been, anger violated Jafari's stomach, climbed into his nose, and nearly suffocated him. And then it hid frozen in his heart. He longed to return to Mariya and the kids. He imagined Mariya standing at the door with hands on hips and mouth agape, watching him as he approached. He wasn't expecting a bear hug from her, coming home deformed. But he had another worry besides Mariya's shock. His long absence must have left her in oestrus. He pondered ways to make up for his lost limb and the sperm spilt into hostages. He could make love to her leaning on one arm. Mariya was old-fashioned about sex. She insisted the man stays atop. He thought of their countless couplings in the flattened, bedbug-infested mattress, his buttocks clenching and unclenching, and Mariya moaning and gulping his sweat. He chuckled at the idea of swapping places now that he was one-handed—a bottom-up position—with Mariya making a song of moaning then crashing down on him like a cow with one last monolith gasp. It sounded like a suicide mission.

Meanwhile, Ekwe became terrified of Jafari after the amputation of his arm. Jafari grew as sore as a beast caught in a trap. The lust to tear and rip with its beak and sharp talons tempted the raptor's palate like a new flavour. Jafari, a raging wildfire, tore a path through the rainforests of Igboland and left a trail of destruction. Their current location—a landscape marked by hills and mangroves—bore every resemblance to Ekwe's hometown of Enu-Ozara. The houses were of a piece, in equal parts tin and thatch, and mud and cement. Ekwe's sense of familiarity became stronger as they walked through village squares where old men sat dressed in rags. The old men stared at the cattle and their drivers with disapproving eyes. They passed groups of young men coming from the farm, their eyes glinting with hostility. Women walked with loads on their heads and babies strapped to their backs or sitting on their hips. Tiredness shone through their sweat-slick foreheads. He looked at the passersby closely for recognition. His family was probably at the habanero farm working without his sister, who was probably now living with a husband. There was a smell, an earthy smell of loam and manure. Ekwe remembered that Enu-Ozara had smelt the same way. Mornings smelt of rich loam, spiced winds blew the aroma of habanero into the nose in the afternoons, and the rhythms of pestles and mortars echoed through nights scented with supper flavours.

ꜛꜛꜛꜛꜛ

Trouble started one afternoon when Jafari stopped to buy cigarettes from a stocky shop owner who at first glance looked like Joe.

"Which Joe?" Stocky shop owner gave Jafari and Ekwe a vacant stare.

Jafari had asked him if he was related to a certain Joe who lived in Central Africa. He lit his cigarette and dismissed the man, realizing that Igboland was a vast nation that spread across many states.

Garba and Mandla were haggling with a motorcyclist when Ekwe and Jafari rejoined them on the village road. It was a common occurrence, cowherds getting into strife with motorists for obstruction, but in this case, it was brewing more tension than Jafari considered necessary. More motorcyclists were arriving, a mob collecting, hostility and aggression growing. And then someone struck a cow with a thick stick. The animal went down on its knees with a great moo of pain. The rest of the mob had been waiting for someone to take the first shot. They darted around for sticks and descended on the cattle like a swarm of angry bees.

The action of the mob set Jafari off like a fully loaded cannon. He craved vengeance. He promised himself that the whole community would pay for the assault. He called Radaminho and spoke with him for a long time about revenge. Ekwe remembered that Radaminho had asked him to call for reinforcement if needed, which Jafari had never considered doing until now, obviously because he had not carried out any assignments that involved complicated planning, like attacking a government institution or blowing up a national installation. They had been in transit to the southeast, and now that they had arrived at their base, Jafari wanted to pull off his first major assignment of bringing down an entire community.

One week after Jafari spoke with Radaminho, reinforcement arrived in the form of a band of mercenaries with cardboard boxes of weapons delivered to Jafari in a trailer load of cattle. The long fourteen-tyre MAN diesel had set off from the cattle ranch in Baga under the guise of transporting cattle to the South. But the trailer was loaded with only half a dozen cattle, making room for a dozen men and several boxes of weapons. The trailer had charged like a bull through the night expressway, its merchandise hidden under a thick tarpaulin cover. The driver had stopped at military checkpoints to shove bribes into the hands of local boys who acted as secret collection agents while the soldiers pretended to inspect the vehicle. The government had replaced police checkpoints with military checkpoints in its desperate effort to combat crime and corruption—monsters it had created—but the soldiers were proving to be more corrupt than the police. After discharging weapons and mercenaries, the truck headed off to a cattle market in Obollo Afor to sell the cattle and return to Baga.

There was no moon on the night Jafari planned the ambush. The community was full of darkness, and then an orange flame suddenly rose, swirled, and then illuminated a peaceful setting punctuated by the sound of sleep—a deep universal snore. The flame lit up a looming of owls. They formed a patch of dark clouds in the sky. As the flame consumed the sheepfold, and a thousand bleats fed from the silence, the night air went rancid with the stench of fleece roasting. Suddenly the raptors descended from their thermal and feasted on the lambs as they half burned, half fled the sheepfold.

Book Three

Bad Omen

A GIANT SPIDER SWAYED INTO FOCUS, A BLACK widow spinning a web between bamboo rafters as Ekwe opened his eyes to the faint pops and cracks of spent holocaust. He felt confused and dizzy. Slowly he came back to life, realized that he was lying on his mat, bathed in sweat, in the room he shared with Mama Ekwe, Oyibo, Azuka, and his twin brothers. He sat up. The room was empty, except for the twins still slumbering. Daylight poured in through countless openings in the rusty tin roof. Was it really a dream? He gasped at its violence, its vividness. In just one night he had traversed the universe, bonding with characters who felt real to him even now.

He came to the door and surveyed the early-morning scene. The clouds hung low and motionless in the hot air. He went behind the house to pee as he did every morning just after waking up, stood under the eaves, and plucked out his penis. As the bright colourless liquid shot forwards with fluid consistency, arced across the water line, and dug a hole in the garden, he shut his eyes. When he opened them, his eyes wandered to the sheepfold, where it lay rusting at the back of the house. It had been in that state of dilapidation for a long time. Some of the wooden poles had caved in due to heavy rain and wood lice. They were crumbling, pulling down the wire-gauze fence. Crows cawed from a baobab tree whose thick canopy hid the line of Papa Ekwe's banana plantation and yam barn in the background.

Mama Ekwe, Azuka, and Oyibo were getting ready for the farm. Ekwe thought about talking to Mama Ekwe about the strange things that happened to him in the night, in the hope that he might be spared working that day. He decided to talk to Papa Ekwe instead. Papa Ekwe was more likely to see that he needed a rest after his epic wanderings.

"Did you touch ekwukwonju?" Papa Ekwe looked at him narrowly after Ekwe finished narrating his experience, surprised that much of it had vanished and he struggled to articulate the few details he remembered.

He was not expecting Papa Ekwe's question. It had not crossed his mind that touching the forbidden leaf could have caused all this. He remembered feeling strange after they went to bed, drifting off into a transitional state of consciousness.

Mama Ekwe overheard Ekwe and Papa Ekwe and came to stand with hands on her hips, reproach burning in her eyes. Ekwe tensed up. Papa Ekwe was more condoning than Mama Ekwe and less likely to spank his first son, who had arrived after several years of marriage and desperation for an heir.

"Answer the question," Mama Ekwe snapped. "Did you touch ekwukwonju?"

He nodded.

Only Papa Ekwe's presence stopped Mama Ekwe from springing at him.

"What he experienced may seem like a dream." Papa Ekwe looked unsettled. "When he touched that mystical leaf, ekwukwonju provoked his ascension to the astral realm. It induced his soul to depart from his physical body and enter the astral body to travel in a plane. Some people who have experienced this have ended up dead because their astral bodies wandered away and never reentered their physical bodies. We are lucky that in his case Ekwe has a powerful chi who guided his spirit back to his body after astral projecting into the future."

"What about the owl that kept following him?" Mama said. "I know that evil bird is a bad omen."

Papa Ekwe looked down. "I am afraid things are not looking good for our community."

The Suitor

THE SUITOR SWALLOWED WHITE HORSE AND scratched his bald head as he narrated the story of how Nimbo fell.

"The ambush was carried out by over five hundred armed militia believed to be Fulani cowherds," he said. "I went there to see things for myself. I met the village in ruins."

Silence fell as softly as cigarette ash.

Papa Ekwe wore a big scowl. His calloused hands were folded under his chin.

Mama Ekwe hissed. A cold and creepy feeling stole up her arms.

Ekwe's big stepmother moaned from the door where she sat in the body of a muturu cow.

Ekwe sat with chin cupped in hand. Going by the suitor's description, Nimbo fell to a holocaust, the same way the sheepfold was engulfed in flames on his astral plane. Papa Ekwe had said that the people Ekwe met were human beings from the physical world travelling through that plane of existence, and the things that happened in that realm were revealed to Ekwe as they would happen in the natural world.

Ekwe knew that Oyibo and Azuka were eavesdropping from the window. This was not the kind of story a girl liked to hear from her suitor on a day he came to propose marriage. What did a girl like Oyibo or Azuka or any other maiden in Enu-Ozara for that matter care about conflicts with cowherds?

"Are there survivors?" Papa Ekwe said in a shrill voice.

The suitor did not think there were any. "The militants were waiting with deadly weapons to finish off those who half burned and half fled."

Papa Ekwe made a gesture of revulsion, something he always did magically with his fingers to produce a rhythmic series of clicking sounds.

Mama Ekwe rubbed the goose pimples that had broken out on her wiry forearms.

Although he suddenly blanked on the details of his astral experience, Ekwe faintly remembered the owls circling in a thermal and then descending to prey on the half-burning, half-fleeing lambs.

"Did you know?" the suitor said. "They sent a threatening letter to your king. The cowherds are coming to attack this village."

Mama Ekwe threw her hands in the air as if to show off the tufts of hair darkening her armpits.

The cow in Ekwe's big stepmother mooed softly.

"Odiegwu," grunted Papa Ekwe. "Is this how we shall end up, ambushed in our sleep and roasted alive?"

Ekwe was thinking of the winged termites they sometimes woke up to find amassing in the middle of the night—swarming around the faintest gleam of light—only to be collected and roasted the next morning for their gastronomic delight.

"No wise king allows cowherds into his community," the suitor said. "They will harvest your crops and feed them to their cattle. And then they will do to you what they did to the people of Nimbo if you try to fight back."

"Aah," Papa Ekwe groaned.

Ekwe's siblings and half-siblings, children aged between four and six, naked with hands on small hips and noses oozing with snot, gathered and stared at the suitor in awe.

"What are we going to do?" Ekwe's big stepmother's voice was bovine with panic.

"We don't have anywhere to flee," Mama Ekwe cried.

"You don't have to flee just anywhere." The suitor's voice was laced with pride and dignity, his laughter fruity as if broken off a twang of blind Nkwa's ukulele. "I have a house in the city. It's large and comfortable enough for your whole household. That's the least I can do for the family of the woman I love in war times."

Ekwe sensed deceit. His sister was not even a full-grown woman. She was only two years older than Ekwe. This suitor was not the first man to want to marry her, he wasn't the only bald old man with a large nose and Adam's apple who had ever wanted his sister's hand in marriage, but he was the only suitor who came to their house in a red motorcar with white seats—a fine big red motorcar with a hot metallic smell—and drank White Horse with Papa Ekwe.

Papa Ekwe summoned Oyibo after the suitor was gone. He wanted a yes-or-no answer to the suitor's proposal.

"No," Oyibo said curtly.

"You have until tomorrow to give me your final answer," Papa Ekwe said.

Oyibo cowered before Papa Ekwe before giving him her final answer again. "No."

"O gini? What are your reasons?"

"I want to continue in school."

"Aah." Papa Ekwe chuckled. "Of what use is school without banknotes?"

Papa Ekwe was right, Ekwe thought. Of what use was school to his sister without a big red motorcar?

"He is old, and his nose is too big. He is ugly." Oyibo wrinkled her nose as if the suitor excreted a bad smell.

Ifugo, thought Ekwe. So that was it. The truth was finally out. She did not want to marry her suitor because of his nose. It was because he had a nose as flat and wide as that of a Sanga cow.

Papa Ekwe said, "My daughter, you didn't have to put on a face like that. We are talking about a human being, not a toad."

Ekwe chuckled.

"Besides, a man is only ugly if his pocket is empty," added Papa Ekwe

"He has other wives," Oyibo protested, and threw Ekwe a glare.

"It doesn't matter as long as he takes good care of them," Papa Ekwe insisted. "If you don't marry a man as his first wife, you will marry him as a second or even a third or fourth wife. The African man has a right to polygamy. My daughter, you will marry him because you will be the most foolish girl in this village to throw away such an opportunity for some other girl to grab. You should be thinking of a good husband and a home full of children for yourself. You don't want to end up like Eliza, the daughter of Orinechi, who eloped and became an okuenu."

Papa Ekwe's voice was curt and final.

Oyibo stomped her feet and pouted, because to have your way with a father like Papa Ekwe, this was all it usually took—stomp your feet and pout—but Papa Ekwe stood his ground, solid as a hill.

Ekwe figured nothing would move Papa Ekwe besides his sister's consent to marry the suitor with the big red motorcar, because their lives were under threat by cowherds, and he had offered them a shoulder to lean on.

Papa Ekwe threw Mama Ekwe an eloquent eye: Woman, talk sense into your daughter.

Mama Ekwe hissed and looked away, as was her habit.

"So, you are not in support of your daughter marrying her suitor," Papa Ekwe said. "Is this what we are going to bed with?"

"I didn't say so," Mama Ekwe said.

"Then say something."

Mama Ekwe hissed and looked away again.

Mama Ekwe normally hissed at Oyibo's peasant suitors when they turned their backs. And then she would follow this up with a greasy sideswipe at Papa Ekwe: "God forbid that my daughter should marry a man who labours in the farm from dawn to dusk." She would pause and look her tall bony self over with disdain. "Look at me! I didn't used to be this bony, but see how the stress of farmwork ate up my flesh, all because I married a poor peasant!"

Papa Ekwe shrugged. "Ngwanu. All right. Go to bed and sleep on it, all of you."

Ekwe went to bed, and, in his dream, Papa Ekwe begged Oyibo to marry the suitor and save the family from cowherds, but Oyibo stomped her feet and pouted, and Mama Ekwe hissed like a cobra, and the suitor formed into a virus in Papa Ekwe's bloodstream, and no matter how hard Oyibo stomped, Papa Ekwe would not bulge.

Fresh-Planed Mahogany

MEN SCRAMBLED FOR OYIBO'S HAND IN MARRIAGE. The endless stream of suitors were attracted to her smooth mahogany skin and large luminous eyes. She inherited them from Papa Ekwe. The suitors were pulled to her the way flying termites drew lizards with their water-coloured wings. Ekwe resented her for running off with the best attributes of their parents. She stole everything good and left him with Mama Ekwe's coarse oil-bean skin and Papa Ekwe's square forehead. While she was growing skywards like Mama Ekwe, Ekwe was circling back to Earth, round as Papa Ekwe. She'd probably grow into a bony woman like Mama Ekwe. Perhaps thin girls like her grew into tall bony women who happily worked in the farm after rejecting a suitor who rode in a big red motorcar and drank White Horse.

"I like his big red motorcar," Ekwe said in a little secret conversation with Mama Ekwe and Oyibo and Azuka in the room they shared.

Oyibo flung him a hard look.

"Mother." Ekwe's eyes sparkled with hope. "Can I ask him for rice?"

"Don't," Mama Ekwe snapped at him. "You will not bring shame to this family."

"Rice, that's all you care about," Azuka spat at him.

"He may be rich, but he is the only suitor who planted malice like a tree in this house." Mama Ekwe hissed.

Ekwe did not know any tree called malice. He knew the neem tree standing in the middle of their compound. Mama Ekwe plucked its leaves and boiled malaria solution for him or anyone who had fever in the family. Papa Ekwe planted many trees long before Ekwe was born. He did many things before and after Ekwe's birth, some good and some bad. He also made many mistakes, like marrying three wives and fathering many hungry children.

"Mother, where is the malice tree?" Ekwe gave Mama Ekwe a puzzled look.

"O bu atu." Mama Ekwe laughed. "You don't know a thing about metaphors."

Ekwe got more confused. Sometimes Mama Ekwe spoke in tongues, like Onukwu the village clown, who said that Mama Ekwe did not need an oil lamp to see around her anymore because Oyibo's skin could lighten up the darkness that covered Enu-Ozara at night like a pod. Driven by curiosity, Ekwe had put out the oil lamp while Oyibo was fast asleep to test her luminosity. He nearly broke his nose on the doorpost as he blundered his way around the dark room. Mama Ekwe laughed long and loud afterwards, because Ekwe didn't know a thing about metaphors.

Onukwu was also the first person to call Ekwe's sister Oyibo instead of Oodo, the name Papa Ekwe had given to her. Because Onukwu had nicknamed her Oyibo after her birth, everyone called her Oyibo up to this time, including those who called Onukwu a clown—that was about the only thing Onukwu ever said or did that stuck. Some people called Oyibo electric nwanyi, saying she was as bright and dazzling as electricity.

Ekwe had seen countless men stopping and staring at Oyibo with the lost look of a goat chewing its cud. Mama Ekwe sometimes scolded Ekwe for staring that way across the compound at his big stepmother's mouth as she ate rice in front of her door. Mama Ekwe had forbidden him from accepting food from his stepmothers, but Ekwe fancied they might offer him something if he continued looking at them like a greedy goat.

Mama Ekwe would be shocked to know that men did not only stare at Oyibo, but they also itched to touch her fine mahogany skin. They always wanted to look into her dark ponderous eyes. Mama Ekwe would be in hysterics if she knew how they became mischievous sometimes and pinched the small pointy breasts that only started to grow on her chest like young coconut seeds. Ekwe figured men could not help themselves when they ran into a girl walking with her brother if the girl had breasts like young coconut seeds. Oyibo merely pouted and sulked. But Azuka grew angry over men's temerity even though it was not her coconuts men touched.

A new man came to Papa Ekwe every now and again to ask for Oyibo's hand in marriage. They sat under the neem tree and drank and talked for a long time, touching on many issues. They talked about Nimbo, and about the letter sent to their king by cowherds. They talked about this and about that. On their way out, Mama Ekwe covertly hissed at them and Papa Ekwe snorted.

Habanero

EKWE FELL IN STEP WITH OYIBO AS THEY WALKED along the wall of the grove. His heartbeat quickened. He did not know how Oyibo would react to what he was about to say to her. He wanted to reason with her and possibly convince her to marry the suitor with the big red motorcar. They never agreed on anything. He figured she turned down her rich suitor to get back at him even if she might end up marrying a peasant and working in the farm from dawn to dusk. Even though she might grow into a tall bony woman like Mama Ekwe.

Suddenly he heard himself saying, "If you marry him, you will ride in his fine motorcar."

She ignored him, probably pretending she hadn't heard him.

"You will live in his big city house instead of our old house with leaking roof." He pressed on, loudly this time. "I can come to visit you. We can all come to live with you, and we won't worry about cowherds."

He might as well have been talking to the sycamore trees.

"You will eat rice every Sunday instead of fufu and ohoyi soup."

She snapped at him, "Rice. Rice. Why don't you marry him?"

"But I am not a girl."

"It is not my fault that you are not a girl and would like to be one, is it?" She chuckled. "Why don't you ask God to remake you into a girl so you can change your name from Ekwe to Oyibo and marry my suitor? Ki lie osikapa. So you can live in his big city house and ride in his fine motorcar and eat rice every Sunday?"

She was making a joke. It angered Ekwe, who hated making jokes out of anything serious.

"Ocha ka omaka," he said, a retort likening her to a light-skinned person who easily appeared flashy from a distance, but whose beauty faded once she drew closer.

She replied, "Black oil bean," referring to his dark skin. And then she threw a glare at him as they walked into the streamlet.

"Papa Ekwe will no longer be angry with you if you marry your suitor." He tried another approach. "Papa Ekwe will no longer reject Mama Ekwe's food. Our family will be complete again."

She paused, then giggled. "Are you that desperate?"

But he saw her indecision in her walk. Defiance had fled from her bearing, slowing her strides. It was true. Papa Ekwe stopped eating Mama Ekwe's food starting from the day Oyibo turned down the proposal of the suitor with the big red motorcar. Papa Ekwe would not answer when Oyibo greeted him. He had snapped at Ekwe when Ekwe had asked him for a new school uniform for this same reason. Ekwe had been sent home because his school shorts had two frayed holes in the back and gave a generous view of his black buttocks. Ekwe had never been eager about going to school at any rate. He trekked something like eight miles to and from school, or something less, and in the end, he sat at the bottom of the class, so he was happy he could stay at home and not go to school by no fault of his own.

At the streamlet Ekwe avoided contact with ekwukwonju. He did not even look in that direction throughout their work as they fetched water all morning like all good children were expected to do. They made many rounds, poured the water into a huge, black rubber cask at the farm where Mama Ekwe and Azuka drew water and watered the plants like every other family did in Enu-Ozara.

Papa Ekwe owned the section of the community farmland closest to Ogele, and had shared his section between his three wives, so that Ekwe and Oyibo walked only a short distance from the streamlet to get to their farm. Ekwe considered his family's luck as he crossed his big stepmother's portion of the farm to get to Mama Ekwe's, which adjoined both his stepmothers'. He could see Papa Ekwe's stooped figure as he ploughed his youngest wife's portion of the farm in the distance. She was heavy with a child and stayed home. His big stepmother got a larger portion of the farm because she had more mouths to feed. Her first four daughters were married, and the remaining five lived with her and sometimes teamed up with her to fight Mama Ekwe.

Every season, Papa Ekwe helped his wives to prep the site where they grew seedlings in a nursery. He then tilled and ploughed each woman's portion. The women and their children did the rest: transplanting and watering, mulching, weeding, and then harvesting. Today everyone was watering. Mulching would soon start. Weeding would follow in a matter of weeks. Because of the drought, mulching would be done in thick layers to protect the plants, and because of the hotness of the weather, the plants drank water like a herd of thirsty cattle. Work would reduce after weeding. Mama Ekwe always insisted they pinch off the first flowers for a reason Ekwe did not know. Harvesting was also a hard job, but the golden yellow chillies and the gifts Ekwe got from Mama Ekwe after she sold the chillies compensated for Ekwe's troubles. Occasionally Mama Ekwe even cooked him rice.

Ekwe sensed Papa Ekwe's resentment of Mama Ekwe even at the farm. He seemed cold and distant and pounded the soil with his hoe as if the parched earth was part of the conspiracy to rob him of a wealthy son-in-law. He got thirsty, and Ekwe confirmed his suspicion, because he drank from his big stepmother's watering can, crossing and ignoring Mama Ekwe's watering can. Papa Ekwe was like that. He would reject Mama Ekwe's food in protest if she annoyed him and eat from his big stepmother's pot instead. If Mama Ekwe and his big stepmother annoyed him at the same time, he rejected both their food and ate from his small stepmother's pot. If all three women angered him, which was rare, he rejected food by all three women and ate his jaw under the neem tree.

Ekwe poured the water into the cask on his tenth round and pondered how he might make the most of Papa Ekwe's mood swings. He was Papa Ekwe's son, his first son for that matter, and was meant to inherit from Papa Ekwe his good side and, well, his bad side; his good moods and bad moods. This meant he had a right to reject Mama Ekwe's fufu for his stepmother's rice to protest Mama Ekwe's many annoyances. This thought put him in a lighter mood.

"Jisieke ooh," Mama Ekwe said in appreciation of their hard work as they rounded off for lunch.

Mama Ekwe's words always strengthened him. The field was now swarming like termites. From where he stood, Ekwe could see the farmland stretching in acres up to the hill. Other children were also marching to and from the streamlet like a column of ants, fetching water for their families. Mothers were working with their babies strapped to their backs, toddlers like Ekwe's twin siblings, running around playing, now laughing, now screeching. Mama Ekwe mostly left the twins at home because they were a distraction. Ekwe's big stepmother always had a daughter looking after the house. Mama Ekwe left the twins in their care.

Now Mama Ekwe started roasting yams for lunch. Other mothers also started lunch fires, a procession of white columns of smoke that provoked Ekwe's hunger. He figured that if he was hungry, other boys his age who were also drawing water from the rivulet and filling a huge black cask must be hungry too. He watched Mama Ekwe as she scraped soot from a roast yam with a knife. He gazed at her with a small smile as she sliced the yam in quadrants onto a plate. The smile broadened on his face as she began to sprinkle palm oil and salt on the slices. She always insisted they wait for the oil to penetrate and yellow the crumbly white insides of the yam. Ekwe swallowed nearly two pints of his spittle waiting.

"Don't salivate onto the plate," Oyibo snapped at him.

He stuck his tongue out at her, too hungry to pursue the rivalry she was fermenting. And then he sank his teeth into the appetizing flesh of roast yam, shut his eyes, and savoured the earthy, salty flavour. Papa Ekwe did not eat with them, which was expected; he ate with his other wife and children. The wind blew Ekwe's big stepmother's laughter over to them at intervals, and each time Mama Ekwe looked in their direction and hissed, Ekwe wondered why Papa Ekwe blamed her for Oyibo's rejection of the suitor with the big red motorcar.

Ekwe climbed to the top of the hill at the end of the day. In the distance, the towns of Ugbene-Ajima, Nimbo, and Opanda were lost in a wild panorama of mangroves. He spied cowherds driving their cattle towards Ogele for a drink of water, a man and his four sons. He climbed down fast and drew near and hid behind a tree, so close he made out the narrow features and braided hair of the young cowherds, their skinny dresses and tight trousers and nose rings. The youngest was about Ekwe's age and was dressed in black kente. They spoke in a rapid tongue. He turned his attention to their cattle. The massive, humped creatures with large dewlaps and drooping ears filled the pasture, countless as swallows in a spring sky.

He spent a long time watching them, trying hard to reconnect with the blurry images of his astral experience. Everything seemed to fade into the dark nothing of his mind as he struggled to recollect the intangible scenes and names and the lost savour of exotic foods. Sadly, he could no longer articulate the elements of that experience. He pondered the harmless look and simple rustic lifestyle of the cowherds against the cruelty and violence the suitor's words imaged. *They will harvest your crops and feed them to their cattle. And then they will do to you what they did to the people of Nimbo if you try to fight back.* He remembered Papa Ekwe's favourite proverb, "Hidden palm nuts bleed copious oil," and his resentment of his sister grew with the still and heavy air as evening drew closer.

Nnamdi Azikiwe

"NNAMDI AZIKIWE IS TO BLAME FOR THE TRAGEDY in Nimbo. If only the man had listened to wise counsel and not allowed his prejudice against Obafemi Awolowo to blind him to reality. But he allowed himself to be swayed by tribal sentiment."

Ekwe looked sharply at Papa Ekwe. And then he stole a glance at the suitor, a look with a bit of a frown in it, for what sane Igboman would talk about Nnamdi Azikiwe in such tone of voice?

"I saw that scowl, boy." The suitor laughed his fruity laugh and sipped his White Horse. "I know what you are thinking. You are young. You know nothing about the politics of this country, the politics of the amalgamation of the southern and northern protectorates."

Ekwe did not understand the long and hard vocabulary. He figured the suitor was a retired government worker, or so he came across. Everything agreed: the eye bags, the loose skin, and the salt-and-pepper beard. A bald pate cut across a thick mix of grey and black hair reminiscent of a country road running across dense bushes, the centre looking fragile, as though made of porcelain.

The suitor smiled. "I am blaming Zik, and I have a good reason for that."

Papa Ekwe furrowed his brow and sat back against the tree. He always furrowed his brow and sat back at the beginnings of his anger, especially when someone said something he did not like, and if there was anything he despised, it was anyone upbraiding Nnamdi Azikiwe.

Imagine the audacity.

"Obafemi Awolowo had suggested, among other things, independence for the protectorate of southern Nigeria since the northern region had appeared not to be ready, a new country that would have Nnamdi Azikiwe as prime minister and him, Obafemi Awolowo, as finance minister.

Ekwe was listening to the suitor with chin cupped in hand.

"Nwammuoemegbunanwammadu, nwammaduemegbunanwammuo," the suitor said. "Wasn't that a fair deal?"

Papa Ekwe didn't answer. The angrier he got, the less he talked.

The suitor sipped his drink again. "But Zik had thrown away such a bright chance of not only becoming prime minister, but also of freeing the South from the scrounging of the North—the northern region had always lived off the budget surpluses of the South—because of personal grievance. Even the Bible condemns an unforgiving spirit."

Aru. Ekwe mused on the abominations uttered by the suitor. For talking about Nnamdi Azikiwe in those reproving terms, the suitor had desecrated the land. Ekwe was certain that Papa Ekwe would chase him away with his marriage proposal for his profanities. Nnamdi Azikiwe had single-handedly wrested the country's independence from the white man, according to Papa Ekwe. He had sacrificed so much for the country—a blameless man, clean as dew. "The Great Zik of Africa," Papa Ekwe would sing his praises. "He is Nigeria's first and foremost nationalist. The greatest man ever to live. Obu Mmuo. He has the gift of eternal youth, the gift of immortality."

Ekwe marvelled whenever Papa Ekwe said those unbelievable things about Nnamdi Azikiwe two decades after his demise. But how can the suitor blame a man who had been dead for two decades for the tragedy that only just happened in Nimbo? Ekwe shrugged in dismay. He did not understand why Papa Ekwe said nothing. Papa Ekwe did not argue with the suitor. He did not say or do anything to the suitor for his audacity, for reducing "The Great Zik of Africa" to a mere tribalist, to nothing.

"The amalgamation of the northern and southern protectorates by the colonial masters was a calculated mistake," explained the suitor. "It was an evil conspiracy. An Igboman has nothing in common with the Hausa/Fulani in whatever way you look at it: culture, religion, language, or even belief. So, the colonial masters also share the blame for our failures as a country, for their shortsightedness regarding the amalgamation."

Papa Ekwe gave him another dumb grin. He was used to giving people a dumb grin if they knew a thing or two more than him. He had never been to school. The small-small things he knew about politics he knew because he had travelled across the country—to the northern region before the war to serve a rich trader, and then to the midwest to work in a cocoa farm after the rich trader got killed in the Nigerian Civil War and his investments were plundered by northerners. Before his violent death, he was the only rich man in Enu-Ozara. He was killed because he could not bring himself to abandon his investments and flee the North.

Ekwe pursed his lips. Enu-Ozara did not have rich men. The only one the village had, it lost to the war, a war blamed on tribalism, tribalism caused by the amalgamation of the southern and northern protectorates, amalgamation the suitor blamed on Zik's tepidness and Western conspiracies. He sighed. He figured his sister said no to the suitor's proposal because the suitor was the type who said last things first and first things last; because of his act of beginning a conversation from the rear, this inverted and annoying way of saying things. For instance, Ekwe remembered to ask the suitor for a gift only about the time the man's rear lights winked and then faded into the encroaching darkness. That was probably about the time his sister remembered she should have said yes to him, so Ekwe blamed the suitor's bad luck on his misplaced priorities: his stories of the tragedy in Nimbo and politics of amalgamation.

Ekwe didn't care about politics. He was more concerned about his Sunday clothes—old and torn as they were—and Sunday rice. Mama Ekwe had promised him new clothes after harvest. She would buy them after she sold her greens, tomatoes, and habaneros. So, he had to wait till after the harvest season unless something happened, unless his sister agreed to marry the suitor with the big red motorcar. Every time the suitor came around, he brought a taste like honey in Ekwe's mouth, but leaving it felt like the bees had fled

Ekwe's mouth with their payloads of nectar. The man might seem a little touched, but Ekwe wanted him to marry Oyibo to improve the quality of their life. He figured his family was the poorest family in the world, a family that could not even afford rice.

Dollops of Fufu

EKWE SAT ON THE BARE KITCHEN FLOOR WITH LEGS wrapped around a clay pot, the leftovers from dinner, now breakfast meant for the three of them: Ekwe, Oyibo, and Azuka. But Ekwe had plucked the clay pot out of fire halfway through heating it up, gripped it tight with his feet as if immune to burns, and, while he greedily swallowed the food, hunched his bare back against Azuka and Oyibo both fighting to wrest the pot from his vise grip. But no matter how hard they pounded him, he would not let go. Azuka gave up and stood watching with helpless abandon. Oyibo sank her teeth into Ekwe's back and drew a yelp of pain, but he held tight to the pot and grabbed more food. Oyibo broke down in tears of frustration as the food went down rapidly. Hearing the commotion, Mama Ekwe rushed in and gave Ekwe a hard, stinging slap to the back. He jumped up with a howl of pain, spilling crumbs from a mouth stuffed with food.

"You greedy goat. Do you enjoy starving your sisters?" she shrieked at him, snatching the almost-empty pot and giving it to the girls.

Ekwe licked his fingers and scowled.

"Ijoka," Mama Ekwe snapped at him. She added that the only time he was not scowling was when he was scoffing food even though scowling did not suit him because he had a face like gunk.

The girls threw him scornful looks as they scratched in the pot for the crumbs left.

"How did I ever give birth to a gourmand like you?" Mama Ekwe raged.

Ekwe stood with hands and feet painted with soot. He could wolf a hot pot of food straight from the fire without a flinch. He had broken many a clay pot in his haste. "I am sick and tired of buying a new pot every market day," Mama Ekwe had moaned with exasperation the last time he broke her pot.

Ekwe was still frowning. He was not scowling at Oyibo or Azuka or because Mama Ekwe's penetrating slap still burned his back. Every so often he came out of a meal with an emblem of their outrage—bite marks, fingernail marks, and all—inflicted on him by Oyibo or Azuka or Mama Ekwe as he guzzled away the food meant for him and his siblings. He was frowning because he was still hungry. He felt cheated. He had been doing fine until his twin brothers were born and stole Mama Ekwe's affection from him. Many of her indulgences on Ekwe she had transferred to the twins. They got their last Christmas clothes, but Ekwe was asked to wait till the next Christmas. Those boys cleared heaps of food before you knew it and cleaned the plates with their tongues. Mama Ekwe overfed them at Ekwe's expense. She rationed the food she dished out to the rest of them just so the boys had enough food, if ever they had enough of it.

"Get ready; we are late to the farm," Mama Ekwe's harsh voice cut into his train of thought.

"But I am still hungry," he grumbled.

"Kitikpa," she swore at him.

Ekwe looked crushed. He despised farmwork. He would lie on his mat every night scratching bumps he got from bloodsucking insects that fed on him at the farm. He fancied his family was punishing him by making him work in the field from dawn to dusk.

"You want me to look as if they stomped on me," he sobbed. "Because I work too much, and I don't eat well."

"I don't care if you look like the lizard's intestine," Mama Ekwe said. "You are quick to finish food meant for three, but you will not have the strength to work in the farm."

Ekwe cut a figure of misery as he stood in the middle of the compound. He figured his family didn't care if too much work stunted his growth. He was only ten and already looking squat, like a table. He believed working from dawn to dusk and swallowing heavy dollops of fufu could dwarf any boy. He did not think it was necessary to copy Papa Ekwe, who did not eat rice unless he was eating it with thick slices of yam. "Rice is bird food," Papa Ekwe would say. "Anyone who labours from dawn to dusk in the farm needs to swallow solids like dollops of fufu the size of a baby's head to stay alive and active."

"But I can't swallow dollops as big as a baby's head," Ekwe had protested.

"You will swallow them when you become an adult," Papa Ekwe had chuckled.

But not every dollop of fufu, Ekwe had pondered, could be swallowed at the size of a child's head. Cocoyam fufu, for instance, was naturally waxy and difficult to pluck and mould to that size. He despised it. Sometimes it stuck annoyingly to his palm like glue.

Of all the things he hated, he despised school the most. The truth was he went to school to dodge farmwork, and then he pretended to be sick to dodge school. Sometimes he went to school twice a week. Some weeks he did not show up at all. When eventually he did, he would have forgotten most of what he had been taught. The school sat at the centre of the community, and pupils coming from the surrounding villages trekked almost the same distance. Ekwe arrived late to school every day; he got whipped by the teacher, the wiry and wicked Miss Clara. Miss Clara had chased him out of her class and insisted he return only when he had the school uniform. Papa Ekwe had shouted at Ekwe when he went to get money for school uniform from him, "Stay at home and help out in the farm or go get it from your conniving mother and sister."

So, now, Ekwe happily stayed back home. Besides, the village school had been closed because of the rumoured cowherds' letter to the king. "They are coming to attack the school and kidnap the pupils," the town crier had announced. Ekwe fancied Papa Ekwe did not really want his children to go to school, but he allowed them to go there because other children in the neighbourhood also went there. He fancied Papa Ekwe allowed his children to do things only because others were doing them. "You have to follow my footsteps," Papa Ekwe would remind him. Ekwe did his best to parrot him, to follow his every footstep. Even though he couldn't by any means swallow dollops of fufu the size of a child's head, he kneaded each dollop to the size he could manage to get past his throat with unthinking ease. You wouldn't think twice about doing things with unthinking ease if you had a sister and a cousin, and the three of you lived in a mud house where food was insufficient, and the three of you needed to fight your way to your stomach. He remembered the good old times when he was Papa Ekwe's only son. He figured that Papa Ekwe used to be a very sad man and scowled a lot before his birth, and it was because Ekwe's big stepmother had mercilessly given birth to girls only. How inconsiderate of her. The scowl had fled from Papa Ekwe's face when Ekwe was born. Finally, an heir *had* arrived. "Your sister cleaned your mother's womb," Papa Ekwe had told him. "That's why you were born a boy, my much-desired heir. And then you brought me good luck with the birth of the twins."

But Ekwe didn't consider the birth of his brothers as good luck, because they stole everything from him.

Sunday Rice

EKWE RESENTED HIS SISTER. THINGS WOULD BE different if she accepted the suitor with the big red motorcar. They would all eat rice every Sunday and ride in the suitor's fine car. He was hoping the suitor would come back to ask her again. He would probably finish the story of "The Great Zik of Africa" and Obafemi Awolowo. Ekwe was curious to know what caused the disagreement between those two. The country was in bad hands because of this disagreement, according to the suitor, and Zik was to blame for what happened in Nimbo. "O kwerom nghota," Papa Ekwe had said. He did not understand how Zik, a man who died many years ago, was to blame for the tragedy in Nimbo.

Ekwe did not understand politics, so he resigned himself to watching people as they passed along the road in their Sunday best. He figured they were going to the Roman Catholic church to hear the Reverend Father's boring sermons and the slow monotonous choir hymns. A few other villagers like Ikpedirichuckwu went to the only hand-clapping church in the village. Ekwe would stop and peer inside the Protestant church each time he passed by the small, matchbox hut from which came stormy clapping and singing. The volume of voices issuing from the hut belied the small congregation.

Ekwe fled to the road as noon drew nearer. He did not want to listen to the hard and soft gasping sounds when Mama Ekwe pounded the yielding, putrid mass of fufu for lunch. It incensed him. Sometimes beads of her sweat, thick as raindrops, fell into the mortar as she pounded away.

Lunch was ready when he returned to the house. He ate and sobbed at the same time. He made sure to make a nuisance of the meal.

"You foolish child," Mama Ekwe hissed. "I cannot steal to satisfy your gluttony for rice. After all, I am not the only poor mother who has ever given birth to a child."

Ekwe paused to swallow a morsel, and then he sobbed harder. Mama Ekwe would have seizures if she knew that he ate aja—the sacrificial jollof rice he found in a small earthen pot at a T-junction in the village, with biscuits, and a bottle of Fanta. Afterwards, he worried that his gluttony for rice might have brought another person's misfortune upon him. Papa Ekwe had said that aja was food or items of sacrifice meant for the consumption or use of spiritual beings. They were kept at T-junctions—playgrounds for spiritual entities—by people seeking a clue for their misfortune in the hope that fairies would feast on them and take away their adversity.

"Ogologo akpili." Oyibo giggled. "I thought you wanted rice. Why didn't you reject your lunch since you wanted rice? You'd have died of starvation."

"You are wicked," Ekwe fired back. "That's why you rejected your suitor, and we have to eat only fufu in this house."

She touched her throat and made a face at him, another way of calling him a glutton.

"Atika," he replied, hinting at her thinness.

"Kwusi. Stop it, you two!" Mama Ekwe shouted at them. And then she faced Oyibo and screamed at her, "Why don't you marry your suitor and stop picking on your brother? Don't you see that everyone is suffering because of you? Your father is mad at me. He accuses me of conspiring with you to deny him a rich son-in-law. Can't you read his body language? I tried talking to him, but it's hard to reason with a man as stubborn as your father. Now he is waging a full-scale war against me to the pleasure of my co-wives. Your brother is becoming affected too." Her voice suddenly lost its sharpness. "I am begging you, my dear, oyoom, please accept this man and save all of us from cowherds and their brutality."

Oyibo stomped away without a word, abandoning the food.

Ekwe climbed the neem tree after lunch and sat alone and sulked. He was not about to let his sister win him at any rate: word for word, sulk for sulk. He sat there for a long time and watched adults stroll out for sightseeing dressed in their fine Sunday clothes. Some went to the motor park to sit and watch Nkwa as he played his ukulele as if he had no worries in the world other than blindness. Others were enjoying Sunday afternoon naps outdoors as if they did not care about the threat of attack on the community. They were coiled up or stretched out on mats under trees in their compounds, enjoying the cool of the shade in the hot afternoon sun, a radio churning out tunes close to their ears.

Ekwe's little ones, the twins, had joined their half-siblings to form play groups. Tired of sulking in a corner of the house, Oyibo brought out a bench and sat under the neem tree. Azuka joined her. Ekwe figured they wanted to gossip and were unaware of his presence up in the tree. Whenever the fever of gossiping caught up with the girls, they sat away from everyone and talked in soft voices—in the same hushed tones as a priest and a sinner at the confessional in the village church—and giggled.

Azuka said, "This malice between Papa Ekwe and Mama Ekwe is becoming overstretched. Why don't you accept your suitor and end it?"

Oyibo sighed. "I don't want to end up like Oyoyo."

Everyone in Enu-Ozara knew the story of Oyoyo, the pretty girl who got married, became pregnant, and died during childbirth.

"Do you think she died because she was young and the man was old?"

"That's what I was told."

"What about our mothers who got married at an age younger than ours to much older men? What about our half sisters who are married and have had their first and even second babies?"

"What about Eliza the daughter of Orinechi?" Oyibo's voice was weak and hesitant.

Everyone knew her story too. Eliza the daughter of Orinechi rejected the suitor chosen for her by her father. She fled the village to the city and became wise in the ways of city people. But parents disapproved of her, saying she was a bad influence. Girls their age only heard about Eliza the daughter of Orinechi in stories. Most of them had never set eyes on her.

Azuka said, "It all depends on life's luck."

"I too I feel like running away."

Ekwe drew a sharp breath at Oyibo's idea of running away and almost gave himself away.

"I heard a sound." Azuka looked around the compound. Besides the kids playing in the sand in the distance, the compound was empty.

"What noise?"

"I thought I heard someone catch their breath."

"I want to flee from my suitor as far as possible. He's too old." Oyibo steered the conversation back to her suitor, to Ekwe's relief. "I have lost Mama Ekwe's support too. But I don't know how or where to run to."

Azuka chuckled.

"So imi. He is all nose and Adam's apple." Oyibo sneered. "I despise that ugly mole on his temple. He disgusts me with the whitish matter that collects at the far corners of his mouth as he speaks."

Azuka giggled.

"Only vultures have his kind of bald head."

Azuka collapsed in giggles against the tree.

"Are you laughing at me?"

Azuka managed to stifle her laughter. "I am not laughing at you. I am laughing at the way you are describing a man who is supposed to be your suitor and likening him to a vulture."

It was Oyibo's turn to giggle.

Azuka's voice assumed a serious tone. "What about the cowherds? They will not get at us in the comfort of your suitor's city house."

"Are you trying to coerce me to marry him? Is that what everyone is doing for their own selfish reason?"

"Oh, no," Azuka said quickly. "I am with you. And if you make up your mind to run away, I will run away with you."

Ekwe was excited and restless up in the tree. He waited for the girls to go in. They were there a long time as night drew closer and the chickens started to retire home in the lively company of their fluffy chicks. Dinner would be eaten indoors because there was no moon. Ekwe would have to go to bed with an empty stomach. The fufu and inine soup he had resented for lunch was also for dinner. He did not think he would be able to get those filthy dollops past his throat again.

Mama Ekwe came out of the room, stood in front of the door with an oil lamp, and called out to the twins, who came scampering back home with their half-siblings.

"Where on earth is that boy Ekwe?"

"I don't know where that wanderer is," answered Oyibo.

Mama Ekwe raised her voice and called out to him a few times. And then she went back in with the twins. Ekwe heard her complaining about a playful rascal who could not tell the difference between day and night, but he sat tight in the tree and waited for Azuka and Oyibo to go in. He felt uneasy. If Oyibo connived with Azuka and they ran away, the family would lose the chance of having a rich in-law who would change their life. That night, he turned this and that way on the mat, his mind working on how he might change things.

Anti-Igbo Riots

EKWE WHISPERED SOMETHING INTO PAPA EKWE'S left ear, Papa Ekwe laughed, the suitor raised his eyebrows.

"My son would like to know the cause of the quarrel between 'The Great Zik of Africa' and Obafemi Awolowo," Papa Ekwe said.

The suitor grinned and took another sip of White Horse. Ekwe leaned on Papa Ekwe's shoulder and peered at the suitor with curious eyes. He savoured the suitor's colour sense. Today he wore a red-brown suit, fine black shoes, and an oval velvet hat. A red car and marching attire.

"The great Zik had accused Awolowo of working against his election into the House of Representatives," the suitor started to explain. "Zik felt humiliated. In anger he came back to the East to become head of the Eastern Region's government at the expense of Eyo Ita. Because he still nursed his anger against Awolowo over the lost election, he did not see the good in Awolowo's idea of pushing for a southern independence with Zik as prime minister and Awolowo as finance minister."

Ekwe stared blankly. The whole explanation didn't make sense. The name Eyo Ita sounded like some kind of grass. The suitor had accused Zik of introducing tribal politics in the country, which now made no sense to Ekwe; however, in his new understanding of politics many years later—when Ekwe had become more enlightened—Obafemi Awolowo, and not Nnamdi Azikiwe, started tribal politics in the country.

The suitor removed his cap, scratched his bald head, and returned the cap.

"Ahmadu Bello had bowed to Queen Elizabeth II and won the heart of the colonial masters with his gesture of submission," he said. "When they were leaving, the colonial masters handed over the leadership of the country to Ahmadu Bello and his northern brothers because they thought them . . ."

A goat bleated into his speech. The suitor paused and glanced at the brown nanny with white feet, and the animal stared back at him with vacant eyes.

"Fa di mfe ighogbu." The suitor's eyes lingered on the goat as if drawing parallels between the animal's vacuous stare and the gesture of the northern leaders. "They may be gone, but the colonial masters still call the shots from across the seas. That's why General Sani Abacha was my best military head of state despite his many atrocities. The West had cut off all ties with the country because he did not allow them to continue milking us."

Ekwe stared at the suitor's White Horse–sipping mouth as it reeled out history. But he looked away as their eyes came in contact.

"I know what's on your mind, boy." The suitor grinned at Ekwe.

Ekwe gave him a blank look, startled that the suitor had addressed him in that direct manner.

"You are probably thinking, Would the country have fared any better if southern politicians had dominated the political landscape?"

Ekwe hid his self-conscious smirk behind Papa Ekwe's broad ear. The suitor amused him by crediting such advanced thoughts to him, a boy who came last in his class.

"Your thoughts are probably the same thoughts that festered in the minds of the country's first coup plotters, in the so-called Igbo coup," the suitor said. "The fear of ethnic domination is what led to the collapse of the country's first republic. The South believed that the Hausa-Fulani would use their demographic advantage to dominate them. On the other hand, the Hausa-Fulani feared that they would lose the contest of the economic and political structures of the federation to the more educated south. So, a bloody coup followed a fraudulent election that brought Tafawa Balewa, a northerner, into power as prime minister. The prime minister and two premiers were murdered in that coup. Then came Major General Aguiyi-Ironsi, an Igboman, whose plan to unify the regions sparked anti-Igbo riots in the North and led to his murder by northern officers who accused leaders of the coup of favouring Igbo domination. These anti-Igbo riots resulted in the pogrom in which thousands and thousands of Igbos were killed along with some other southerners. This led to the Nigerian Civil War."

Papa Ekwe's eyes grew alight with interest. He was probably hearing new and original versions of the country's history, original because they were coming from the suitor with the big red motorcar.

"How can they call a coup meant to release Obafemi

Awolowo from prison and make him prime minister an Igbo coup?" the suitor asked. "But I'd feel the same way if I were a northerner. It is easy and believable. How can it not be a conspiracy? The man who led the coup was an Igboman and the casualties were senior northern politicians. The man who took over the reins of power, General Aguiyi-Ironsi, was also an Igboman and he didn't send the coup plotters to the firing squad."

Ekwe did not know that Obafemi Awolowo had been in prison. The suitor kept opening broad new leaves of history. He was happy when the man started to talk about something else. The conversation about tribal politics had become a kind of monologue with Ekwe and Papa Ekwe only listening, knowing very little or nothing at all to contribute.

"Our one big weakness as a country is tribalism," the suitor said. "We do not trust each other. It's all about us and our relatives. We are all nepotists." He paused and took a sip. "Enough of politics. This old mud house does not befit this large compound and a man of your status." He gestured towards the vast empty space. "A modern house should be sitting in place of this old house. There should be a courtyard, a large, landscaped frontage encompassed in a fence, with a gate and a driveway."

Papa Ekwe's shoulders shook with laughter. "I am not about to build another house, I am a poor, old, village man."

"A man who has a rich son-in-law should not consider himself poor. He deserves to live in better surroundings."

Ekwe wished the suitor had added, A boy who has a rich brother-in-law deserves to eat rice every Sunday.

"We can start with renovating the old house," the suitor

said. "You know what they say about sleep deepening and finding a rhythm in snoring."

Ekwe looked lost. Oyibo always accused him of snoring. She said when he snored, he croaked like a frog. He'd deny it and they would fight over it. But he knew nothing about what snoring signified in proverbs.

"Give me time," Papa Ekwe said. "My daughter is still very young and needs time to come around."

"I am a patient man." The suitor shrugged. He removed his cap again and gave his bald head a few light pats. "But do what you can to hasten the marriage ceremonies. No one knows when the cowherds are going to strike again. You must get out of this village as soon as possible."

"The vigilantes have risen to the occasion," Papa Ekwe said.

The village had tightened its security operations and expanded its network. Ekwe had seen young men patrolling with long guns and swords. They wore mean faces and bloodshot eyes. Sometimes he'd hear them baying at those perceived to be intruders, their voices aggressive, rupturing the silence of the night.

The suitor laughed. "The vigilantes cannot stop the militants who come in their numbers armed with dangerous weapons." He lowered his voice. "There is a strong suspicion that some people in the government are their sponsors, and they get all the arms and ammunition from their brothers who are in power. Besides, they are invincible. They wear amulets with powers to transform them into cows, trees, or even grass."

A shocked look mounted to Papa Ekwe's face.

"They will strike any moment. It could be tomorrow; it could be in two months or even in six months. The time is unspecified, but one thing is sure: they will keep to their promise. So, it's dangerous to underestimate them. The people of Nimbo made that mistake and paid dearly for it. Their village is now a heap of charred remains."

When the suitor finally rose to leave, his joints crackled in protest. His legs were a bit unsteady as he walked to his motorcar, and as the bright yellow lights of his headlamps illuminated the night, a burst of Oriental Brothers' highlife music filled the night air. Ekwe stood in the compound and watched the okwuotoekeneze float into the surrounding darkness. He desired to be rich. He wanted to own a car that churned out highlife rhythms. He wanted to play music a little too loudly and to talk about politics and "The Great Zik of Africa" with impunity and swagger, with the overconfidence of a man who knew all there was to know. The music filled his lungs like a gulp of fresh air. He retired only after the light and music faded into the dark nothing of the night. But he continued to hear the vibrant vocal notes of the song in bed as he lay down with a smile. The track "Obi Nwanne" was Oriental Brothers' best song, as far as he was concerned, although he did not quite understand the nasalized Igbo lyrics. The music always made him think of a marriage ceremony in which people were eating pounded yam with ogbono soup and others were dancing while highlife music screamed from a large horn speaker tied to the top of a tree.

He woke up with a clear head the next morning, not one filled with thoughts of music, rice, and Sunday clothes. Smoke rose in slow coils over the three thatched kitchens sitting across from the tin house—one for Mama Ekwe, one for his big stepmother, and one for his younger stepmother—as breakfast was being warmed. Before the start of rancour, they were a large and not unhappy family. Sometimes Ekwe's stepmothers and Mama Ekwe bickered and displayed acts of petty jealousy. Sometimes the household sat in the moonlight and shared stories. Ekwe was fond of the stories, especially the tale of theft by the goat and the tortoise in the farmer's barn, as told by Papa Ekwe. The tortoise and the goat snuck into the barn to feed themselves on the farmer's yams during an acute famine that showed in their high, defined ribs. The tortoise ate wisely, going every now and again to check that he did not overfeed himself and grow too fat for the size of the barn door in an emergency. But the goat greedily and foolishly devoured the delicious yams until her stomach filled out as though pregnant. When the barn owner surprised them with a visit, the tortoise easily fled through the gate, but the goat's fattened body got stuck. The goat was caught and slaughtered by the farmer, who used her meat to make pepper soup.

Papa Ekwe once told a new moonlight story every other night. He shone in conversations and storytelling, but Ekwe figured he was not the kind of man to start a conversation inversely on the day he had proposed to Mama Ekwe or any of his wives, like the suitor. Even if he did go a bit off the point, he would never have discussed tribal politics or electoral malpractices and things of that nature. He didn't think Papa Ekwe had ever talked about corrupt politicians or the police taking bribes or judges perverting justice. He had not been to a city in many years. He had spent his life here in this village pounding fufu and chopping firewood for his youngest wife.

Perhaps he was fond of her because she didn't criticize him, unlike Mama Ekwe and Ekwe's big stepmother, who made him eat his jaw in place of swallowing baby-head dollops of fufu.

Papa Ekwe had gathered his farm tools around the foot of the neem tree, and now he chatted with his youngest wife, who stood in front of her door and threw spittle like a vulture, a picture of nausea and bouts of listless depression. A wrappa was tied loose and short around her body, heavy with pregnancy. Ekwe figured she was at least thirty years younger than Papa Ekwe. Papa Ekwe was ready to leave for the farm, but he was waiting to eat breakfast. He was waiting to swallow dollops of fufu to fill up his expanded stomach. How he got those huge balls past his throat baffled Ekwe. It seemed his life revolved around it: working from dawn to dusk on the farm and swallowing child-head dollops of fufu. Sometimes he belched. Ekwe was not sure how many times he belched during a meal. He presumed he belched after each dollop thundered down in his stomach. At times he indulged himself with a drink after a meal, a few shots of cheap kinkana. He drank White Horse only when Oyibo's suitor came around.

Azuka, thin, dark-skinned, and pimply, stooped into the low thatched kitchen holding a pot of soup. She was going to warm the soup for breakfast before they left for the farm. She threw Ekwe a wary but daring glance, a look warning him to keep away from the pot of breakfast. He loured at her and walked away, hating himself and everything that found its way into his sight and thoughts: the pot of soup layered with soot, habanero and the waterside farm, his ration of meals that only scratched his throat and made worse his hunger, his inconsiderate sister and conniving cousin. The exhaustion he felt after working all day at the farm and the pain that racked his body when he woke up the following morning crowned his self-disgust.

Ekwe hated pain. He hated trekking. He figured he might die one day from trekking. But he didn't think anyone ever died from trekking, or did they? He didn't suppose the man who trekked from Lagos to Aso Rock in support of the president of the country died. He didn't know the distance between the two cities, but it sounded like trekking from one end of the earth to the other. The trekker saw the president after the impossible trek, according to the suitor, and even shook the president's hand. The president even had a gift for him.

The trekker got Ekwe thinking, What if I trekked from Enu-Ozara to Aso Rock to see the president and get my own gift? Ekwe had trekked all his life, eight miles to and from school, and four miles to and from the farm. He figured if he added up all his life's trekking, it was enough to take him to the president to get his own gift. But he didn't even know who the president was or what he looked like. Besides, another man had started to trek from Lagos to Aso Rock to protest the president's poor leadership, according to the suitor.

Mama Ekwe came out of the room and went into the kitchen to share breakfast. Ekwe didn't fancy that she rationed their food. He figured he was the one being cheated. Everyone knew he had a large stomach, a larger appetite than Oyibo and Azuka put together, so Mama Ekwe was doing him an injustice sharing their meals with equal proportions.

He went and collected his own share of the breakfast grudgingly. The food was far from enough for him, only a few morsels that awakened his hunger.

"I want more," he said after he cleared the plate and licked it clean.

Mama Ekwe flung him a hard look. "You are not getting a morsel extra. The food left in that pot is for the twins, for their lunch while we are at the farm. And hurry up, we are running late."

Oyibo giggled, pursing her lips at him.

They set off to the farm shortly. The morning was brightened by a rising sun. Ekwe wished his family would grow rice instead of habanero and tomato and cassava and yam. He figured the soil in Enu-Ozara was incapable of growing rice. He prayed for the rain to start falling. It was long overdue. "This community hasn't seen such a drought in years," Papa Ekwe had said. Ekwe wanted rain because it would reduce their work at the farm. There would not be any need to water the plants if it started raining. But then the rain would help the weeds flourish and soon it would be time to weed the farm. He hissed. He was always going from one task to the other, from one trouble to another. He fancied he had seen too many troubles for a ten-year-old boy. No reasonable human being would believe him if he told them that he worked all day on a habanero farm and ate rice only three times a year, only on Christmas Day, New Year's Day, and Easter Sunday.

He wished things were different.

Shehu Usman dan Fodio

WHEN NEXT THE SUITOR VISITED, HE DIDN'T TALK conversely about politics, and he didn't drink White Horse. He simply gave Papa Ekwe a wry smile and said, "I am sending workers to begin renovation of the house, as promised." Papa Ekwe was in the middle of a meal. He belched and pushed back the food. And then he called out to Mama Ekwe in a loud voice. Mama Ekwe rushed out of the room, heard the good news from Papa Ekwe, and broke into a song. Her voice attracted Ekwe's stepmothers, who joined her in singing and dancing and laughing loudly.

Ekwe did not understand women. One minute they were laughing like best friends, the next they were quarreling and exchanging unprintable words like sworn enemies.

"I am short of words." Papa Ekwe rubbed his wet hands on his shorts and dried them on his hair. "May Chukwu Abiama pay you back for your good heart."

"It's nothing." The suitor waved it away. "It's my pleasure to have the opportunity to help my in-laws in a small way."

"You have the full support of the family," Papa Ekwe assured him, and glanced at Mama Ekwe for assent.

"Yes," she agreed.

The suitor brightened up. He went to his car and returned

with a bottle of White Horse and a few glasses, resettled in his seat, poured himself a drink, and invited the women to share the drink. They accepted and drank it in the performatively shy way of women and retired to their kitchens. The suitor and Papa Ekwe then drank and chatted. Ekwe drew closer to Papa Ekwe as he started to tell the story of what happened earlier at Jerome's bar. Papa Ekwe imported many stories and rumours from Jerome's bar. He unloaded them when the family relaxed at the neem tree after dinner. He did so mostly on evenings when he half lurched home and polished off a large plate of food, which he evacuated with a thunderous belch. Some of the stories were adult stories, but he would ignore the stern eye contact from Mama Ekwe and his other wives while he reeled out amorous stories men freely shared with their bar friends. Stories of how they related with their wives sexually. Stories of how wives took turns to sleep with a husband, and how most domestic fights were caused by one wife trying to shortchange the other in the bedroom.

"A cowherd came in to buy himself a drink," Papa Ekwe said in a lively way. "The conversation was all about cowherds after he walked out. There was tension in the bar. Some said the king had allowed them to graze their cattle in the pasture and even took money from them, some said they were in transit and would only stay for a short time, others said they could settle in this village permanently. No one knows which to believe."

"Your king would be a very foolish man to take money from the herders in exchange for a place to pasture their cattle in this community," the suitor said. "He obviously has nothing positive to offer his subjects as king."

Ekwe caught his breath. Firstly, the suitor was disrespectful to Zik, and now he called the king a foolish man.

"He has something to offer." Papa Ekwe's voice was heavy with sarcasm. "He has a pair of thick lips to offer."

The suitor laughed. "I have a problem with our tribesmen. We seem to have a short memory, and we treat things passively while allowing too many others to go unnoticed. We only react after we have been snagged from all sides. How quickly we seem to have forgotten Nimbo. I think the question your king should ask himself is why are many of the cowherds pouring into this land? I will tell you why. They are not ordinary cowherds. Do not be deceived by their looks, their innocence. They are sponsored militias who are trying to insinuate themselves into as many southern communities as possible. They will continue to attack our communities because they are here to finish what their master Shehu Usman dan Fodio started."

Ekwe whispered into Papa Ekwe's ear. He wanted to know who Shehu Usman dan Fodio was and wanted Papa Ekwe to help convey his question to the suitor.

"Shehu Usman dan Fodio was the founder of Sokoto Caliphate," the suitor explained. "He was an ancient warrior who fought on horseback. He conquered many northern Nigerian communities and forced his religion on them."

Ekwe was thrilled by the story.

"That's why the Fulani have dominated Hausaland and are the rulers of this country today," the suitor said. "They want to do the same thing to us. They want to create an emirate in Igboland and impose Islam on as many Christian tribes as they can subdue. The same thing the Ottomans did to wipe out Armenian Christians in Turkey, the same way

Hitler wiped out six million Jews—that is the same method they want to use in wiping out our people."

Ekwe was getting confused. The conversation was becoming too complex for him.

"By the time they are finished with the Christians, those who are lucky to survive the onslaught will be hitting their foreheads on the ground."

"That's not good." Papa Ekwe shook his head.

The suitor finished his drink and stood up. "That's why you must resist the cowherds in every way possible. But first you must leave this environment for a safe place. The earlier the marriage ceremonies are done, the better. Think about it."

After he left, Ekwe thought about the suitor's jihadist theory, although it made little sense to him. The cowherds didn't look dangerous to him. They were seen wandering about all over the place. Their women and girls came to Orie Ejuona market square to buy things or to sell their fura da nono. They seemed friendly and exchanged greetings with the villagers. They even tried to speak to the villagers in the local tongue, though they knew only a little of the language and spoke it with funny diction, assuring the villagers that their cattle would not eat up their crops, the only line they seemed to have committed to memory. Some of the villagers were starting to get used to them and even patronized them. Ekwe had nosed out the area of the forest where they lived in grass huts. He would hide behind trees and watch them as they lived their simple forest life, expecting them to transform into butterflies or cows or snakes.

One day, unable to resist his curiosity, he approached two herdsgirls on the village road. They were sisters, and each had a calabash on her head; they were in the company of a little girl, a baby sister, pretty with large eyes and a thin nose. Ekwe pointed at the calabash and showed the note in his palm. The girls exchanged glances and giggled. They lowered the calabashes. One calabash contained fura, and the other nono.

"Anyi ghotara Igbo ntakiri," the one with nono said, implying he should not make gestures at them all the time to communicate because they understood a smattering of Igbo.

He understood them clearly even though they spoke Igbo with a strange intonation. He figured they were about Oyibo's age or a little older. He wondered if they were twins. They looked alike, though not in the striking way of identical twins, light-skinned and pretty in their sleeveless half tops and short wrappers. One was triangle-faced and the other had a round face.

"Fura k'obu nono," said the round-faced one with fura, and giggled.

"Nono."

"Ego ole?" the second girl said.

"Fifty naira." He showed the crisp one-hundred-naira note in his palm again, a gift from the suitor.

She collected the note. She wore large, dangling copper earrings. Her braids were long and beaded, stopping short of reaching into the calabash of nono as she bent over and ladled nono into a small bowl. She handed the bowl to him. He took it and drank while they watched him and giggled.

"Ke afa gi?" One asked after his name.

"Ekwe."

They giggled.

"A bum Rukaitu," said Round Face.

"Munwa bu Maimuna," her sister said.

Rukaitu pulled the little sister to her and introduced her. "Aha ya bu Aamaal."

They gave him his change, lifted their calabashes, and waved at him with hands covered in mehndi patterns.

He watched them as they walked away giggling, a vague feeling of familiarity washing over him.

The Palace

EKWE LOATHED HAVING TO GO TO THE FARM BEFORE everyone, but it was his inheritance. His grandfather used to go to the farm before everyone, according to Papa Ekwe, and he was always the last to go home. After his grandfather passed on, Papa Ekwe inherited the legacy of going to the farm first before the entire village, and he did not leave until everyone left. It was the family heirloom. But Ekwe did not fancy this heritage. He did not see any good in this early-bird patrimony. He figured being the first to go to the farm did not make Papa Ekwe's plants any greener. It did not make his potatoes turn into yams. Indeed, if Papa Ekwe had not come to the farm this morning before everyone, he would have been spared the anger that enlarged his nostrils and made them gape like wells at what he stumbled on.

"We have to go and see the king." Papa Ekwe's fist tightened around his machete.

The neighbours agreed.

"But who will be our spokesperson?" someone asked.

"We shouldn't behave in an unruly manner before the king," another said.

The cowherds had let their cattle loose upon the community farmland. The animals had stamped through, annoyingly grabbing a mouthful of plants here and there. Papa Ekwe had found their hoofprints everywhere as soon as he had stepped into the farmland this morning.

"I will be your spokesperson." A dark angular man stepped up.

Ekwe knew him. His name was Otonjo. He was notorious in the village for his drunkenness, his pluck.

"I suggest we make Papa Ekwe our spokesperson," said a woman's voice.

"I am in support. Papa Ekwe we shall make our spokesperson," another female voice said.

"We all are in support," chorused many voices.

Papa Ekwe was made the spokesperson, and, singing a revolutionary song, the crowd marched off to the palace. The king's palace was enclosed by an old fence. Ekwe had never visited the palace. He did not think he had been to an important place. He fancied there weren't many important places in the community. It was probably only the king's palace. And he was not sure there were important people in the village other than the king. Papa Ekwe had once told him of a man from Nrobo, someone big in the state government. The man was born on the other side of Adada River, if Ekwe correctly remembered the way Papa Ekwe had put it, and the man's parents had lived and died as peasants who grew corn there. Their farmhouse was probably still there in the farm settlement, overtaken by neglect. Ekwe reckoned the man-who-was-someone-big-in-the-state-government did not visit home. The road to his village was probably too bumpy for his expensive cars. Maybe he had no use for the farmhouse where his parents died. Why bother about a farmhouse when he probably lived with his family in a fine large house in Enugu city?

Moss grew on the low palace walls, soft and furry in the rainy season, like a cat's wet coat. But in the dry season, the moss died, and the begrimed walls looked like vomit on the old brickwork fence. A large cement house wearing brown paint stood in the wide compound. The king and his family lived in the brown house, but his official duties were carried out in his obi, a thatched, round reception hall with a conical roof.

Ekwe looked around the compound. His eyes settled on a flower hedge around the door of the brown house. The hedge looked untrimmed, bursting with deep orange blossoms. The protesting farmers waited for the king outside the reception hall. He was wearing his king's long robe when he finally came out of the large house and walked down the paved way to the thatched reception. Tall, with thick drooling lips, he walked with regal strides and urgency in his steps. Ekwe copied Papa Ekwe and others who bowed to the king as he settled on his throne. Mama Ekwe and other women genuflected.

"Your Highness." Papa Ekwe started to tell the king about the invasion of the farm while the king's thick lower lip hung like a kilo of meat as he listened to firsthand accounts of the invasion.

"I have heard your complaints," he said. "I am going to investigate them. I will seek out the cowherds who have come into our land and ensure their cattle don't trespass into your farmland again after I have met them, I assure you. Do not raise dust over this issue any further. Don't forget we have a tradition of hospitality in this village. We must be nice to our guests. We must learn to tolerate them. Egbe belu, ugo belu. The tree will accommodate different birds; therefore, no bird should deny the other her perching right."

"We understand your proverb, our king, but a man should not come to another man's land at the peril of his host, so that he will not grow a haunch when he is leaving." Papa Ekwe returned proverb for proverb.

"The insects of the hill have resolved to sit on each other's back not because the blade of grass they share is the last one standing on the hill, but because they have love for each other," King Okosisi said with a slight note of irritation in his voice.

"Shall we then use our testicles as seats in our own homes at the risk of crushing them?" Papa Ekwe returned.

"Have you people come here to trade proverbs with me?" King Okosisi flared up. "I am your king, and I decide who comes into our land or not. I expect you to understand when I assure you that the cowherds and their cattle won't go near your crops again."

A ripple of protest passed through the crowd. Angered by the king's offhand manner, opinions rained from the protesters.

"We won't tolerate total strangers coming into our land uninvited to destroy our crops with their cattle," thundered Papa Onukwube, a short man with a stutter whose farm was next to Papa Ekwe's.

"We couldn't believe our eyes," another man who was even shorter than Papa Onukwube said, his anger rising and inflating his chest as he spoke. "Even a swarm of locusts could not have done more damage to our crops."

More protesters reacted. Papa Ekwe's efforts to stop them went unheeded.

"Those cows are worse than peach-potato aphid."

"We will accommodate our guests, but we certainly won't do that at the expense of our comfort and well-being."

"We will not allow them do to us what they did to the people of Nimbo."

"Yes. We want them out of our community."

"We heard you leased out our land to them." Otonjo pushed through the crowd and stood before the king. "What happened to the money realized from the illegal lease?"

The king looked furious. His lips protruded, stung like wasp on the mouth by the accusation.

"Gbaghalu. I apologize if anyone of us has said something that offends you, Your Highness." Papa Ekwe cut into the storm of protests. "Fellow farmers. We have never had cause to doubt the king's words and his good intentions for us, his subjects. Let us give him the benefit of the doubt, I entreat you. Let's leave the decision of what to do about the cowherds and their cattle to his wisdom."

A weak murmur of protest tapered off as Papa Ekwe bowed to the king. The protesters repeated the king's salutation, bowed one by one following Papa Ekwe's example, the women bending their knees as the small crowd left the palace.

Ekwe was overwhelmed with an eerie feeling of déjà vu.

A New Calling

EKWE WAS DRAWN TO THE ROAR OF AN ENGINE, BUT when he dashed outside, what he saw forced him to take a step back into the room. Water covered everything. Everywhere. The compound was a surging ocean, the waves so high they were about to crash over the house. Breaking through the water was a fish, the biggest fish Ekwe had ever seen, a giant fish caught in a fine breaching arc, in a large splash of water. He felt himself drowning in the blue and glacial water. If Ekwe could read, he would see how imaginative the artist had been with his paintbrush, how brilliantly the painter had captured the sea themes on the gwongworo's tailboard in deep blues and greens, and succeeded in turning the name of the gwongworo, "Go Slow," into a breaching fish.

Go Slow gave a shrill honk as it drew to a stop in the compound. It was loaded with iron sheets and timber. Everyone came rushing out of the house. The family had been expecting the delivery: roofing materials and workers sent by the suitor for the renovation of the house. Papa Ekwe had asked everyone to stay home. The women would cook for the workers and the children would help in whatever small ways they could. There was widespread excitement.

"Nno nuo." Mama Ekwe, intoxicated with happiness,

greeted the workers as they alighted from the gwongworo and set to work at once, unloading the materials.

A pink-faced black monkey was jumping from plywood to plywood. The monkey calmly surveyed the landscape from a height. Ekwe and his siblings and half-siblings shrieked with joy as they gathered to watch the monkey, who soon attracted other children from the neighbourhood.

"Her name is Chilo," announced the angular driver who laughed a little too often.

"Chilo, Chilo, Chilo," the children chanted. They threw her palm kernels and nuts and giggled. The monkey caught the gifts and put them away in her cheek pouch but made funny faces when she lost a gift.

"Get moving, everyone." Papa Ekwe shooed the children away from the monkey. "Go get things out of the house. Bring everything out."

The children went to work grudgingly. Ekwe, Oyibo, and Azuka quickly brought out things in Mama Ekwe's room. Ekwe's half-siblings also emptied the rooms they shared with their mothers. They rushed back to play with the monkey. Ekwe threw her a ripe palm nut. The monkey missed it and pouted. He threw it again. This time she caught the nut and gave him a broad, wrinkled grin.

The children giggled.

After unloading the materials, the driver jumped back into the gwongworo and fired the engine. The guard, a slight man with a square forehead, removed a thick wedge from the back tyre and threw it into the empty lorry as it started to move. The children waved at Chilo, who paused from eating a palm nut to wave back at them with a sad look. The guard was casually chatting with the workers, completely ignoring the gwongworo now gathering speed. The children stared with wide wondering eyes. The gwongworo was leaving the guard!

Suddenly he turned and sprinted towards the lorry like a madman, momentarily disappearing in a helix of smoke the gwongworo coughed out of its exhaust pipe. Ekwe peered through the umber screen of smoke. Now the gwongworo was at full throttle, and the guard was visible again in the fading film of smoke. Ekwe relished the rhythmic slap-slap of the guard's slippered feet as he sprinted. And when he finally caught up with the lorry, he slapped the tailboard three times, which did not make any sense to Ekwe. The smoke had almost cleared up to give the children a better view of the spectacle. Now gripping the tailboard, legs thrashing in fluid motion, the guard sprang. He swung across the tailboard like a gibbon, using it to lever himself to a height above the gwongworo's body. At that bird's height, he cartwheeled dangerously but felinely to the awe of his watchers, and when he landed in the lorry on his feet and smiled and waved at the children, they broke into spontaneous applause for his unbelievable acrobatic display.

"Oh, God, please let that be me someday!" Ekwe groaned after he lost sight of the gwongworo.

He admired the display so much that he yearned to become a guard himself. He wished he knew how to pray as persuasively as Oyibo and Azuka. But prayer worked for him like a sleeping pill. He dozed off no sooner than Oyibo or Azuka started their bedtime prayer. He crossed himself only when he wanted to eat. It was not even a real crossing, but a mechanical wiggle of his fingers, a caricature of crossing by a boy who was always too hungry for a proper prayer, Oyibo had mocked him.

Later, Ekwe walked to the stream thinking of his new calling. He closed his eyes and replicated the guard's wild and dangerous somersaults. He saw him again slicing through the air like a blade, his slight body manipulating the airflow around him. Ekwe's eyes shone as he wondered how he might become a guard with the ability to take to the sky.

At the stream, he stood away in awe of ekwukwonju and mused over the precognitive power of the leaf. He rummaged through the blurred lines of his astral experience. He remembered Papa Ekwe's words: *When he touched that mystical leaf, ekwukwonju provoked his ascension to the astral realm. It induced his soul to depart from his physical body and enter the astral body to travel in a plane. Some people who have experienced this have ended up dead because their astral bodies wandered away and never reentered their physical bodies. We are lucky that in his case Ekwe has a powerful chi who guided his spirit back to his body after astral projecting into the future.*

Back home, Ekwe smelt the room's unfamiliar new smell, faintly metallic after hours of the sun roasting the new iron roof. In the night, he lay down on his mat in quiet recollection of the day. Mama Ekwe's oil lamp illuminated the room. The light gave the ceiling a curious shine because of its newness. Now the smell was warm, earthy, and reassuring—the scent of wood fresh from the mill. The darkness, when Mama Ekwe blew out the oil lamp, was figurative, but it was the suitor and not Oyibo who lit up the scene. Ekwe saw the eventful day again in cinematic glimpses as the workmen ripped off their shirts and almost re-created the guard's aerodynamics, their skills holding them aloft as they peeled off rust zinc like layers of skin from an old wound, and as they uncovered raffia beams untouched by wood lice. Ekwe focused his mind on the muscles of the carpenters as they hammered the new iron sheets into the woodwork. Gbam gbam, it resonated through his mind, the overlapping sounds of hammering that gave the new iron sheets their name. At lunch, the carpenters had plucked fufu with those callused hands and dunked their balls into Mama Ekwe's bowl of ohoyi soup for lunch. The same toughened hands had cupped around Papa Ekwe's gourd of palm wine at the end of their work.

But Azuka and Oyibo would ruin everything if they ran away, Ekwe thought. He did not think that the suitor deserved such treatment after his act of generosity. He might withdraw his favours from the family. Ekwe did not want to spit this honey, which the bees in the suitor's apiary had deposited in his mouth, so he resolved to tell Mama Ekwe of the girls' secret plot to run away. He tossed and turned. Mama Ekwe's snoring kept him awake and interfered with his powers of concentration. He hissed. Mama Ekwe stirred. A pause in her snoring amplified the momentary silence, and then she vroomed like a CG motorcycle. He lay still with eyes closed but unable to sleep. A barn owl pierced the night with her classic call, dark and foreboding, as exhaustion slowly overcame Ekwe and a feeling of emptiness descended on him, a sensation of walking out of his own body. His encounter with the herdsgirls had evoked in him a strong sense of nostalgia. The reason he went to the stream earlier was to pluck ekwukwonju and hold the forbidden leaf in his palm long enough to invoke its powers.

Azuka's Treachery

EKWE DID NOT UNDERSTAND THE CURVE OF MAMA Ekwe's anger when he told her of Azuka and Oyibo's secret plot to flee. Her anger moved like the wind, which swept Ekwe's tome-tome away from the goalpost and caused the ball to miss its target.

"How convenient it is for you to hide your hypocrisy." Mama Ekwe's anger alighted on Azuka. "Did you think I wouldn't find out, how you tried to goad my daughter into running away from her suitor? Such a good schemer you are. A good pretender. You are the innocent one, the quiet mouse that gnaws hard but blows comforting air to the wound. Ki ife mmelu. But what is my offence? Have I committed an abomination because I want my daughter to settle down? How could you bite the finger that feeds you?"

Azuka's cheeks were rouged by Mama Ekwe's hard words. Her pimples all stood in protest, tipped with pus. Suddenly she turned with a sob and fled towards the road. Ekwe hissed, thinking, Why can't Mama Ekwe's anger move like an Adidas ball, which hit the target when kicked in the right direction; instead it derailed like a tome-tome and hit Azuka, who was not even the person who had suggested running away. A thought steeled him, brushing his mind away from Mama

Ekwe's anger against Azuka. What if he asked the suitor to buy him an Adidas ball? He longed to kick a real ball instead of a tome-tome.

"This is all your fault." Oyibo lunged at him for blowing their secret. "You open your mouth like an anus and excrete things that stink."

Ekwe crossed his arms, put his hand to his jaw, and searched himself for any guilt. He had only reported what he saw and heard, so why dump the blame on him? He always reported things to Mama Ekwe. When he noticed that the tissue at the base of the habanero plants were browning and shriveling at the farm, he reported his finding to Mama Ekwe. The whole farm would have been ruined had he not, and together they had pulled out the affected plants and thrown them far away from the good ones.

Ekwe thought that Oyibo deserved to take all the blame. All this would not have happened if she had ignored the suitor's nose and Adam's apple and married him. If only she could think of his fine red motorcar instead of thinking of his bald head, which shone like glassware when he took off his hat. Ekwe chuckled despite himself.

Mama Ekwe hissed and stamped in and out of the house after Azuka fled, needled by a song Ekwe's big stepmother sang loudly and derisively. Papa Ekwe was leaving for the farm, a hoe hanging over his left shoulder, his back arced against Mama Ekwe. Later at the farm, Ekwe and Oyibo drew water from Ogele and watered the plants in hostile silence without Azuka. Even when they ate roast yam, they ate it in malicious quiet. Ekwe missed working with Azuka at the farm. He sensed that all would not be the same again in their cheerful little room now that Azuka had left. As night drew near, he sat under the neem tree expecting her to show up among the trees widely spaced and nutty brown in the setting sun. He shifted his gaze to Mama Ekwe. Her anger fully spent, she was no longer stamping the ground as if it was complicit in that secret plot to run away. She sat outside her kitchen and peered regretfully down the road as if expecting Azuka to simply walk home.

"We can eat the meat now that the maggot has been removed from it, eeh?" Papa Ekwe said at supper.

Tufiakwa! Ekwe spat furtively into a corner. He would never eat meat with maggot in it no matter how hungry he was. What kind of gluttony was that, and how could Papa Ekwe suggest it?

Ekwe knew nothing about metaphors.

Zaram's Obssession

EKWE WENT OUT IN SEARCH OF AZUKA THE NEXT morning. His guilt started to eat him up when he realized that Papa Ekwe had metaphorically called Azuka "maggot in the meat." Azuka probably fled to Umulokpa, the farm settlement where her father lived with her stepmother and her half-siblings. They had lived there right from the time people started moving away from the bight towards the headwaters. Long periods of droughts had dried up the back-waters and hampered manual irrigation methods. They had resettled around the foothills and started to grow their crops there. The settlement had blossomed with more migrations, and though the basin occasionally dried up during severe droughts, the human tributary continued.

As Ekwe rounded a curve at the T-junction where he had found and eaten aja, he came almost face-to-face with Azuka in the company of a young man named Zaram. Ekwe ducked out of sight. He had seen the young man Zaram in the village before and admired him for his refinedness but wondered why he began all his sentences with "Umm . . ."

"Umm, my name is Zaram." Ekwe overheard Zaram speaking to Azuka from where he hid in a thicket. "Umm, please can you show me the way to my grandmother

Orinechi's compound? I am her grandson visiting the village from the city and I can't seem to find my way."

Zaram came to the community not only to see his grandmother Orinechi, but also to see the necklace of hills with a pendant of villages. On his way back to his grandmother Orinechi's house after one of his excursions, he lost his way in the warren of village paths. Visitors always got puzzled in the community connected by a twisted matrix of paths looping around compounds and gardens.

Azuka studied him, a thin village girl looking flustered. She seemed to think, If this boy is Orinechi's grandson, then he must be Eliza's son. She knew all the grandsons and granddaughters of Orinechi except the two grandchildren by Eliza, who lived with their mother in the city. They had never been to this village.

"Come, let me show you," Azuka said.

He followed her. He didn't have many options in any case. She led him through the twists, zigzagging, easily meandering. Ekwe followed, ducking behind trees and shrubs. Grandmother Orinechi was well known. She was the mother of Eliza, the most successful woman in the village by any standards.

Azuka stopped and pointed naively. "That's her house."

"Umm, thank you." His face lit up with recognition.

She waited, wondering if she should talk to him and take him into confidence for Oyibo's sake. As far as one could tell, Zaram's mother was the most controversial figure in the community. She left Enu-Ozara and married a city man, broke free and married this boy's father, like a dove freed from a cage, soaring high and exploring the space it never could before.

"Umm, do you want to say something?" Possibly he saw her indecision competing with the pimples on her face.

She started to tell him about the suitor with the big red motorcar, her cousin's suitor. "After my mother died when I was still a little girl, her sister took me and raised me. I grew up with my cousins Oyibo and Ekwe doing everything together. Many suitors have been coming for Oyibo's hand in marriage. She is a great beauty! Everything changed when the suitor with the big red motorcar materialized. Papa Ekwe wants him to marry her because of a dream my cousin Ekwe had about cowherds attacking our community, but I think it's also because of the generous bride price he would get from the suitor. My cousin doesn't like him because he has a large nose and Adam's apple. He's old, ugly, and polygamous. Her rejection of the suitor created rancour at home. Things started falling apart. My cousin considered running away. She had my support, so Mama Ekwe accused me of backstabbing. She accused me of ingratitude to the family that gave me life. 'You were only three years old when your mother died. I took you in, a good and kindhearted aunt who cared about a poor helpless baby whose mother had died and left dry. I sheltered you, fed, and clothed you. I brought you up like my own daughter. But what did you do? You repaid my good with evil. You grew jealous of your cousin because she has a suitor who drives a red motorcar with white seats and drinks White Horse. You vowed to frustrate the suitor. You are evil.'" Azuka paused.

Zaram stood frowning at her. He understood her dialect with some difficulty. At times the Igbo/Wawa dialect sounded like swear words to him, sometimes like percussion from a long, endless roll of thunder. "Umm, what are you going to do now?" He spoke his Igbo with a musical twang.

"I am going away. I don't want to plague Mama Ekwe's eyes again with my thin, ugly self. But I feel for my cousin. She is going to leave school and marry a man her father's age. Her beauty is going to go to waste. I shouldn't be bothering you with my problems, anyway. Thank you."

She made to walk away, but he stopped her. He invited her to his grandmother Orinechi's house, a large cement house with a sit-out, burglary-proof, and sliding-glass windows. The house had no rival in the village, Ekwe thought. It was a modern house befitting a woman of Eliza's status. Zaram's uncle Anango sat outside and oiled his hunting gun. His bald head shone as if he had oiled it too. His second wife, Ozioma, was arranging her nchu-anwu in a raffia basket to take them to Eke Enu-Ozara. She was a little woman with quick, impatient movements and disheveled hair. In a chatty mood, her voice rang through the neighbourhood.

Zaram led Azuka into Grandmother Orinechi's room. She lay on her iron bed, shriveled as a rag, small mouth set like a pout against the hollow of her cheeks. He sat at the edge of her bed and fondled her wrinkly fingers. He talked with her for a while about her arthritic legs while she stared at him with milky, unblinking eyes.

"Tell your mother no need bringing those medicines," Grandmother Orinechi said, the words gently parting the curtains of her thin-lipped mouth. "This body is too old and impervious to medicines. No need wasting money."

Grandmother Orinechi went on to list her complaints: Uncle Anango delighted in inflicting pain on her, which was why he kept inviting nurses who pierced her skin with needles. And did Zaram know that his uncle's wife starved her? And did he also know that even though she preferred ora leaves in her egusi soup and resented ugu leaves, that wife of her son's still cooked with ugu leaves? That eating that woman's food made her feel like a goat eating grass? On and on she went, her words taking a slow but dignified flight as if through a well-lubricated windpipe.

Zaram tried to convince her that Uncle Anango and his wife meant well for her, that the injections were meant to cure her arthritis, that the doctor had forbidden her from eating food high in cholesterol because of her diabetes and her daughter-in-law wanted her to eat more vegetables because vegetables were good for her body.

Azuka sat in silence and listened to the mild argument between the grandmother and her grandson.

Amadi

EKWE REVEALED HIMSELF TO AZUKA WHEN SHE came out of Grandmother Orinechi's house. She was surprised to see him but rejected his plea to return to the house because everyone was missing her. He then begged to follow her, which she granted him. He accompanied her to Amadi's house. Zaram had advised her to seek help from Amadi, a very enlightened man, a man too much education made headstrong. He lived in isolation in an old family house, a cottage Ekwe and Azuka approached with caution in the emphatic silence of the treed surroundings. Ekwe caught sight of Amadi through an open window. As one would expect, Amadi was sitting on a threadbare cushion in the furniture-challenged room. He was reading a book. Ekwe wondered if Azuka's heart was beating as fast as his as the two crossed themselves at the door before knocking and entering the house.

The book Amadi was reading had *The Green Wall* as its title. He was immersed in the book, sure enough, one leg thrown wildly over the arm of the cushion. He closed the book, swung his leg down, and scowled at them. Amadi's fierce eyes and bearded face unnerved them. But then he relaxed his hard, questioning stare.

"Azuka," Azuka said when he asked for their names. "This is my little cousin Ekwe."

Amadi waved them to a seat and rubbed his bald head that was not as glossy as that of Oyibo's suitor. The house smelt fruity, as might be expected. When Ekwe looked out the back window, he saw a garden with a banana plantation and many trees. He saw several seed trays with young plant shoots carpeting the underwood.

"So, what brings you here?"

"My cousin is about to be forced to marry a man older than her father against her will."

Ekwe was startled by Azuka's accusation, her boldness.

Amadi chuckled. "Is that not the culture in this community? Why is she objecting to the marriage?"

Ekwe felt his hopes rising to his chest.

"She wants to continue in school," Azuka said.

"School?" Amadi laughed. "It's interesting to learn there is a young girl in this community who will choose school over marriage. Tell me more about her."

She told him everything about Oyibo: her beauty, the suitor, and the dispute in the family.

"I had a niece," Amadi said. "You may know her story. I grew up with her father in this house. But we were different. He was a son of the soil. And he cherished family life. I was not cut out for family. I was adventurous. I wanted to see the world. I wanted to leave this village at all costs. It felt like a cage. But I had no idea where to go." He paused, grinned, then continued. "I have heard the village pupils complain of trekking four miles to school. Back then I used to trek seven miles to an urban school because there was no school in the whole of this province. I was the only student from the province who went to the urban school. And then the opportunity came, one day, as I was listening to my father's transistor radio. I heard of an essay competition whose winner would receive a scholarship. I took the opportunity to write about poverty and the agonies of education in this part of the world. My essay won the competition and a scholarship to study in one of the unity schools in the country. The success of my essay also attracted an elementary school in Enu-Ozara. Then I left Okposi for Utah to study for my bachelor's degree. I spent my years outside teaching human resource management and development at various universities. Like I said, I am not a family man. My earnings went into charity. After those many years outside, I'm finally home for good. The good news is, I am partnering with UNESCO to set up a scholarship scheme for indigent students in this region. So, you see, it's still possible for your cousin to realize her dream of going to school." He rubbed his bald head and fingered his oily beard. "We have talked about your cousin. Now let's talk a little about you. Tell me about your dream. Have you got one?"

She would like to become a teacher, Azuka said.

Ekwe wanted to hiss, but he suppressed it. How could Azuka want to end up a teacher, a stereotyped miser who measured a tuber of yam with a ruler to make sure she ate just enough to keep her going?

"In that case the scholarship is for you," Amadi said. "But you will have to work for it because only those who top their class will receive it. But they must have proof of having planted a tree. Have you ever planted one?"

She shook her head.

Naturally he started to talk about trees: how they provide fertility to the soil, protect it from water and wind erosions, take up carbon dioxide from the air to give oxygen in return, improve humidity by putting moisture in the atmosphere, which aids the buildup of cloud cover and rainfall.

"I am sure your teacher has taught you all that at school, hasn't she? Unfortunately, people are getting increasingly obsessed with activities that reduce the number of trees and disturb nature's balance."

Azuka kept nodding, but Ekwe looked blank.

Amadi threw his hands out in a wild shrug. "That's all. You may go now."

They left.

"I will see what I can do about your cousin," he called after them.

▲▲▲▲▲

The long walk to Umulokpa left Ekwe and Azuka winded. The sun burned. Azuka did not want to be dragged back to her aunt's home. After her supposed act of betrayal, she could not face her aunt just yet. She had lived with Mama Ekwe since she was three years old, since the death of her mother, who, she was told, died during childbirth along with her unborn baby brother. She would have treasured the faintest recollection of her mother's image, but her memory of the woman that gave her breath was empty. The walk took them over the bald brow of the hills and past the blackened remains of the Aguowuru Forest after the recent fires. They crossed parched melon fields and sunbaked plains dotted with cottonwood. Azuka rarely visited her father. In the fullness of her rage, her aunt had hinted at how she had saved Azuka from her stepmother by taking her away after her mother passed. According to Mama Ekwe, her stepmother had tied her father into the knot of her wrappa; he acted at her bidding. Now that she was finally going home to her father, the thought of living with a dumpy and grumpy stepmother dissolved into a watery sensation in her stomach.

After a long trek on a track that tore through the country, they emerged onto the main road. They had completed the journey by half. Ekwe cast a long look to the east. In the distance, the wide, untarred road crested a small hill, then disappeared into a mesh of greenery. He looked the other way where the road descended a valley, cutting through a thick wood. He wondered how much time it took a traveller from Enu-Ozara to get to the city of Onitsha as a smoking gwongworo emerged out of the leafage. They watched the cargo lorry as it rolled down in a cloud of smoke and dust, then clattered past, its angular woodwork filled with baskets of produce. They stood and watched until they lost sight of the cargo in a fine white haze of smoke. If they turned left and started walking in the direction towards which the gwongworo had come, the road would lead them past the village school and over the bridge, but instead of the motorway, they took a cross-country route across hills and valleys. At last, a dark and broody stream loomed ahead. They clambered down into the spongy water to wash their faces and limbs.

Refreshed, they continued the last lap of the journey.

The mountain rose in a cloak of mist in the distance, a broad and crouching animal. The more they walked towards the range, the farther away it moved, taking the shape of a beast lunging at prey somewhere in the clouds. In the distance, the snaky path skirted timidly around the ridge in much the same way as a weaker opponent would avoid a more powerful and threatening enemy. The path fled from them until they felt as though they had walked the full circumference of the land, then the village sprang into view in a chaos of huts.

Marriage Proposal

THEY ENTERED HER FATHER'S COMPOUND LIKE TWO chickens stepping into an unfamiliar territory, three huts set in the shape of a triangle. Ekwe was meeting Azuka's family for the first time. Her stepmother was a large, peevish woman fighting her arthritis-infested limbs with the help of her grandchildren and the village quack. All her children were married, all two sons and six daughters. She was mostly confined to her hut. Her grandchildren helped her to the housefront every afternoon, where she sat and watched them as they played with other children. Some were the children of her much younger co-wife and others the children from the neighbourhood. They made her laugh, made her snap, and made her screech with their adventurous acts of play.

Azuka's second stepmother, Mama Ofor, was a quiet and alienated mother of five who spent all day at the farm. While making dinner, she sang songs as stringy as her wiry frame. Ekwe did not know if Mama Ofor's melancholy manners had to do with her careworn relationship with her co-wife. Sometimes they chatted and laughed, but their laughter did not seem to go beyond their incisors. The only time their laughter reached deep down to their guts was not when they laughed with each other, but when they laughed at each other. The house was almost frozen, with the stepmothers minding their space. The icy relationship left Ekwe and Azuka confused and ambivalent.

Azuka's father was a man hardened by overwork. He looked as dry and toughened as a bullwhip. He was rarely seen at home besides when he dozed on a back chair in the housefront after dinner, stirred, took a drowsy sip of a hot drink in a bottle by his side, meant to unlock all knotted joints and free them for the next day's work. But things had changed since the attack on Nimbo. Militants had infiltrated the forests. They ambushed the villagers in their homes and farms. A woman of the village was raped in the loneliness of her farmland only a few days back. It became unavoidable for him to raise a small hut for Azuka and Ekwe. Azuka had left too early as a child and needed to acquaint herself with life in the village. There were new friends to make on the path to the market, the track to the farm, and during a bath by the river. And there was farmwork to be done. But she was not afraid of work. She had been well trained on the farm.

"Don't go to the farm or the river alone," her father warned. "It is no longer healthy. Always go in the company of others."

Making new friends posed a new kind of conflict for Azuka. Most of her age-mates were married. Some already had babies and looked a decade older than her. They could never understand her thoughts and desires, especially when she talked about her dream of becoming a teacher like Miss Clara, the village schoolteacher, instead of starting her own family.

"I will wear lipstick and painted fingernails, and I will

walk like this." She mimicked the ladylike way Miss Clara walked.

Her friends looked away without interest. Miss Clara ought to have been married, they said. At her age, she should be running a home full of her own children. But no, she was wasting her life fussing with a bunch of children who would soon abandon her class to become wives and mothers, shepherds, and farmhands. She was wasting her precious life wearing flowers and skirts. They mimicked the way she painted her lips and walked on her toes. They would rather talk about their husbands' likes and dislikes, strengths and weaknesses, temper, generosity, and passion. They gushed over the number of children they wished to have.

Azuka's obsession with school and Miss Clara and teaching bored Ekwe. Miss Clara sent for her weeks after she returned to Umulokpa. Ekwe accompanied her and listened to Miss Clara talk about Amadi's scholarship.

"Amadi wants you to take part in the scholarship exam," Miss Clara said. "The scholarship is fully funded. It comes with a full tuition scholarship and a fellowship grant for your living expenses up to university education."

Scholarship and fellowship and university sounded so unfamiliar to Ekwe. At the time Miss Clara was posted to the school, the pupils had studied under the shade of a tree. They were sent home whenever the clouds had gathered for rain. But a few years later, someone who did not wish to have his identity disclosed had built a school block and equipped it with benches, chairs, and tables. Miss Clara's school became structurally complete, but she had faced a different and bigger challenge: the classrooms were empty. She was forced to go from house to house to beg parents to allow their children to come to school. Some parents had been reluctant, but most were outright hostile. They did not want to lose their children, who were farmhands and shepherds, to school. The class had thinned down instead of growing, with parents steadily withdrawing their female children and giving them out in marriage.

▲▲▲▲▲

One evening, a man from the community named Agugwu visited Azuka's father. The old and haggard man was not familiar to Azuka. He ate dinner with her father, drank wine and talked about crops and greenflies and cowherds. Agugwu became a frequent guest of the house. And then he came with some relatives a few weeks after his first visit. They came with a goat, a few tubers of yam, a bag of potatoes, and palm wine.

"Agugwu has shown his interest in you as his bride," Azuka's father said to her.

Azuka was told that the items were for her bride price. She glanced at Agugwu, who showed a pair of missing incisors in a smile at her, the rest of his teeth begging to be scraped of some soft, pulpy, yellow coating. She opened her mouth, but the will to protest deserted her. Suddenly she was overcome by a feeling of fatigue. She did not feel anger, did not even feel self-pity; what she felt was closer to anguish. Her father hadn't had the least decency to discuss her suitor with her before accepting her bride price. What was the use of protesting? It would only serve to confirm her badness. No good daughter questioned her father's decisions on matters of her suitor. She felt as unwanted as a mole growing on a prominent side of the face. As worthless as flatulence. But where was her father's obligation in fairness to her aunt who brought her up? What she felt against him—disappointment rather than anger—was not as much for his lack of obligation towards her, nor for his unfairness to her aunt who had raised her, as it was for the urgency to get rid of her for only a few tubers of yam, a few mouthfuls of wine, and a sickly looking goat.

Azuka followed her suitor home, seen off to the road by her stepmothers, who left her with a sense of celebrity. Also on the marriage train were Agugwu's oldest daughter and his sister, with the obligations to accompany the bride home. The women were parroting a wedding song, their tones decrepit and obligatory. They were expected to deliver the bride safely into the hands of her co-wives—her suitor's wives—who waited at home. The songs would have had more vitality, the event more vibrancy, if the bride were Agugwu's first. Still, he was hailed in each compound across which the train went. He had himself a brand-new wife, a delicate tendril of a wife, to add to his other wives. The train arrived home to the halfhearted cheering of Agugwu's wives and a swarm of neighbours. As the women sang and danced, Azuka glimpsed her future in the hollows of their cheeks and in the sway of their withered hips.

The City Beckons

EKWE DID NOT FOLLOW AZUKA TO HER SUITOR'S home. He slept alone in their little hut and ate with Azuka's father, whose fufu balls dwarfed Papa Ekwe's dollops. Ohoyi was the big man's favourite soup, and Ekwe believed it was because the slimy soup helped his outsized balls to slide easily down his throat. He huffed like a cat after throwing down each ball. A vein protruded from his left temple, stood watch while he ate, and disappeared only after the meal. But he was a kind man and allowed Ekwe generous portions of meat from his kills. He always went to the farm with his long dane gun, partly to kill antelopes and grasscutters, and partly to protect himself from dangerous cowherds.

Ekwe was excited when Azuka returned on the fourth day, in line with tradition. She told Ekwe secrets she would tell only Oyibo. She returned untouched. Fate had been on her side. Her blood had come on her first night in her suitor's house, kept her company for the four customary days she had spent in his house, and followed her back to her father's house at the end of the rite. Agugwu could only stare at her and swallow. Ekwe felt shy hearing Azuka talk to him about femininities he considered sacred. He could imagine how much her youth had entered Agugwu's eyes while she was in his house for four days. He knew that Agugwu would be back in no time to finalize the marriage and take her away. Ekwe was sorry for Azuka to have to marry a man even older, uglier, and poorer than Oyibo's bald suitor.

Ekwe and Azuka went to harvest cassava. They followed a group of villagers to the community farmland by the river. While they worked, Ekwe spied a figure in the high rock bluffs on the far side of the canyon and alerted Azuka. They gazed up until they lost sight of the figure in the fluffy white clouds. Azuka grew scared and approached a woman in the neighbouring farm.

"We saw a figure in the rocks," she said.

The woman peered up anxiously in the clouds, shading her eyes in the intense sun. "I can't see anyone."

"I know what we saw."

Normally the first person among the villagers to sense danger would raise the alarm; a long, piercing cry that travelled across the expanse of farmland and warned everyone of danger. But people had raised false alarms before, causing everyone to flee and abandon their work.

"I am sure it's your imagination." The woman sounded dismissive as she went back to her work.

Azuka and Ekwe also returned to their work, got busy again, and forgot about what seemed to be an optical illusion. Her father's was one of the many farms spreading in acres over the lowlands up to the foothills. Her father planted cassava, yam, and corn mainly. Some others planted melon, beans, or groundnuts. When they finished with the harvest, Ekwe and Azuka loaded the robust brown tubers into raffia baskets and quickly moved into the river to wash. The apparition materialized and faded again among outcroppings of rock. They did not see it glide out of the last shelf of rock and vanish once more as they hurriedly headed back to their baskets of cassava. Suddenly the shadow reappeared again in the rift valley. They were going to flee as he kept on towards them, but then Azuka held Ekwe back by the hand as she recognized the familiar languorous gait. She stared at him as he approached in disbelief. He too stared at her, recognition dawning in his eyes and making them grow as round and big as watermelons. Azuka would never have thought she would ever meet Zaram again after they parted ways, of all places in this remote mountainside. He was excited to see her, took her hand and led them to the riverside, where they sat on a rock and talked.

"You mean you came all the way just to see the country?" she said.

"Umm, I have enjoyed the best possible country views." He came to see the mountain because he was leaving for the city the next day.

"We almost fled, thinking the figure that emerged out of the rock was a killer, a dangerous cowherd."

He laughed, his voice plumy. "Umm. Why don't you come with me to the city where there are no cowherds?"

She giggled. She told him she had a suitor, like her cousin Oyibo. She was tired of everything. Her misery told him everything he needed to know about what had happened between when they first met and now.

"Umm, you can come with me to the city if you want," he repeated. "I am serious about it."

"Can my cousin come along too?"

"Of course."

Ekwe cocked an ear as Azuka raised startled eyes and looked at Zaram. The thought of following her to Zaram's city lit Ekwe's face in a smile. He threw stones into the river as it wound its way slowly through a mangrove forest. Down the far right the water thinned then swept out of sight.

Zaram was equally startled. The offer to take Azuka and her cousin to the city came from nowhere. It was a wish. An impulse. But now that it was out, he did not know how to take it back, did not want to take it back. He refused to ponder the consequences of taking them to his home in Enugu to save her from her suitor. His life these past few days had been governed by impulses. The decision to go back to the city had come this morning as he had set out on a walk.

"How are you going to explain me to your mother?" Azuka said.

"My mother." He chuckled. "Umm. Is my mother not the most educated woman to have come out of this bush? The most notorious?"

The mere mention of his mother made her heart skip a beat. His mother was a household name in the community. She was famous for all the wrong reasons. Her name came up whenever a parent scolded a daughter they considered wayward. "Do you want to end up like Eliza, the daughter of Orinechi?" a parent would say while pulling the ear of a daughter who had rejected a suitor. The story went round: Eliza, the daughter of Orinechi, had rejected her suitors and fled to a place illuminated by electricity to sell her body to all kinds of men. Old and tired out, she had sunk her claws into one unfortunate man who would never hear the cry of a baby in his house because she was long past her menopause. The two children she claimed were her children—Zaram and his sister—she had adopted later in life. When he said his mother was educated and notorious, he left Azuka wondering if he knew the full story of his mother, Eliza, the daughter of Orinechi. Although her name was the subject of many conversations, Azuka, like most young people in the community, had never seen her. And though she did not know her in person, Eliza, the daughter of Orinechi, remained her role model.

Eliza, the Daughter of Orinechi

AZUKA'S CURIOSITIES GREW TO ANXIETIES ON A BUS to Enugu with Ekwe and Zaram. She tried to distract herself with conversations with Zaram. Ekwe entertained himself with the views that rushed past the window as the bus rolled across mangroves, hills, and plains. And then he began to see houses wearing shiny paints and colourful roofs. The smell of city filled his nose, different from the sometimes-loam-sometimes-iodine smell of the country. The vegetation was disappearing, and the houses were growing in close numbers, taller and more beautiful, and then the road opened out to tarred streets with wide signboards welcoming them to the city of Enugu.

Azuka's heart started to beat fast as they approached a large cream house with a white fence and black gate after alighting from the bus. A woman opened the door, smiled and hugged Zaram, frowned at Azuka and Ekwe, hesitated for a moment, and then stepped back to let them into a large white sitting room with big seats upholstered in black tiffany. Ekwe stole curious glances at the woman and her son. He thought he found a resemblance only in their slimness. Mama Ekwe had said that Eliza, the daughter of Orinechi, was born as dark as the ripened seed of an African olive. But now her skin blazed like fire. Azuka watched the son reuniting with the mother in utter disbelief. Was this Eliza, the daughter of Orinechi, for real, this woman who looked petite in a light house gown, with her Jheri curl cascading down her back, and barely drawing level with Zaram's shoulders?

Azuka soon found herself alone with and sitting squarely across from Eliza, the daughter of Orinechi—a moment Azuka both awed and dreaded. She saw a woman who was advanced, a middle-aged woman in the skin of a young lady. Gripping her seat tightly to keep her hands from shaking, she listened to the soft, throaty voice speaking in fluid dialect.

"My son has done something very foolish bringing you here without seeking my approval," she began.

A moment of silence followed, punctuated by the hum of the air conditioner, but the thumping of her own heart was all Azuka could hear.

"I have zero tolerance for disobedience. You didn't have to flee home without the knowledge of your parents. It is inexcusable. You both were stupid."

The large room suddenly became a closed, incubated space with Azuka gasping for air.

"I shall take you and your cousin back to your parents tomorrow morning."

The humming of the air conditioner grew into a din. The room started to reel slowly, forcing Azuka to grip the edges of her seat tighter.

"In the meantime, feel at home, take a shower with your cousin, eat dinner, and get a good sleep to regain strength for tomorrow's travels."

Daddy, Eliza's husband, was a thickset man with lustrous

grey hair and a big incandescent smile. His laughter rang clear like a new bell and when he returned from work the house seemed illuminated by the bright fluorescence of his smiles.

Ekwe had jollof rice and fish for dinner and slept on a large bed with blankets. Sleeping in that big, comfortable bed didn't give him nightmares as sleeping in Papa Ekwe's old mud house did. But then he became sad when he realized that Eliza, the daughter of Orinechi, was determined to repatriate them from the beautiful house. He cringed in the back seat of the flashy motorcar as Eliza drove very fast the next day. Azuka had spelt the name of the big motorcar as LANDROVER while tracing the stainless lettering on the shiny body of the car with her fingers. Eliza looked different this morning, girlish in an orange blouse and a short black skirt. As the journey progressed, she cheerfully told them about her daughter Miranda, who was a year older than Azuka. Miranda was in a boarding school, and literature was her favorite subject, and green her best color, and singing her favourite pastime. She also had a passion for painting and poetry.

"Shakespeare's sonnets are her favourites." Eliza laughed a soft and benign laugh. "She has pictures of *Mona Lisa* pasted all around her room, that great painting by Leonardo da Vinci. You missed her. She was home by the weekend, but she spent a sulky Sunday. You know why? Instead of the yellow ribbon she had asked for to go with her new black church gown, I forgot and bought her a large red rose."

Azuka giggled.

Ekwe wondered what they were: poetry, sonnets, and *Mona Lisa*. He and Azuka warmed up to Eliza's conversations even though they did not understand most things.

They pondered, in the intervals of silence when they heard only the tyres rolling on the tarmac, how different two people can be, how different two places can be: from streets and avenues edged with fine colourful houses to miles and miles of bush bordering dusty roads, from jollof rice and fish to fufu and empty ohoyi soup. The feeling of unease that had enveloped them lifted as they sat back and enjoyed the stories and the receding view.

At last, the car laboured up the rough country road, and following Azuka's direction, turned left into a wide approach bordered by stretches of farmlands and stopped in her father's sunbathed compound. Eliza alighted smartly. She walked towards the triangle of huts with Azuka and Ekwe cowering behind her. Azuka's stepmother sat on her favourite spot and nursed her swollen legs. She was surrounded by a flock of hungry, clucking chickens. Azuka's father heard voices and came out from his hut, boredom and exasperation heavy on his face.

Eliza declined the seat her father offered. "I am the one you call Eliza, the daughter of Orinechi from Enu-Ozara." Her tone was soft and polite.

Azuka's father could not have reacted more strongly to a sudden punch in the face.

"I brought your children back to you because I am sure you have been worried sick about them. I apologize on their behalf for running off without your knowledge. But I did not bring your daughter back for you to give her out in marriage. I brought her back to ask you in the proper way to let her live with me because I know it was wrong of her to flee from home."

Azuka was surprised at her directness. It took her father and stepmother a while to find their voices. They spoke to Eliza in a polite voice. He would have been very mad with Azuka and Ekwe had Eliza not brought them back herself, her father said. He would love to grant Eliza's wish to take them back to the city to live with her, but a man had made commitments on Azuka towards marriage.

"I will give back everything the man spent," Eliza said. "Marrying off a maiden of her age without her consent is child abuse and punishable by law."

Her father scratched his stubbly chin and gave a weak smile. He seemed lost for words.

"I shall return tomorrow to take them. I hope you will oblige me this request."

Azuka watched Eliza drive away.

"I don't know how you managed to get yourself entangled with a woman like that," her father started as soon as Eliza had driven out of sight. "Do you realize what you put us through when you took your little cousin and left without telling anyone?"

Azuka sulked.

"What are you fleeing from? You fled from your aunt's house after you created problems there. And then you vanished again only to reappear with Eliza, the daughter of Orinechi. And now you are going to live with a woman like that when you should be in your own home having and nursing babies for you and your husband. Is this the kind of wayward life you want for yourself?"

Azuka smiled furtively, at peace with herself, and certain of victory.

Cold Feet

AZUKA AND EKWE WERE ALL SET WHEN ELIZA ARrived the next morning. She had passed the night with her mother, Orinechi, in Enu-Ozara. She fired the car engine and tooted the horn to announce her presence. The neighbours rushed to their housefronts to stand and watch, children cringing naked behind mothers, with noses running and bellies protruding. As she drove away with Azuka and Ekwe, Azuka's father and her stepmothers stared after the forbidden blackness of the car until it slid out of sight with its tabooed passengers. Eliza did not drive straight back to Enugu. She drove to the village school. Miss Clara came out and hurried over to meet her as she pulled up under the large canopy of a mango tree. They walked into an empty classroom.

"The pupils are all gone," Miss Clara said with a helpless gesture. "Parents kept withdrawing their children for fear of the cowherds. A town crier had gone round to warn parents of the threat of an attack. I come here every day to wait for them."

The last time Eliza had come to the school, the pupils had numbered about fifteen. They had sat on benches and stared sleepy-eyed at her, their bare feet buried in the dusty floor.

"The children had started dropping out of school even before the fear of attack, especially the females," Miss Clara explained. "They were being given out in marriage. Even the boys were inconsistent as pupils and farmhands."

"What can be done to stop this menace?"

"I went from house to house to speak to them, but it didn't yield any success." Miss Clara's pain defined her thin frame. "I think you should speak to the priest. They listen to him, the ones who go to church, and their number is growing. He can speak to them through his sermons. But that should be when tension falls."

"I will see the priest," Eliza said. "I will also send materials and workmen across to take care of the floor."

"Thank you, ma. It will take care of the ticks eating into the pupils' toes." Miss Clara walked them to the car and watched them drive away.

"Amadi is a gift to the community," Eliza said on their way to the city. "He might seem a bit weird, but that is not important. What matters at this point is gaining from being kin with a man like him. I have the privilege of chairing the selection committee of a scholarship fund he is central to."

Ekwe would have loved to sit back and enjoy the drive and fantasize with eyes closed about going to school in the city, wearing crisp uniforms and leather sandals and being driven to school instead of trekking miles barefoot and getting his soles burnt on hot sand. But he was worried. What would Mama Ekwe think of his running off to the city with Azuka? He didn't even say goodbye to them. He suddenly realized that he had missed them. He had missed home. He wanted to be with his family when they relocated to the city after

Oyibo's marriage to the suitor with the big red motorcar. He knew that Oyibo would not withstand the pressure on her for too long. There would be nothing better than the family living together in a beautiful city house and eating good food without having to work from dawn to dusk in the habanero field.

"Kwusi! Kwusi!" he cried suddenly.

"O gini?" Azuka swung round in alarm.

"I want to go home. I am missing my mother and my father and my sister and the twins."

"You no longer want to go to school in the city?"

"No." He rocked his seat in defiance.

Azuka and Eliza conferenced briefly while he continued to throw tantrums.

"Okay," Eliza said, and turned the car towards the road to Enu-Ozara. "I am going to take you home."

A Marriage

MAMA EKWE AND OYIBO DASHED OUT OF THE HOUSE as Ekwe walked into the compound. Eliza had dropped him off near his father's house and driven away with Azuka. Mama Ekwe swept him off his feet and held him tightly to her bosom. And when she released him, Ekwe and his sister embraced, clinging to each other for a long time. The commotion drew Papa Ekwe and everyone out. Ekwe got more hugs, felt like a hero.

"We thought you were lost," Mama Ekwe said.

"We missed you so much," Oyibo said.

Mama Ekwe at once cooked a delicious meal of rice and stew for him from the bags of foodstuffs the suitor had supplied to the family. Later, as they ate dinner, Ekwe narrated his experience with Azuka, her family, and Eliza, the daughter of Orinechi. He was happy to be back home now that Sunday mood and the sound from the kitchen had changed to the hissing of stew from the annoying kpokonyapia of fufu pounding.

"Ekwe, my heir, we are happy to have you back," Papa Ekwe said in the middle of the meal. "We are also happy that Azuka is safe. But I must remind you all that this family is lucky to have a suitor like Chief Agubata for our daughter

Oyibo. This is a man who can have his choice of a wife anywhere at the click of the fingers, but he chooses this family. He spent a large amount of money on the renovation of our house. Look at how well we eat now. As his in-laws, he has promised to accommodate us in his house in the city if the militants should strike. What else do you expect from an in-law?"

Mama Ekwe's look was softened, but Oyibo's countenance was still rebellious.

"I am happy we have finally come to an understanding." Papa Ekwe cashed in on the frozen silence to press home his resolve. "I am going to send a message across to the suitor first thing tomorrow. I know he would want an urgent ceremony, so you better be prepared."

The air around the house thickened with expectation as a date for the marriage ceremony was announced. Mama Ekwe suddenly became the most envied woman in the village. She set Sunday afternoons zesty with her onion and crayfish stew. The suitor's aura followed her everywhere she went, framing her face in a light-catching aureole. His generosity lulled the hisses and sarcastic songs Ekwe's stepmothers and Mama Ekwe traded. Ekwe accompanied her to the market to make purchases for the Idego ceremony. He stood by as Mama Ekwe paid for the purchases with the suitor's crisp currency notes, which caught mirror reflections.

"My daughter has a suitor, the timber merchant from Aku," Mama Ekwe said at the table of each market woman with a smile as shimmering as the suitor's new bills. "They are coming tomorrow to bring her bride price. You are invited."

"I'm happy for you," the women would say, and they

would laugh, Mama Ekwe's voice rising like the rhythmic notes of a flute.

Ekwe's tongue felt like it had tasted nuggets of sugar on their way home from the market. Mama Ekwe had a large basket of ingredients on her head. He was carrying the remnant of her purchases in a walkie-talkie bag. He was happy to help Mama Ekwe since Oyibo had refused to accompany her to the market. She was still acting bad-tempered.

Ekwe spent the afternoon at the neem tree savouring this sweetened taste in place of food, too happy to care about lunch. He no longer remembered to ask God to make him a guard before going to bed every night and first thing every morning. The prospect of going to live with his sister in the city now overshadowed his dream of becoming a guard. The night seemed endless. Sleep fled from his eyes. Now and again, he went and peeped through the keyhole and scowled as darkness confronted his eyes. And then he went back and lay on his mat, afraid the new day might never come.

The day finally dawned with a fluorescent glow in the morning sky—the day of the ceremony. One of the suitor's boys, a young man with thick muscles, arrived with a ram in tow. Ekwe and his siblings gathered and watched him as he wrestled and tethered the big, brown, bearded beast to the neem tree. The ram looked around the strange surroundings with wide and hostile eyes. Its balls hung low like avocados from a tree branch. They were nearly touching the ground. The rough beard reminded Ekwe of Amadi. It held inside its coarse texture a gleam of Amadi's fierceness.

Ekwe and his siblings weighed the ram. They went about the animal in roundabouts, gauging its mood, its temperament.

Papa Ekwe approached with a knife, shirtless, his face and forearms bronzed after many years of hunching his back against the sun burning out in the field. He used to have skin like planed mahogany. He had passed it to Oyibo, but now his wrinkled brown body shook like cassava mush as he moved towards the ram, whose hair stood on end, either with fear or fury as he approached. Papa Ekwe ordered Ekwe and his siblings to grab hold of the beast as he got ready a pan to collect the blood. The ram backed away, alert and suspicious, head lowered in battle readiness as they circled him. They closed in on him slowly. Suddenly the animal went for them, picking on the boy directly facing him, Ekwe's little halfbrother. The boy doubled back with a yell, tripped, and fell as others fled. He would have been caught in the ram's dangerously curved horns had the leash not restrained the animal from charging at him. Others were laughing at him as he struggled to his feet and scampered to safety, his small rat face a picture of fear.

They started regrouping, closing in on the ram again. The animal was now looking wild and upset, and danger lurked in the loop of his horns. He sprang forwards again, forgetting the leash around his throat in his blind fury and self-survival instinct. But he doubled and hit the ground with a thud, legs up and balls wobbling like half-filled sacks. He kicked out as they rushed in and grabbed him. And then they held his legs for Papa Ekwe, who grabbed one of the horns and reached for his knife.

After slaughtering the ram, Papa Ekwe set up a fire at the back of the house, where he burnt and flayed the carcass. He then set up a table and cut the meat up into lumps for the soup. The children fell on a bowl of the pepper soup he had made and ended up fighting over it. Mama Ekwe and Ekwe's stepmothers were cooking for the guests. The marriage ceremony seemed to have united them, but Ekwe figured it would not last long before malice set in again.

The suitor arrived flanked by relatives who were clenching jars of wine and crates of beer and soft drinks taken out of their car. The bride price was the first public event. The traditional wedding would follow, and, if the suitor were religious, a white wedding by a priest in the local Roman Catholic church would crown the process. The suitor was wearing a long black ishiagu gown and a red chieftaincy cap, the kind of attire Ekwe had seen members of the king's cabinet dressed in. He wondered if the suitor was a cabinet member in his city.

Ekwe watched as Papa Ekwe ushered the suitor and his relatives in with a grin that stretched from one end of his jaw to the other, and Mama Ekwe genuflected so many times the whole place started to scent like a palace. Papa Ekwe had set seats under a canopy for the guests whose arrival sparked a burst of activities. Kola nuts were eaten. Talks were made. Food and drinks served, with Oriental Brothers blasting from horn speakers. Ekwe ate himself sick. He bit into barbecued mutton, rinsed it down with a big drink of palm wine, and let out a belch like a low gruff from a rainy day's sky. His younger siblings sullied their clothes with food and scum. Their bellies protruded. Papa Ekwe and Mama Ekwe brownnosed and waited on the suitor as if they had spent weeks practicing it. Oyibo kept to herself until she was summoned by Papa Ekwe. She had to surrender to curious stares and the suitor's gawking eyes. Ekwe figured she felt like a sheep up for bargain at the market.

"This man and his people have brought wine to ask for your hand in marriage—should we or should we not drink their wine?" Papa Ekwe said to her.

The question sounded ridiculous, coming when the jerry can of wine had already been half drunk. Mama Ekwe had schooled a sulky Oyibo on what to say and what not to say when answering questions before the guests. "Your answer should be an assent, nothing more, nothing less."

Oyibo was silent, head bent.

The suitor and his relatives smiled to fill up the embarrassing silence as she stretched it until their smiles froze in their faces. Even Papa Ekwe and Mama Ekwe started to shift in their seats. If she said no, it would be the height of embarrassment. But she was not expected to reject her suitor publicly, and no one ever gave such an answer. No good daughter would embarrass her family with no for an answer to such a critical question asked publicly.

Suddenly she fled from the laughing and clapping that greeted her "Yes" into the room to continue her sulking. She refused to show herself again for the rest of the ceremony. Mama Ekwe was all teeth, all pride and dignity. The compound was flooded over and quaking with voices as greedy neighbours pounced on the food and drinks, ate, drank, laughed, got drunk, and sang.

"Thank you for giving us this much food and drink," a haggard old woman said to Mama Ekwe.

"If your daughter's suitor can give us so much to eat and drink for only knocking on the door, I wonder what he will give us at the wedding proper," another with sunken eyes said.

"Maybe he will give us the flesh of an elephant," said

yet another who looked so thin Ekwe felt pained by merely looking at her. "And the ordure of a witch bird for wine."

They rocked with laughter.

Their praises swelled Mama Ekwe's head. "My son-in-law is equal to the task. He will give you all that and more."

Papa Ekwe was half drunk already. His words had begun to jam. Whenever he got drunk, he spoke his bad English. Azuka had said that Papa Ekwe's English was like a head twisted to face backwards, but Papa Ekwe insisted it was correct, insisted education and Catholicism today were nowhere near what they used to be during his own time—the days of Aloysius Muller.

Some drunks started to beat a rhythm with bottles, tins, and pans. They sang the suitor's praises in scratchy voices. They caroled until they wore out, and then they started to lurch towards their homes. Voices tailed out as calmness reclaimed the night. The ground was littered with bottles, cups, plates, and spoons and shivered with heat and exhaustion. Papa Ekwe continued mouthing his broken English alone in his room long after he retired. Completely knocked out, Mama Ekwe succumbed to a dreamless sleep, deep shadows of hardship forming rings around her eyes, sunken cheeks highlighted by the yellow light of the oil lamp that fell like benediction on her face. Ekwe saw something new on that face, a lustre on the forehead; between the confluence of light and the old ruins of her face hovered a connection. Ekwe thought that the connection stood for Oyibo—the power to make or mar Mama Ekwe's happiness lay in her palms.

A Dream Come True

OYIBO FOLLOWED THE SUITOR HOME. THE REST OF the family would join her in the city after the traditional wedding. Ekwe missed her soft snoring that reeked of exhaustion after working all day in the field. He did not know that Oyibo wielded such power—despite the feeling of wooziness that sank its claws into him after the few cups of wine he had drunk—to make him so restless.

The days following Oyibo's final departure to her new home were fine days glorified by early spring sunshine. The rolling green floodplains flaunted a rich meadow pasture. Ekwe was starting to feel the full effect of having a wealthy and generous in-law. He had nothing to complain about with school perpetually suspended and Sunday rice assured. The marriage ceremonies done and dusted, the land of Enu-Ozara still trembled with the stomp of a thousand feet, still sucked up the human precipitation.

After the wedding, Ekwe, Mama Ekwe, and the twins rode with the suitor in his fine motorcar to his large and beautiful city house. Papa Ekwe did not go with them. "I cannot relocate to the city." He had made a U-turn. "I will not abandon my compound and my other wives and children for cowherds to feast on them."

"His wives rejected the offer to come with us out of envy," Mama Ekwe said to Ekwe. "It would have been better to swallow their pride and join us than to be ambushed by the militants."

Ekwe enjoyed the drive. He sat by the window where the breeze fanned his face. He cherished the soft seat of the motorcar as highlife music fled with trees and bushes towards the opposite direction. And now they drove along a narrow highway at the cliff edge of Milliken Hill. The city hid behind the hills, but as they descended, it sprang into view with a big warm tectonic smile. A delightful gasp escaped him. The more they pressed forwards, the more the cars and people walking the streets multiplied, and houses grew taller and more colourful. At last, they drove into a large compound in Uwani via a long drive with trimmed hedges. They alighted and entered a beautiful one-storey house looking more metallic than stone. Ekwe had never been in a house so large and baffling, with many bedrooms and sitting rooms and built-in toilets and bathrooms and kitchens. In his village people stooped over pit holes to shit. Others did it in the bushes.

His first night in the suitor's house was sugared with sweet dreams.

▲▲▲▲▲

Oyibo was the queen in this new home. She had the city house all to herself, chaperoned by a doting husband and a maid. Her life revolved around shower baths, gas-cooked meals, and a drink of cold juice. It revolved around motion pictures:

fast cars crashing against each other with loud screeching sounds as men in all black pursued and shot at each other and half-dressed women walked around with long hair and high heels. Oyibo had started to look like a city woman, sloughing her sun-bronzed skin from the days of tomato and habanero. Now her skin shone, pure manila, like it used to back when Onukwu had described her in luminous adjectives and metaphors. She had gained some flesh and a bit of roundness around her hips, no longer skinny, but delicate and shapely.

The roundness progressed slowly about her abdomen, her stomach sphering, curving out as if she had had too much to eat, and slowing her movement. And then it ballooned out of her body. She started to lose weight and became so thin her rib cage protruded. As the days wore on, she became heavier and nauseous, now sick, now well again. And then she put a baby boy to bed. The boy right from when he slithered out of his mother was the very ochre of a fresh-planed mahogany, but his thick nose defined his patrilineal features.

Baby Beluchi

SOMEONE KNOCKED ON THE DOOR, AND WHEN EKWE answered, a well-dressed man who wore glasses stood there. Ekwe fancied the glasses made him look like an owl as he walked in. As if he read Ekwe's mind, the man took off the glasses. Solicitude kindled in his eyes, kindness loitering in the back chamber.

"Nno." Mama Ekwe waved Dr. Ezenwa, Oyibo's gynaecologist, to a seat.

Oyibo came quietly out of the bedroom, greeted him, and sat around the bedroom door. Ekwe figured that sitting around the bedroom door would make it easy for her to flee into the room when incontinence set in suddenly.

"How are you doing, ma'am?" Dr. Ezenwa said.

Oyibo sighed.

Baby Beluchi suckled noisily on his feeding bottle, snug in Mama Ekwe's arms.

"I am here to speak to you again about the need for an urgent treatment."

Ekwe knew why Oyibo was refusing to see a doctor no matter how hard anyone pressed her, no matter how much Mama Ekwe pressed her. More than in protest of the injustices and conspiracies against her, which had resulted in her marriage, it was to avoid shame and embarrassment. She had returned in tears the first day she had been to see the gynecologist. She had fled from wrinkled noses and fingers pressing against nostrils as curious eyes followed the furtive movements of her hand, which concealed a small towel for soaking up the urine running down her legs and forming a small pool on the floor at her feet. People had fled the hospital lobby to evacuate ponds of spittle from their mouths in a way that stitched up her humiliation.

"I will not go back there," Oyibo insisted, defiant.

While she was giving birth, she had developed a complication because of a long and difficult labour. It took from her the power to control the passage of urine and stool from her body. She had returned from the hospital a different person, the ruins of her succulent old self.

"Fistula is not an incurable condition, but if left untreated, it could result in sepsis," Dr. Ezenwa said. He said *sepsis* in English and explained its implication in Igbo. "Sepsis will lead to low blood pressure, organ damage, or even death."

Mama Ekwe looked alarmed at the mention of death. "You will go, nnem," she pleaded with Oyibo.

Ekwe glanced from Mama Ekwe, who was feeding the baby, to Oyibo, who had a sad, listless look on her face. Mama Ekwe's postnatal obligation to Oyibo had redoubled. It became twice as demanding after the maid resigned. Besides the regular omugwo chores—bathing and caring for the baby and its mother—she made sure Oyibo did not lack the emotional support of a mother needed in the current situation. And the twins still needed her attention.

After the doctor left, Ekwe went to the window. It was

sunset. Houses and streets looked beautiful in the brilliant kaleidoscope of a skyline. If hit at the right angle by sunset, the Holy Ghost Cathedral was a beauty to behold in the distance. The stained glass of the Greco-Roman architecture picked up the subtle nuances of the changing light, but Ekwe was unaware of the breathtaking shades of orange. He did not understand why the suitor rarely came home since the birth of baby Beluchi. The man popped in and out. He still drank White Horse, and he still talked in reversals. For instance, rather than talking about Oyibo's refusal to go to hospital and her fear of facing the crowds that surged outside, he talked about cowherds and their relentless attacks.

"They attacked a settlement in Opanda," he announced as he hurried into the house one afternoon.

"Oh, dim oma," Mama Ekwe said in a small voice. "My beloved husband, I am afraid for you. Why have you allowed your envious wives to lead you astray?"

Ekwe was also worried about Papa Ekwe's safety and the safety of his stepmothers and half-siblings.

"I want to go to the village to see my father," he said to Mama Ekwe.

"Nwantakilia. People are fleeing out of the village, and you are going back to it."

Ekwe insisted he would go.

"Who will take you to the village, assuming I give my consent?" Mama Ekwe said, and snapped at the twins, who were worrying her about food.

"I can find my way. It's simple. I will walk to the park

and get on a bus to Nkpologu. I will then get on another bus going to the village from Nkpologu."

"Let him go," Oyibo said tautly. "He can't miss his way."

▲▲▲▲▲

Ekwe threw a few clothes in a plastic bag the next day, after reassuring Mama Ekwe that he could travel to the village from the city all by himself. When he got to the motor park, he climbed onto a waiting bus and sat down. He waited until the bus filled up, and then a sweaty, aggressive conductor leaned in to collect the fares. He smelt something toxic, the conductor. Ekwe quickly handed him the fare. The conductor snatched the money, glared at Ekwe one last time, and withdrew with his moist manure smell as the bus coughed to life. Ekwe sat in his favourite position by the window. He enjoyed the view spiced with adult conversations, hiding his laughter in his plastic bag of clothes. At Otigba Junction, they ran into protesters blocking a whole side of the road with placards. Cars were squeezed together on the free lane. The protesters were women—mothers. The placards read STOP EMBEZZLEMENT OF PENSION FUNDS, SENATORS HAVE MERCY ON PENSIONERS, ENOUGH IS ENOUGH TO PENSIONERS' SUFFERING. Ekwe did not understand any of it. He was enjoying the commotion resulting in blaring of car horns and exchange of swear words by drivers as the crowd surged forwards and crippled traffic.

"I know an old man who collapsed and died while standing on a queue, waiting endlessly for the verification and payment of his pension entitlement," a woman's voice said from the back of the bus.

"What pension? Is it the one already stolen by government officials?" another female voice lent support. "Now that the man is dead, his family had better look for money for his funeral and not lace their hopes on his entitlement, because they will never get it."

"A case of dog eating the bone hung around its neck," a male voice said, and the passengers laughed.

"What have we not suffered in this country at the hands of the so-called government officials and politicians?" This time it was the man sitting next to Ekwe who spoke, a thin man with a deep voice. "This is the only country where snakes eat money."

The passengers reacted with an exclamation of surprise.

"Did you say a snake ate money?" someone said doubtfully.

"Have you just heard it for the first time?" replied a sneering voice.

"A snake entered a government office and swallowed enough money to last us all a lifetime," explained the deep voice.

"What kind of snake eats money?" someone asked. "Tell us how it happened."

"I don't know if it was a python or an adder or a cobra."

"It is government snake, a new species of snake," someone said, triggering a burst of laughter.

"How does a government snake look?" a female voice asked him.

"It has a bald head and a potbelly where it is able to store all the money."

The passengers roared with laughter as the protesters swept past and traffic started to flow again. Ekwe wondered if protests were part of the daily life of city people. When had he moved about in the city without witnessing a protest march? If they were not protesting a hike in fuel pump price, they were whining about high electricity tariff in a city in perennial darkness. The bus ran into another congestion caused by cattle travelling in their dozens around Abakpa Junction. There was a flourish of horns as cars crammed together and tried to squeeze through the congestion. The cattle were driven by a thin boy in layers of dirty clothing who was taking unconcerned bites at a stick of sugarcane as he walked along. His nonchalance enraged both drivers and passengers. An impatient motorist drove his taxi straight through the herd of cattle, horn blaring, headlights full on. The man kept up the pressure as the cows panicked and jostled for safety. The scene thrilled Ekwe. In the end, it was the impatient taxi driver who got his windscreen smashed when a cow, maddened by the frightful crush, rammed into the windscreen horns first.

Freed at last, the bus clattered on until it got to Opanda. Ekwe changed buses and headed home. Somewhere close to home they ran into a police checkpoint half barricaded with empty drums along the bumpy village road. The bus driver swore at the policemen, four in number, as a scrawny-looking officer waved him down with a scowl. The officer wasn't carrying a long rifle like his colleagues, who were watching from a distance, but a truncheon was tucked under his arm as he stretched a palm to collect the money the conductor rudely shoved at him.

"They were sent to help protect the communities from militants," someone said in a voice heavy with sarcasm as the bus clanged off.

"With what are they going to face the militants? With those sticks they are carrying?" a tight voice said behind. "Besides, the cattle those cowherds drive around belong to top politicians in the country who invest in large herds of cattle. They will do anything to protect their investments."

They came across two other checkpoints and went through the same ritual before arriving at the village park. Ekwe got down and walked home.

Ambush

"THE FARMS ARE NO LONGER SAFE," PAPA EKWE said. "Men have been killed and women raped in their farms. We now depend on whatever we can get from our little gardens around the house for food."

Ekwe stared at Papa Ekwe. Seated in his customary position under the neem tree, Papa Ekwe looked emaciated, almost gaunt. The children were playing in the compound, looking skinnier and dusty. Ekwe's big stepmother was brooding around her door. The south end of the house had remained quiet and dark since Mama Ekwe left for the city, although there was still the unmistakable hint of irony in the air.

"Your small stepmother was birthed of a stillborn shortly after your departure to the city."

The news shocked Ekwe. "Where is my stepmother?"

"She is not home. She went to the market."

"Was it a boy?"

"It was a girl."

His tone of voice left Ekwe with a grim sense of familiarity.

"The cowherds are not even our major headache." Papa Ekwe changed the subject. "The Ishiawo are the real terror now. Ishiawo is a gang that specializes in kidnapping and robbery. They started as a vigilante group set up to fight off the militants. They started off well and even repelled the militants when they tried to attack the community. But then they changed to goats that eat the owner's yam. Eche, the community youth leader, is their mastermind. They decamped into the forest from where they terrorize the villagers."

Ekwe remembered the long nights broken by the deep notes of their bell while the vigilantes barked out orders in their stentorian voices as he ate roast yam with Papa Ekwe. The yams were looking shrunken when Papa Ekwe had fished them out of the crumbling barn before roasting them.

"We are halfway on the last line of the barn posts," Papa Ekwe explained. "These ones are among the last few tubers left. We would have finished everything soon, and then we would all die of famine."

"Why don't you come with me to the city? There's plenty of food. Plenty of rice."

"I can't leave my wives and your half-siblings here by themselves to starve to death." He declined. "We would all have moved happily to the city had your stepmothers accepted our in-law's offer, but women find it hard to get along. And, in any case," he added, smiling, "rice is not my thing, you know."

Ekwe decided to tell him about his sick sister even though Mama Ekwe had asked him not to. She did not want Papa Ekwe to worry himself to death over Oyibo.

"I couldn't have known." Papa Ekwe looked worried. "Our in-law has not been here again since he completed the marriage rites and took his wife away. I do not blame him though. He seems a very busy man, and with the whole family there with him, there's really no urgency in coming to see an old man like me in this herdsmen-infested village."

The compound was empty of chickens, Ekwe observed, empty of the usual throng of hens and their fluffy flock of tweeting chicks.

"Your mother's chickens are all gone. I fed them every morning after letting them out of their coop, but they returned from their daily forage with a chick less, given up as meal to some famished raptor."

Ekwe enjoyed the roast yam in a thoughtful silence. He hadn't eaten roast yam since he left the village.

"Sorry I had to be frugal with oil." Papa Ekwe's tone was apologetic. "I try to manage the little we have left. Our palm nuts are wasting away at the farm. It's too dangerous out there to try to harvest them."

For a workaholic like Papa Ekwe, it must be torture to sit at home and do nothing. And for some reason, Ekwe had a vague notion that the diminution of Mama Ekwe's poultry was a dark foreboding.

The classic story of Enu-Ozara.

ııııı

Ekwe went to the motor park when it was time to return to the city. He boarded a bus waiting for passengers going to Enugu. Some six passengers were already seated in the bus, the same old rickety Nissan that enjoyed a monopoly of the desolate park and the dusty country road. A dirty-looking tout was screaming for passengers in the hot sun. Loading seemed very slow, and the sun blazed down with remorseless ease. Every so often the boy, the tout, grabbed "pure water" from any of the girl-hawkers at the motor park, tore the sachet with his teeth, and gulped down the water. And then he tore another sachet, poured it on his round forehead, and took a deep breath, enjoying the coolness of the water as it ran down and soaked him through his worn polo shirt and dirty shorts. Idlers sat at shop fronts and gazed into a sweaty afternoon or played draughts with their shirts hanging over their shoulders.

The number of passengers had shot up to nine when Ekwe dozed off. When he woke up, the number had fallen from nine to six. He pondered the puzzle with a yawn—the plus and minus game going on—realizing that the young men who had vanished from the bus were motor park touts who would sit in the bus and pretend to be passengers. Most travellers fell to this deception, this the-more-you-look-the-less-you-see-motor-park riddle. Ekwe was sure that the man now playing draughts in a grey shirt at a shop front was one of the people he had met in the bus. The passengers were starting to fuss over the long wait when the bus finally coughed to life and began the journey, groaning its way out of the park and clattering up the long, untarred road in a cloud of dust.

Back in Enugu, Ekwe told Mama Ekwe about his stepmother's stillborn and how hard life had become in the village.

"I know what it means to lose a baby. I have been there twice." Mama Ekwe crossed her arms. "When next you visit home, you will take some foodstuff to them."

Ekwe saw the worried look in her eyes and wondered if she missed Papa Ekwe. It was probably natural for people who didn't say anything good about their spouses to miss them after a long time of absence.

ııııı

The days rolled by with uneasy calm. Ekwe enjoyed waking up, eating breakfast, and watching TV every morning. And then he would spend the afternoon at the window watching the dazzling kaleidoscope of the city. The suitor hardly came home, and even when he was around, he kept to his room upstairs. He probably kept to himself in protest of Oyibo's refusal to see a doctor. On second thought, Ekwe wondered if he could no longer stand her odour. Oyibo, whom men had stared at with the lost look of a goat chewing its cud, now stank to the point that the suitor could no longer stand her. Ekwe remembered how men had itched to touch her fine mahogany skin with their crooked hands.

One morning, the suitor blew in and ordered her to pack a bag. "Pack your personal effects; we are going to the village to spend a few days."

He sounded brusque. Mama Ekwe started to pack their things. Ekwe had a premonition about the suitor's sudden idea of taking his family to his hometown in Aku to spend a few days.

"I don't want to go with you," Ekwe said to Mama Ekwe. "I want to go to our village to see my father again."

"I don't know why you prefer going back there to danger,"

Mama Ekwe said. Still, she packed some foodstuff into a bag and gave it to him. "Give this to your father and his family."

As the suitor drove away with Mama Ekwe, the twins, Oyibo, and her baby, Ekwe headed to the motor park to board a homebound bus. He arrived home with the bag containing the foodstuff and his personal effects sitting on his head. Papa Ekwe was surprised to see him again only a few weeks after his last visit.

"Why do you have a big bag?" Papa Ekwe helped ease the bag off Ekwe's head.

"I have foodstuff for you," Ekwe said.

He told Papa Ekwe the full story after he rested. Infected by a strange lackluster air, Papa Ekwe stared ahead, engrossed in the depressing story. A brown he-goat strolled up and made himself a part of the storytelling audience. He stood next to Ekwe and stared at him with a cocked ear. But then the he-goat lost interest in the story and started to walk away, dark brown pellets raining from his anus.

Later, Ekwe sat around the door of the village house and pondered how quickly the family's fortunes had switched from bad to good, and now things were worse. His big stepmother had no shame showing her festering teeth as she laughed at the news of how the suitor had maltreated Oyibo. How he had whisked her away to the house in his village and dumped her there among the disfavoured wives. And now the rumour that he was planning to take a new wife scented the air in place of Mama Ekwe's mesmerizing stew. Ekwe gave a deep sigh and glanced at Papa Ekwe seated at the neem tree, remembering the countless times the suitor and Papa Ekwe had sat under that tree drinking White Horse and discussing politics and "The Great Zik of Africa." Would Oyibo have fared any better if she had married any of the other suitors who didn't drink White Horse or talk politics? He figured she would have been better off if she hadn't married at all

Death hovered over the village in place of a dream house in the city. Nimbo and Opanda had fallen. Enu-Ozara awaited the long, piercing voice. Ekwe threw Papa Ekwe another glance and saw his father's guilt in the slack of his shoulders. It crossed his forehead like a birthmark. Papa Ekwe now sought solace in snuff and alcohol and had a little bit too much of both. Ekwe felt it too, this nagging sense of guilt. It snuck up on him whenever he was alone. He felt it mostly in the night, when everyone had gone to bed and the "hoo-h'HOO-hoo-hoo" of an owl calling from the fallen barn provided a woodwind soundtrack to Papa Ekwe's drunken snores.

Ekwe lay awake and listened to the haunting acoustics.

The Tribunal

EKWE WAS SHAKEN AWAKE AS IF BY A FORCE RE-entering his body. He opened his eyes and gazed into low-hanging clouds. Slowly, the white clouds mutated into the silver metallic brilliance of the new gbam gbam that now capped the house. Its silver glare hurt his eyes. He blinked a few times, surprised it was already daylight. He lay still in utter prostration and relived yet another long night of exhausting astral experience. He tried to save it in his memory before it washed away again down the shore of time.

At last, he walked out into a bright new ivory dawn, thinking of Azuka's successes and Oyibo's abominable marriage in the astral realm. The aura of the suitor still scented the air. Mama Ekwe was already cooking in the kitchen this morning. Azuka and Oyibo were helping her prepare breakfast of akara and akamu. The twins were playing in the compound. Papa Ekwe sat at the neem tree. He entertained himself to the sight of passersby. He had announced a work-free day at dinner to fully savour the suitor's gift. This morning, there was something new and different about his posture. He was reclining with legs stretched out and crossed in front of him, regaling himself in his new status, in the penumbra of his newly renovated house, which silvered the rust-coloured neighbourhood.

"Edi ura," Azuka teased Ekwe for sleeping like a toddy cat.

"I do not blame Ekwe for forgetting to wake up," Papa Ekwe said, and laughed heartily. "We all had a dreamless sleep last night under the cool sheet metal, deep and peaceful. Ibini Ukpabi will reward our in-law for his large heart."

Ekwe could hear Oyibo grumbling in the kitchen. He wanted to share the revelations he had about Oyibo and Azuka. But he knew that Papa Ekwe would demand to know why he went to the stream when everyone was home resting after the renovation yesterday. Mama Ekwe would insist he be punished for being hardheaded. Her hands were itching to spank him at the littlest opportunity in lieu of the first time he was spared punishment for touching ekwukwonju.

Ekwe swallowed a whiff of Mama Ekwe's akara as he spied a familiar figure approaching. He hissed as Papa Ekwe's kinsman Omeje walked towards their compound with his nose. Nwoke a, o saka. The man had the annoying habit of appearing when a pot of food was singing on the fire, staying until the food was done, and not refusing when he was invited to a meal. Ekwe was upset with Papa Ekwe's habit of always inviting people who came to their house for a meal. He figured it was civil of them to decline, to say they had just had their meal before leaving their houses even if they were starving. But not a glutton like Omeje. He would never turn down an invitation to a meal. The man had a gigantic appetite and always left his host in serious food shortage. His talent for nosing out where and when food was being cooked was legendary.

"You should have been better off as his son," Oyibo sneered at Ekwe in a fierce whisper as Omeje approached, "so that both of you can have one big, fat nose for smelling food."

Tufiakwa! Ekwe did not wish to become Omeje's son for all the rice in Adani. The man didn't seem like a father who would spare his son a tiny morsel of food, like Papa Ekwe would always do when Ekwe ate with him.

"You have been summoned to the tribunal of kinsmen to defend an allegation brought against you by Amadi," Omeje said in his loud, annoying voice as he settled on the bench with Papa Ekwe.

Mama Ekwe rushed out of the kitchen and stood with hands on her hips. "I si gini? What are you saying?"

"What for?" Papa Ekwe found his voice.

"It is about your daughter's suitor."

Mama Ekwe flared up at the news of the summons and rained curses at Amadi. "I wonder why that okokporo will not mind his business," she sneered. "At his age he does not have a wife and children and is not even bothered about it. He can never give a woman attention because he is always lost in a book."

Amadi was the subject of much gossip in the village. He read all the wrong things in a book and said things that offended the ears. He did stupid things too, like fighting a man for felling a tree in his own farm, and planting trees everywhere in a community with too many trees and bushes already. He had been away to some distant land doing God-knows-what. He was probably retired. He had a bald head and an oily beard. Perhaps the death of his niece Oyoyo had provoked him, and he had vowed to fight underage marriage anywhere.

The day the kinsmen summoned Papa Ekwe was the same day Oyibo began a hunger strike and the same day Ekwe's small stepmother gave birth to a stillborn. Papa Ekwe dug a small grave near the barn and buried the baby. But Ekwe's stepmother's belly still hilled in front of her, making Ekwe wonder if another baby lived inside it. Oyibo started a hunger strike because she had lost the support of Mama Ekwe. Ekwe didn't want his sister to die of hunger. He could never go on a hunger strike no matter how much anyone provoked him. He figured he would die if he didn't eat for a whole day. He wondered how much longer his sister could carry on. He had his own worries, anyway. He still wanted to be guard in a gwongworo, to swing from chipboard to plywood. He preferred to be guard than to be farmer or government worker or even ukulelist.

On the day of the tribunal, Ekwe accompanied Papa Ekwe to the village hall. The kinsmen encouraged their young sons to go there to bring them closer to tradition. Ekwe had been there a few times. He liked watching the kinsmen argue, their nuances of expression, their tones of voice, and casts of mind. He had come to know the kinsmen one by one by their names beginning with Amuta, the village head. Amuta moderated the meetings but fell asleep and snored soon after setting things in motion. He slept like a giraffe through the meeting, opening his eyes to stare at the kinsmen, then snoring again. His voice, though small and almost incoherent, had an automatic effect on the kinsmen—this old man with a pointed chin and white hair. Another interesting character was the iconoclast Ikpedirichukwu, who adopted a new surname—let God be the judge—for himself because he considered Ishiwu, his ancestral name, heathenish.

Ekwe and Papa Ekwe set out to the hall as the deep notes of the village's timber drum floated in with the light mid-morning wind. Ekwe was named after the slit drum, which the village publicist struck to announce the tribunal, a low rhythmic tune that travelled across the village and beyond. Ekwe was anxious to know how the case would go. He fought his conflicts. He wanted the suitor to marry his sister so they could eat well, but the things that happened in the astral realm, which now played back in his mind like film footage, left him in doubt. They scared him.

Papa Ekwe walked with quick, agitated steps. He smelt of nicotine. He had done nothing but snuff since he got the message of his summons—snuff and blow his nose so fiercely it sounded like the suitor's motorcar horn. Ekwe ran out of breath trying to catch up with him as they rounded the large udala tree towering over the village square. And then they walked down a long approach between farmlands to the hall. Trees enclosed the village hall purpose-built by the kindred for such meetings and tribunals. Kinsmen and even fighting couples were summoned to settle land or spousal disputes. The cracked mud walls told a story of age—a time when the ancestors were installed in a sanctum within the hall. Good historians like Omeke could identify the relics one by one, but that was before heretics like Ikpedirichukwu fought to have the artifacts evacuated because they were idols, according to him. The hall's double entrances had no doors. They gaped at and admitted Ekwe and Papa Ekwe into the cool interior. There were no windows. The only light came through the beams. They entered like everyone else, sat on the mud bench built into the walls along with some twelve men already seated. Ekwe was the only boy of his age in the hall. And now he glimpsed Ikpedirichukwu as he approached with his bicycle in tow, always in a coat, threadbare and oversized, and towing a bicycle, the same bicycle he rode to the Protestant church every Sunday morning.

The meeting started shortly after Ikpedirichukwu arrived and latched on to it like fish to a hook even without being formally invited to lead the kinsmen in an opening prayer. The business of the day followed the same rhythm and flow. Kola nuts were broken and eaten with a loud, crunchy melody. Sharing followed the same pecking order, in order of seniority. Although Omeke sometimes inadvertently broke the sharing rule, he was immediately recalled by the kinsman so bypassed. Sometimes the offended kinsman felt slighted and blew things out of proportion or even took things personally with Omeke even though he retreated at once with a quick apology.

The village secretary Madu started to read the minutes from squiggles on an old notebook, his writing all swirls and loops. His Adam's apple bobbed up and down in rhythm with his enunciation as he interpreted the impossible English to his itarigba, awed kinsmen who listened attentively. He listed the cases before the tribunal to include Odum vs. wife/brothers-in-law. Odum had beaten up his wife again. He was a notorious wife beater. His irate brothers-in-law had descended on him with their fists in retaliation, prompting the kinsmen to summon Ezinne and her brothers. The case had passed through a first hearing. The latest conflict was between Amadi and Papa Ekwe. Amadi had brought a case of underage marriage against him, accusing Papa Ekwe of forcing a rich old man on his way to the grave on his young daughter for a generous bride price. The kinsmen would plough into the case at once as a matter of urgency.

Ekwe watched Amadi with awed eyes. The man would have been a fine man but for a set jaw covered with a rough beard. He spoke with a gleam in his cat eyes, his voice strong and passionate. The hall fell silent to the hard, metallic timbre of his voice. As he was talking, Ekwe studied the facial expressions of the kinsmen one by one. He started with Odum, the brawny kinsman known for his loud voice and exaggerated stories. Odum sat next to Papa Ekwe and scowled in the middle distance. A vein snaked across his temple. Because he always wore a scowl, it was hard to know if he was angry or not.

Ekwe was also interested in Okoboyi and Ikoh. As a team, he figured that Okoboyi and Ikoh could influence the verdict of the kinsmen if only they could come to terms. He moved his eyes and rested them on Okoboyi at the far-right corner. Okoboyi was staring out the doorway, where sunlight pooled and made a light dance around the entrance, face blank, fine lines of wrinkles frozen below his forehead like water waves. Ekwe shifted his eyes to Ikoh's pale, sagged face. His lips glistened like roast maggots, swollen and raw from drinking too much kaikai. Ikoh did not know how to pretend. If he did not like you, it showed on his face, as it did now. He was glaring at Amadi with bloodshot eyes. It was clear whose side he was on.

Amadi sat down after he finished speaking and blinked in the slow, confident way that Ekwe's big stepmother's cat blinked. Ekwe imagined that Amadi was a cat, a fish-stealing, mouse-chasing cat cornered while trying to steal fish in Mama Ekwe's kitchen and given a beating. It was now Papa Ekwe's turn to speak and address the allegation against him. Ekwe sat up with expectation. He watched Papa Ekwe as he stood up and walked across the floor to the door where you must stoop to address the kinsmen. His shoulders were slouched. Ekwe saw doubts in his eyes. When he started, Papa Ekwe did not speak with the confidence with which Amadi had spoken. His gestures betrayed his helplessness, his uncertainty. Where Amadi spat threats, Papa Ekwe groaned in self-pity, his speech far from a riposte, more like a lamentation. A ripple of disappointment rose in the throats of the kinsmen and greeted his speech. The air grew tense again as the babble died down.

Ekwe scanned the hall and rested his eyes on Okoboyi again. As if summoned by his anxious stare, Okoboyi rose to his feet. His walk had the swagger of a man who always took initiative, a man gifted with words and idioms. As he started to speak, his critics looked away, but Ekwe knew that they were listening with attentive ears and picking holes in the speech.

"For me, the bone of contention in this case is not that Ngwu is trying to give his underage daughter's hand in marriage, for who among us kinsmen has not given a daughter of that age or even younger to a man in marriage? I suppose the actual conflict is that the said daughter does not approve of the suitor who is being foisted on her."

His admirers nodded to the cadence of his speech, but

Ikoh was quick to react, quick to limp across the floor, a grouchy young man who had a bad leg and often requested to be allowed to make his speech standing rather than stooping, as was customary. His body language was rebellious. As he crossed, a waft of familiar smell tormented Ekwe's nostrils. At times Papa Ekwe smelt like that when he returned from Jerome's bar. The smell would sleep and awake with him the next morning. Usually, he would be too unwell and queasy to go to the farm or even to eat.

"We did not gather here to oil our language or to show how good an orator we are." Ikoh shot Okoboyi a hard look to drive home his sarcasm. "My kinsmen, we ought to carefully review cases brought to us to know which ones to investigate and which ones to throw out. I can't imagine the audacity of a man working very hard to stop the marriage of another man's daughter. What concerns Amadi in the business of another man's household? How does it affect him? The reasons he gave us for his prayer were all flimsy ones. We have a standard way of doing things in this village. No sensible daughter declines a suitor chosen for her by her parents. I'd advise the kinsmen to throw this case out for lack of merit and attend to more important businesses."

Ekwe did not know if Ikoh's position was meant to spite Okoboyi, who stood with a shocked look at being rudely interrupted. Sometimes the kinsmen traded malice at the expense of reason. Sometimes they acted like schoolchildren in a classroom. Amuta intervened in the face-off brewing between the two men, reprimanded Ikoh for cutting in on Okoboyi in the middle of his speech, and asked both men to take their seats, take a deep breath, and relax.

Papa Ekwe seemed to be gaining support. As Odum raised his bulk from his seat, Ekwe hoped he would speak in favour of Amadi. Odum and Ikoh were allies and often backed each other. Odum might not shine in the art of speech making, but the aura around him was compelling. It was contagious, his alliance with Ikoh watertight. He dragged himself across the floor. He walked with a shuffle, chest puffed out and arms thrown wide in his exaggerated gait. He started his speech with a chuckle. It was short, but it had a clear note of scorn.

"I get provoked by people who take their fellow human beings for granted," he rumbled. "It's capable of putting me in the killing mood. No man dares to try such with me. They know the weaklings they pick on."

Ekwe glanced at Papa Ekwe. He looked pathetic, chin cupped in hand. Odum did not seem to have stirred up any emotion in Papa Ekwe by insinuating that he was a weakling.

Odum continued, "I have six pretty daughters. I have given out four of them in marriage. Why didn't anyone try to stop me? I would have made their skull my drinking vase. I still have two daughters to give to suitors. I dare anyone to interfere in my family's business." He finished with a scowl directed at Amadi.

Ekwe wondered if Odum ever got tired of reciting his litany of threats. Amadi looked calm. Odum's threats seemed to wash off him like water poured on the shell of a snail. The kinsmen had learned to tolerate Odum's bombastic nature. Ekwe was sure they tolerated him to avoid chaos. After Odum resumed his seat, the man who took the turn to speak, Ogwo, was partially white-haired. Ekwe did not know him well enough to rate him: his clout, his power to influence.

He was a calm and reticent man, had been sitting in silence, laughing when there was something to laugh about and whispering his criticisms of those who had spoken.

"With due respect to the last speaker, I do not think he has said anything at all." Ogwo started his speech with a denunciation of Odum's.

Odum threw a riposte at him, threatening to crush his bones and drink his blood.

"I dare you to touch me," Ogwo returned hotly in his tinny voice. "You will be devoured. What your brothers-in-law did to you will be nothing compared to what you will get."

They warmed the hall once more with a quick verbal exchange, Odum's voice drowning Ogwo's thin voice, but Ogwo was the leathery and unyielding type. Ekwe concentrated his gaze on the veins protruding from Ogwo's neck as he haggled relentlessly. Omeke warned the combatants of incurring a fine if they carried on. The threat had a sobering effect on them. Odum sat down, but he continued to scowl at Ogwo. Ekwe watched Odum out of the corner of his eye. He liked the way Odum spoke with authority and conviction, the way he entertained his audience with his exaggerations and intimidated his opponents with his muscular body. But only a very few people knew that beneath his brawny exterior, Odum was a milksop who easily fled from a determined opponent, according to Papa Ekwe.

"I too have given out daughters in marriage." Ogwo continued with his speech after tendering an apology to the kinsmen. "Some I gave out at a much younger age than Papa Ekwe's daughter. You, my kinsmen, came to witness the ceremonies. You ate and drank, and everyone was happy. But here, we have a different case. The bride in question vehemently rejects her suitor. This is what brings about the conflict in Papa Ekwe's household. When a family disagrees over dinner, the menu would be made known to neighbours who gather to resolve the conflict. This case is already before us kinsmen; therefore, it'd be wrong to throw it out. In my opinion, there's only one way to resolve this crisis—summon the young woman in question and hear from her."

This motion by Ogwo sparked off a fresh round of argument. The hall grew noisy. Sideswipes flew like pelts. The ones that stoned Amadi showered the floor as if his body were made of armour plate. Odum and Omeke took things personally and were within inches of coming to blows. Ekwe was getting more nervous. He did not like this idea of summoning Oyibo to this place. As if he read Ekwe's mind, Okoboyi stood up and took the contributor stand.

"I am not in support of summoning Ngwu's daughter in our midst," he said. "We must not subject the poor girl to such misery in the presence of her father in a matter we can easily resolve."

Ikoh snapped, "Tell us how we can resolve it, then, and stop wasting our time."

"I don't know why you get easily irritated with everything I say, but I will not be intimidated into silence by anyone," Okoboyi said resolutely. "I shall always speak my mind. You may trash my speech if you think I have not spoken to your taste, but do not cast me away as well."

Ekwe was impressed with Okoboyi's skill in handling malice from a kinsman, his composure, his oratorial skill.

"The day is far gone," Okoboyi said, and faked a yawn. "The squirrel does not pluck the whole bunch of palm nuts at their disposal but feeds on the ripe nuts while placing their tail over the unripe ones to secure them. I think we should adjourn to give us more time to digest this case."

Amuta agreed that the tendril of Okoboyi's speech did not need detaching, for it sprouted well, and, on that note, the tribunal adjourned. In his closing prayer, Ikpedirichukwu prayed for Chiokike to save the village from the violence of cowherds and save idolators from eternal damnation.

The Alarm

EKWE CAME OUTSIDE TO A CALM, CLEAR SUNDAY. He had indulged himself so much sleep in the night; it filled his palate like food. Mama Ekwe allowed him a full dose of sleep only on Sunday mornings because the villagers did not go to their farms on Sundays. It was a day to go to church for some, and a day to go to village meetings for others, but mostly it was a day to rest and prepare for a new week. Ekwe walked into the broadness of the day, his bare body tickled by the warm stroke of sunlight. He felt the breeze cool his nose. The softly scented wind brought a smell like freshly laundered clothes as the aroma of Sunday redolence settled in the sky. It swelled at noon as Mama Ekwe's kitchen hissed loudly, punctuating the rhythmic kpokonyapia kpokonyapia as some woman in the neigbourhood gave her fufu a good pummeling. Ekwe felt the synthetic energy of the pounding, but wished the hissing would go on forever. He sat under the tree and inhaled the aroma of lunch. Just then a frantic voice peeled into the percussion, drowning the voice of the pestle and the warm lunch notes. Ekwe knew that the voice rose only in an emergency: if a man walked in on a thief in his goat pen or his yam barn or if fire leapt up a neighbour's thatched roof in the thick of harmattan. This time it was the herdsmen's cattle that broke into people's farmlands and were causing widespread destruction.

Papa Ekwe snatched a machete and dashed out. Mama Ekwe followed, abandoning her cooking. Ekwe ran after them, angry at the voice for interrupting lunch, but excited at the drama that was unfolding. The scene was moderately crowded when Ekwe got to the farm. His eyes ranged over the field with widespread destruction, terrible to look at, with large areas of people's farms completely flattened, habaneros and tomatoes stamped to a pulp, cassava foliage beheaded, their stems broken, and their roots uprooted and devoured. Papa Ekwe scanned the damage with the demeanor of a lion faced with a foe. The sight of the uncontrolled cattle still grinding vegetables and corn into the ground with their hooves and chewing on yam tubers drove him wild. He gathered himself and went after them. One large cow trailed behind, too engrossed in her chewing to sense the threat. Ekwe watched Papa Ekwe deliver a furious blow to the animal's thurl; the cow sprang forwards in a great moo of pain, Papa Ekwe gave a hot chase, caught up with her, and delivered another machete blow to her rib. The cow buckled and crashed down to her knees. Papa Ekwe, seized by a terrible rage, the kind Ekwe had never witnessed before, unleashed another blow. The cow rolled over on her back and threw her legs up. His next blow sank viciously into the cow's neck. And then he rained several blows to the head, stopping only when he saw that the animal was no longer moving. He went after the next cow within sight.

More villagers were arriving. Men raced up with machetes like lunatics and descended on the cattle. Women wept and mouthed curses. Children giggled as their fathers crumbled onto their stomachs while chasing after the cattle. At last, the large herd of riotous animals was driven out of the farms. Papa Ekwe had dropped on his buttocks, exhaustion hitting him after slaughtering as many cows as he could catch up with. He was bathed in sweat. And now he brought out his snuffbox and began inhaling fiercely, his anger trickling out of his nostrils in dark brown liquid. Mama Ekwe was devastated by the scale of the destruction. Tears and snot glistened on her face. Ekwe was crestfallen, not so much for the realization that there would be no harvest now that the crops were ruined as for the cattle ruining his dream lunch. He felt like a baby whose mouth was suddenly plucked away from its mother's nipple. Ekwe had sucked his mother's breastmilk up to the age of four. The twins had not been born, and he was pampered as Papa Ekwe's only son. He would grab a stool, pluck Mama Ekwe's breast out of her bra, and help himself. And right after that he would descend on a bowl of fufu. To stop his obsession with breastmilk, Mama Ekwe tried the bitter leaf stunt. She would grease her nipple with the bitter juice to put him off. Ekwe would grimace at first contact with the bitter nipple, but he soon found a way around Mama Ekwe's trick, which he did by tonguing the nipple clean and spitting out the bitter juice to reclaim his sweetened breastmilk. "You little mischief!" Mama Ekwe would vent her frustration.

Ekwe resented the cowherds and their cattle. He watched Papa Ekwe as he blew his nose, his anger spraying the air in fine brown droplets. And then he got up and walked off, his machete in his tight grip. Papa Ekwe did not notice Ekwe trailing behind as he made for the road to the king's palace.

King Okosisi sat around the courtyard door, a black dog at his feet. As Papa Ekwe stamped in with a machete, the dog started to bark, provoked by the glance of steel in the afternoon sun. The king recalled the little scabrous thing inching timidly towards the armed man as Papa Ekwe stepped back and leaned the machete on the dwarf fence. For the first time, he noticed Ekwe stalking him but did not mind.

"I wasn't sure if I should remain seated or take to my heels as you approached with a machete that looked as if it's coming straight from a visit to the whetstone," King Okosisi said jokingly.

His joke was received like muck plastered on Papa Ekwe's face. The king called for a seat, but Papa Ekwe declined.

"I would rather say what brought me here standing."

"Why do you come charging into my palace like a tempest?"

The dog growled and wagged her tail at Papa Ekwe as he gathered himself.

"You won't recognize the community farmland," he said brusquely. "It's as flat as a football field after the herdsmen's cattle finished playing a match there."

"Tell me, what happened?"

Papa Ekwe recounted the scene: shock, grief, and bravado contending with one another in his voice.

"You took laws into your hands." The king's voice assumed a monarchical tone as the dog went back reluctantly and sat at his feet in the company of flies. "Why run to me after you have taken revenge? You confessed to killing some of the cattle, which makes you as guilty as the cowherds. You should have come to me before taking revenge."

Ekwe felt like punching the king on the thick slab of his lower lip. The lip, caught in the light of the sun that streaked across his face, looked like raw meat. He wondered how the king would look if stung by a bee at the lip and stifled a chuckle. He would probably resemble a camel.

"I lost control of myself." Papa Ekwe's voice trembled, his hands formed fists. "It was a terrible sight to behold."

"The first time you came here with other members of the community to complain about the cowherds, I pleaded with you to be tolerant." King Okosisi's voice migrated from magisterial to sheer indignation. "I was trying to avoid the sort of violence witnessed in Nimbo. I expect you to cultivate a broader perspective on life. The land of Enu-Ozara is not known for its inhospitality to its guests. But you allow acrimony and intolerance to get the better of you. Your heart is bitter with hatred against men whose only offence is coming to your land to make a living. You seem to forget you have brothers and sisters who are also living in other lands. What if the owners of the lands in which they live are as hostile to them as you are to the cowherds?"

Papa Ekwe did not look satisfied with the king's position, but he did not want to disrespect the throne with a retort. He turned, grabbed Ekwe's hand, and started to walk away. At the fence, he picked up his machete and ignored the resentful dog that began barking again.

As he was being towed straight back to the farm, Ekwe wondered why Papa Ekwe had softened like cocoyam fufu before the king.

▴▴▴▴▴

"Yes, I saw the king. He blamed us for killing the cattle and said there was nothing he could do since we had taken revenge," Papa Ekwe said to a group of villagers who crowded around him with curious eyes as he sank his machete into the soil and lowered himself onto a ridge.

They were working in solidarity, the villagers, trying to save what they could. They picked tomatoes and habaneros strewn about the farm and fed soil to the plants that were not completely torn up by the roots. Not many of the tomatoes and habaneros were ripe. They were still green, still some time away from full maturity. They would have to be preserved in the hope that they might ripen. Sadly, it was supposed to be the first harvest of the season.

"How can he not know what to do?" The man who spoke had a face covered in ugly white hairs. "Is he not the king of this community? And how can he blame us for killing a few cattle out of dozens feasting from our farmlands?"

"I would have finished off all the cattle if I had arrived in time," said Papa Onwulie, a frail, squint-eyed old man.

Ekwe hid a chuckle. The old man sounded like Odum even though he looked incapable of killing a fly—incapable of even seeing well through a squint. Ekwe noticed that Odum was nowhere within eyeshot.

"Let's all march to the palace to tell the king how displeased we are with his stance," a hoarse-voiced man said as he wiped his sweaty face against his shirtsleeve.

"I have always known that our king is no good." It was a woman's thin, sardonic voice. "He blames us for slaughtering the enemy's cattle instead of holding the cowherds responsible and making them pay for the crops they have destroyed? Why is he being so lenient with those people? Is there something he is hiding from us?"

"How can a complete stranger occupy another man's land and destroy his crops, and no one does anything about it?" another female voice scoffed. "What is the matter with our men? Are they so weak as to allow total strangers to dominate us in our own land? They better step aside and allow us women to do it since it appears they do not have the balls to face those people."

The women applauded.

"Nowadays women are the ones with balls. They fight the wars and men tell the tales. It's no longer the other way round," another woman said, inverting a popular mantra and drawing support from other women.

"The palace is not the best place to bring this war," a voice fumed. "We can't fold our arms and wait for the herdsmen to attack us. We must confront them in the forest and beat them back. We must chase them out of this community."

Half the crowd seemed to disagree with the voice, but the other half seemed determined to take the war into the forest.

Guilt Gifting

THE STORY OF CATTLE DESTROYING THE COMMUNITY farmland continued to reverberate throughout the villages. Men gathered at Jerome's bar to talk about it over a drink. The place was full and smelt of hot spice and sweat: the odour of bare-chested men sipping hot drinks and spooning from bowls of dogmeat pepper soup, which sent out a spicy steam in front of them. They paid for the drink in turns. A big Lucozade bottle refilled with kinkana stood on a wooden table from which they poured into a glass shot, sipped, and chattered. Ekwe sat some distance away and drank from a small bowl of pepper soup in the same measured way as the men. Papa Ekwe took him to Jerome's bar from time to time. Mama Ekwe didn't exactly jump up for joy when he took Ekwe there and bought him spicy dogmeat pepper soup. She would nag about a father who exposed his little son to the affairs of men. Ekwe didn't think there was anything wrong with it. Mama Ekwe wanted Papa Ekwe to sit at home and mourn the family's loss instead of going to a bar to spend the evening. Was he celebrating his misfortune? Papa Ekwe insisted on going there probably to take advantage of the sympathies of others who were luckier. He enjoyed free drinks in addition to a flood of sympathies from neighbours whose farms were not terribly affected.

"The only language cowherds understand is violence," Odum said. "God knows they would have had a full dose of it if their cattle had touched a leaf in my farm. I am sure they know this, that's why they avoided my farm and chose to strike on a day when I was out of the village."

Ekwe imagined Odum grabbing two enormous cows, one with his right hand and the other with his left, and throttling them until their bodies went limp and then grabbing another two and another and another until the farmland was littered with the bloodied, stinking carcasses of cattle. The men did not argue with Odum even though a furtive voice wondered if Odum had not been taking refuge in his house on the day the cattle broke into the farmland. They seemed addled to ponder his unreasonableness. But violence, they all agreed, was the only language the cowherds seemed to understand, and violence they must get.

▲▲▲▲▲

The verdict of the tribunal appeared to be going Papa Ekwe's way, but Amadi did not strike Ekwe as a man who would easily give up a fight. He remembered that Amadi spoke only once at the first hearing, when he cast his accusation at Papa Ekwe like a stone. When the kinsmen adjourned, he simply stood up and walked out of the hall without another word, but he said so much in the silence of his glare. It was safer if a man voiced his thoughts, Ekwe thought. Odum would howl and threaten to rip his opponent to pieces, drink their blood, and chew their bones. He expended his strength in words, but a man who refused to speak had cocked his energy and anger within him like gunpowder capped in a bottle and kept near a fire.

Oyibo had broken her hunger strike. She was forced to break it after Mama Ekwe joined her in sympathy, in solidarity, but Oyibo was still full of defiance. She was still full of fight. Mama Ekwe's branch of the family tree ate together with Papa Ekwe for the first time in a long time after the hunger strike was broken. They had the meal outdoors under the neem tree—Papa Ekwe, Mama Ekwe, Ekwe, Azuka, Oyibo, and the twins—in the circle of an oil lamp light that threw a conciliatory yellow patch around them, leaving Ekwe's big stepmother in the sulky umbra of her corner.

"I am still wondering why Amadi picked on us," Mama Ekwe said in the middle of the meal. "Are we the first parents to want to give their daughter out in marriage in this village?"

"He did not pick on us," Papa Ekwe said. "He is a madman. A man made mad by too much book."

"What if the kinsmen rule in his favour?"

"They cannot do that. I challenge any one of them who has not given out a daughter in marriage at our daughter's age to come out and prove me wrong."

"I am nervous," Mama Ekwe said. "What if they insist on hearing from our daughter as basis for their judgement?"

"I leave her to you. Talk sense into her. I am not going to take lightly any public humiliation."

Ekwe sensed a note of anxiety in Papa Ekwe's voice. Ekwe himself was nervous. But he wanted Amadi to win at the tribunal. His experience in the astral realm had opened his eyes to the danger his sister was exposed to if she married now and had a baby. He was scared. Things were unfolding in the exact same way he had experienced them. Amadi had stepped in to stop the marriage even though the appeal was made by Azuka in the astral. Despite it all, the verdict seemed to be heading the suitor's way.

The suitor came the next day to know what the kinsmen had resolved. His windscreen picked the light from the setting sun as the big red motorcar glided in like a falcon and Ekwe was dazzled by star-shaped flashes of affluence. The suitor climbed out and walked in with a big bottle of White Horse. He set the drink down on a low stool as he settled next to Papa Ekwe. They started to drink. Ekwe moved a wooden stool to the neem tree to listen more closely, sensing Oyibo's quick movement as she snuck out through the backyard. As usual, the suitor poured himself a shot of drink and started the conversation from the endmost.

"I have it on good authority that your king sold a portion of the community land to the cowherds to graze their cattle." He sipped his drink.

"He sold it?" Papa Ekwe said.

"I heard he conspired with some community leaders to sell the land and share the money. He will probably sell off the entire village to the strangers under your nose."

A rooster crowed into a ponderous silence as bits of the puzzle fell into place. Now Papa Ekwe understood why the king was quick to jump to the defence of the cowherds.

"There will be consequences on the throne if what you just said gets to the villagers." Papa Ekwe broke the silence.

The suitor shrugged. "Tell me, how did the meeting of your kinsmen go?"

"The kinsmen adjourned without arriving at a decision after a heated debate."

"I think I have something for your kinsmen in the car boot," the suitor said.

Suddenly, as if by magic, the boot of the motorcar started to open, to Ekwe's amazement. He was entranced by the sight of the boot closing again on its own after the suitor lifted a carton of White Horse out, dropped it at Papa Ekwe's feet, fished out a neat wrap of currency notes, and dropped it on top of the carton of White Horse.

"This drink and the money are for your kinsmen when next they meet."

"All these things are for my kinsmen?"

"Yes. Tell them it's for their refreshment."

Papa Ekwe thanked the suitor and asked Mama Ekwe to carry the carton of drinks into the house.

"Tell me," the suitor said. "Which way do you think the verdict will go?"

Papa Ekwe sipped his drink and made a harsh savouring noise in his throat. "I believe the kinsmen will rule in our favour."

"What if they rule against you? That kinsman of yours Amadi seems to me a very troublesome man."

"He may be troublesome, but he is certainly not the father of my daughter."

"If you concede victory to him, your entire clan will suffer in his hands. He is a widely travelled man with ideas that are foreign and very unsuitable to life in this rural community."

Ekwe frowned as a recollection of Oyibo's doomed marriage to the suitor in the astral realm flashed through his mind.

The Verdict

EKWE WOKE UP IN THE FIRST DULL LIGHT OF THE morning on the second day of the tribunal. Anxiety streaked across his heart like lightning as they walked to the village hall. This time Mama Ekwe accompanied them to help carry the carton of White Horse to the hall. Odum's voice was heard from a distance, as clearly as a town crier's gong. The air felt oaky as they approached the hall, Odum's voice rising in a scissor to axe a woodpile of threats, but the air grew light again as they entered the hall. The cadence of the kinsmen's laughter changed dramatically as Mama Ekwe eased the drink down before them. She was treated to acts of chivalry as she genuflected and exited the hall. Women were not part of the tribunal except when summoned. After she left, Odum resumed his narrative of how he had spent weeks in a trench with other Biafran soldiers without food during the Nigerian Civil War.

"The choir of artillery fire sang through the forest with a vicious melody," he said. "Bullets flew about like swifts. We shared the swampy trench with snakes and other dangerous reptiles. You dared not stir or cough or you would have yourself bitten to death or your brain shattered by a bullet."

Ekwe was enjoying Odum's story. He watched Ikoh from

the corner of his eyes as Ikoh gazed at Odum in rapture, his face as softened and mushy as a rotten fruit. Ekwe chuckled at the thought that Ikoh's face might burst open and spill gouts of pus if pricked with a needle.

"I was the sole survivor of that ordeal." Odum thumped his broad chest. "The other soldiers died inside the trench, some of snakebite, and others of hunger."

"Which means your claims have no witnesses," Okoboyi said in his critical manner. "I am always hesitant about stories that have no witness."

Odum swallowed a riposte that rose like bile in his throat as voices trailed off into silence. Amuta had called for silence, and he got an almost automatic response from the kinsmen, but not from birds singing from the surrounding trees, the audacious notes of a parakeet that came clear.

Ekwe's anxiety over the verdict returned as Papa Ekwe whispered into Amuta's ears, then moved the carton of White Horse to the centre of the floor.

"My prospective son-in-law brings you this gift, my kinsmen, for your relaxation," Papa Ekwe said.

The kinsmen applauded, but Amadi kept a straight face. Amuta started to make a small opening speech after the ovation died down, but Ikpedirichukwu insisted on beginning the day's business with a prayer. Scrawny in his filthy oversized coat, he merely gave Odum a pious, self-righteous smile when Odum warned him not to keep them from starting by prolonging the prayer as usual. Odum had said that Ikpedirichukwu did not pray, he barked at God as if God were hard of hearing. And now as he prayed, Ikpedirichukwu's voice seemed to fill the lapel of his coat, so that he appeared to hang on the coat like a scarecrow. Kola nut was shared with the usual slight bickering and eaten in the mouthwatering way that made Ekwe stare and swallow. He was considered too young to eat kola nut, and Omeke always bypassed him during sharing, but now Papa Ekwe gave him a pinch from his own lobe. The taste was disappointing, nothing like the crunchy rhythm it made in the jaws of the kinsmen who insisted on a round of drink before continuing, much to Ikpedirichukwu's disapproval. His church forbade the consumption of alcohol, but Ikoh walked to the carton of drinks, and, swinging his bad leg as if it were made of rubber, he took out a squat bottle, kissed the bottle, and hugged it to his chest as a mother would hug her long-lost baby. The kinsmen started to sing the suitor's praises, listing the gift as one of his many acts of generosity. Ekwe looked to see Amadi's reaction as Omeke drank the very first shot, frowned, listened, and gave a nod of approval.

"The drink is good, my kinsmen," he said, and started to share the drink with the kinsmen in a shot.

"My kinsmen, I don't know why we are sitting down with arms folded and doing nothing to stop the influx of cowherds in our community," Okoboyi said chattily. "Are we waiting until we are completely surrounded with no way for escape before we realize that another civil war is about to begin?"

"Nimbo has fallen," Amuta said. "Are we waiting to be the next?"

Odum stood up and thumped his chest again. "Attacking our community will be their worst mistake. They will be asking for war. My kinsmen, I beg of you, give way when the war begins. I will face them alone. I don't need help from anyone.

You will know you have a lion for a kinsman. This body you are looking at is bulletproof. With this head I will nod their bullets away as though a football. What other weapons are they going to use that are worse than guns? Is it machete or arrow? But I tell you, it's easier for an arrow to pierce through steel than for it to penetrate this body you are looking at, and machete cuts are like fingernail scratches to my body."

The kinsmen laughed and washed Odum's words down with more drinks. Ekwe expected Amadi to speak on the cowherds. He ought to know more about things than the average village man, but Amadi said nothing, rejected the drink as many times as Omeke offered him a shot, and sat scowling, unstirred by Odum's unbelievable bragging.

Papa Ekwe allowed Ekwe a sip from his shot. Ekwe shuddered as it stung his cheek with the suddenness of a slap, clenched his teeth, and swallowed it down with a shiver. He felt his eyes bulging. After he took more sips, with more ease this time, the air grew weightless, and the room started to swing slowly. He leaned on the wall and shut his eyes to savour the honeyed taste as voices grew distant, then faded into the dark void of his vision.

Ekwe started to hear the faint clash of voices again. When he opened his eyes, the hazy shapes of bottles and shots lay empty on the floor, and a thick aroma hung in the air over the kinsmen who had collapsed in sleep as he came fully awake. Amuta was far gone. Spit crawled like an angleworm down his pointed chin. Ikoh nodded, met Ekwe's gaze, then dozed off again.

"Wake up, they are here, they are here! The killer herdsmen are here!"

The scramble that followed Ikoh's frantic voice left Ekwe stupefied. The kinsmen were awake in an instant. Odum was the first to leap towards the door in escape. He collided into Omeke and both men crashed to the ground, struggled again to their feet, and joined the frightful crush at the doorway as every man fought their way out. Amuta, Papa Ekwe, and Ikoh seemed to be at a disadvantage owing to age and bad legs.

Ikoh suddenly burst into laughter and started to limp back to his seat. Slowly, it dawned on all that he had played a prank on the kinsmen who stopped scrambling at the door and started to return to their seats, much to their relief.

"Odum, is this how you are going to fight the militants when they come?" Ikoh rocked with laughter. "Is this how you are going to strangle them two at a time, by running away like a schoolboy at the first hint of trouble?"

"Suddenness will beat even the strongest," Odum said.

"Have you not heard of the saying that the ability to tackle suddenness defines a great man?" Ikoh said.

The kinsmen roared with laughter as Omeke resumed sharing White Horse.

Amadi had been unmoved by the false alarm. He was furious at the kinsmen who got drunk and turned the tribunal into a bar.

"This is sabotage." He suddenly rose to his feet. "This is a conspiracy, and it is unacceptable."

He stormed out.

"He is going to involve the police," Omeke said in a panicked voice. "I know him too well."

The fear that Amadi would involve the police forced the kinsmen to disperse. Ekwe did not know that even old men including Papa Ekwe feared the police. He imagined Amadi and a gun-wielding policeman in a scary black uniform marching in to arrest the kinsmen. He always crossed a police post on his way to school. Whenever he passed there, he walked very fast and refused to look towards the small tin house with a policeman always standing in the frontage, a rifle slung over his shoulder.

War Beckons

A BODY WAS LYING NEAR PAPA EKWE'S FARM IN A pool of blood. The body wore a nose ring and braided hair, according to Papa Ekwe, who saw it. The corpse belonged to a boy about Ekwe's age, he added. Ekwe wanted to see the body. He didn't think he had seen a dead boy before, but Mama Ekwe frightened him, said a boy's cadaver was nothing like the carcass of a cow, and if Ekwe saw the body, he would see ghosts in the night. Ekwe wasn't fond of ghosts as a ten-year-old boy, so he kept his curiosities over the dead boy confined to what information Papa Ekwe passed at home. Mama Ekwe grieved for the dead boy even though she did not see the corpse. He was not sure Mama Ekwe had grieved this way for anyone before. He figured the reason could be because no boy of Ekwe's age had died in a pool of blood at the farm before to elicit her grief. It could also be because she was against the slaughtering of children. He imagined himself as the boy who lay dead on the farm. Mama Ekwe would cry. He did not like to see Mama Ekwe cry. When she cried, she could not control her runny nose, and runny noses disgusted him. He did not know if Papa Ekwe would cry. The only time he ever saw him in tears was when he took fierce sniffs of snuff and looked up with engorged, watery eyes.

People would pour into their compound to console Mama Ekwe. She would cry buckets of tears, her nose running until the ridges underneath flushed pink like a rabbit's.

"You must not go to the farm in the meantime." Papa Ekwe sounded a clear note of warning to all. "Whoever killed that herdsboy has created a big problem. They will want to avenge his death on anyone they can lay their hands on."

Ekwe figured the neighbours would not go to their farms either. Mama Ekwe and other village women should have been harvesting their vegetables by now. They should have been reaping what was left of their greens, pumpkins, and squashes after the cattle invasion. After harvesting them, Mama Ekwe would tie them up in handfuls with the help of Oyibo and Azuka. And then she would wrap the bundles away from the harsh clutches of the harmattan. A woman came from the city to buy the vegetables, a fat, fair-skinned woman Ekwe thought rich and gorgeous but who had a smell about her. Ekwe didn't know if it was a good smell; he didn't think it was a bad smell either. He gulped a thick waft of it whenever she passed by or came close to him. He would watch her as she dished instructions to the pickup truck driver, who conveyed her vegetables to the city, and then he would steal glances and chuckles at the upslope of her large buttocks. What amused him was not the size of her buttocks, but how they swung inside her gown. Ekwe didn't know that mothers wore gowns. Mama Ekwe tied a wrappa around her waist over a blouse whenever she was going out, but when she was at home, she tied the wrappa around her chest and left her angular shoulders bare.

▲▲▲▲▲

One afternoon, Mama Ekwe hurried home from the market with news of unfamiliar faces materializing in the village. The strange men were believed to be spies sent to the village ahead of a planned attack. People were pointing fingers at Papa Ekwe, according to Mama Ekwe. The cowherds had fingered him as the boy's murderer because the body was found between the stream and his farm. Papa Ekwe sat scowling while Mama Ekwe and his stepmothers talked in apprehensive tones. Ekwe had never seen Papa Ekwe so withered by a rumour. He wondered if Papa Ekwe murdered the herdsboy. He remembered those times when Papa Ekwe had left the house with a sharpened machete and a face like a pugilist. Could he have gone hiding in the bush near the farm? Could he have sprung at the boy and cut him dead?

Papa Ekwe started to stay awake every night. He kept vigil over the compound. He would sit late into the night under the neem tree with a machete by his side. Ekwe woke up to pee every night and heard the deep resonant notes of the vigilantes' bell. He heard them crowing like masquerades, but despite their reassuring presence, the villagers slept with an eye open.

The suitor came again. He pulled up in the compound and strolled in as if he had no worries in life, as if cowherds did not exist in his world. He had an aura about him, indigo in colour.

"Too bad." He shook his head when Papa Ekwe told him of the rumour making rounds in the middle of their conversation. "If they suspect you of killing the boy, they are likely to begin the war from here."

"The young men of this village have reinforced their vigilante duties."

"I have said this before; setting up a vigilante patrol will not stop the militants from attacking." He took a sip of White Horse. "Do you think the people of Nimbo had folded their arms and waited to be attacked? The militants will always attack when the village is caught napping. Besides, your vigilante reinforcements are nothing compared to their advanced weaponry. They are not the sort of militants you go after with machetes and dane guns. The best anyone can do to help themselves to safety in this situation is to flee."

"My mother came from Nrobo and I married my first wife from there," Papa Ekwe said in an anxious voice. "I married my second and third wives from Abbi and Ugbene-Ajima. I have thought of taking my family to any of those communities, but they are like nose and mouth with Enu-Ozara."

"The entire neighbourhood is not safe as long as the militants are out there in the forests, especially after the murder of the boy," the suitor said. "You will need to get away from this area at once with your family, possibly go to the city." He laughed, his voice deep and musical, his aura spreading around and surrounding the compound. "I told you I have a house in the city, a newly finished house. I meant it when I said it was all yours."

Ekwe caught Papa Ekwe and Mama Ekwe as they exchanged glances.

"The wedding will have to be done at once." The suitor glanced from Papa Ekwe to Mama Ekwe as if daring any of them to object. "Let me have an estimate of the costs of the bride price and traditional wedding. The white wedding will be held in the city. I want my city friends to be in attendance. After the bride price and traditional wedding, we shall all move to the city for the white wedding. And then you will move into the new house and be far away from the killers."

Ekwe glanced at Papa Ekwe again and saw a look of relief and self-vindication.

Mama Ekwe summoned Oyibo after the suitor left. "As things stand, we have no choice other than to allow the suitor to have his way." She pleaded with her. "This is the only way we can escape the militants."

Ekwe shot Oyibo a piteous glance. Her look was lukewarm, between a simmering defiance and a tepid submission.

Sabotage

THE FIRST MARRIAGE RITE IDEGO WAS FIXED TO BEgin amidst the crisis. Women gathered as soon as it was dawn and started to cook. They washed gigantic pots, plucked vegetables, ground things, and started huge log fires. They chatted and laughed loudly. Papa Ekwe sent two kinsmen to Enugu Ezike to purchase palm wine.

"Look for the best wine," he said. "I don't want to give my in-laws bad wine. They deserve nothing but ohuesual."

"Is ohuesual the name of a type of wine?" Ekwe asked.

Papa Ekwe laughed. "Ohuesual is palm wine tapped and taken straight from the palm tree and drunk fresh without adulterations."

Ekwe kept throwing glances down the road, regretting but not regretting what he had done. He could not believe that Papa Ekwe was giving his sister's hand in marriage to the suitor with the big red motorcar, as happened in the astral realm, and they were all supposed to go to Enugu to live with the couple, and they were supposed to be safe there with no fear of the militants. Oyibo's marriage to the suitor was a narrative destined for a catastrophic ending, and everything in him now rebelled against it. He threw another look towards the road and at Papa Ekwe, who was busy making the best pork kebabs for the guests, and guilt stabbed Ekwe through the heart for his betrayal. But he could not watch his sister fall into the bottomless pit the suitor had dug for her. He himself would be the worst loser if the marriage did not push through, doomed to eat only fufu for the rest of his life. No more akara and akamu, much less rice.

Ekwe's heart gave a lurch as a white van suddenly appeared. At first, it seemed the in-laws had arrived, and all eyes were fixed on the van as it nosed its way into the compound, but then Amadi and some gun-wielding police officers jumped out and started to march in. The sudden appearance of the police officers left hands hanging over chores. Papa Ekwe left the fire and started to walk towards the officers. His bare body was covered in soot smudges. Something seemed to have snapped in him, something more than anger as he stomped straight to Amadi. Ekwe had never seen him in such captivity, his usual soft mien having fled from him and in its place a belligerent look. He stopped in front of Amadi with fists balled to his sides, eyes blazing. For a moment, Ekwe thought he was going to punch Amadi, but then Lance Corporal Okute, sensing violence, moved in.

"You are under arrest," Lance Corporal Okute said to Papa Ekwe.

Instead of punching Amadi, Papa Ekwe put out his hands meekly in surrender. He was handcuffed. Mama Ekwe and his stepmothers wept and shouted pleas to Amadi, even knelt before him, but the man kept a straight face. As Papa Ekwe was cuffed and led into the police van, Ekwe regretted sneaking out to Amadi with information about the hastily arranged marriage in the hope that the man would put an end to it. But

Amadi had taken it too far by bringing policemen with guns to arrest and cuff Papa Ekwe like a common criminal. They were even pushing him roughly into their van and cocking their guns. What if they shot him, Ekwe thought with alarm, and he became a fatherless boy?

The police were far gone when the in-laws arrived and met everywhere in a mournful mood.

ııııı

Lance Corporal Okute was probably the only person from Enu-Ozara who was in the police force. He worked in the Nsukka Urban Police Division. Ekwe sat close to the police officer, who was now dressed in plainclothes. He had looked different in a police uniform when he came to arrest Papa Ekwe, lank with a tough, angular demeanor. Without his police uniform, the man looked ordinary, thought Ekwe, like any other young man who casually went around the village drinking palm wine or playing draughts at the motor park. Ekwe listened to the corporal's deep voice as he narrated Amadi's experience at the police station nestling on a hill, how Amadi met a female inspector at the counter on arrival, who was busy writing and did not give him attention until she finished and pushed the notebook away.

"Yes?" She looked up at Amadi with a frown.

"My name is Amadi. I am here to report a case of underage marriage."

Inspector Agatha's eyes dilated with interest. The officer nicknamed Iron Lady for her toughness looked him over and concentrated her gaze on his oily beard.

"Underage marriage, kwa," she said. "How old is the bride?"

"A precocious twelve-year-old."

She chuckled. "Gentleman, where are you coming from, and how is this girl related to you?"

"I don't think how we are related is important. I am only a concerned person."

Iron Lady burst into laughter. "Is that why you are wasting your time? Men do worse things in those bush communities than marry twelve-year-olds. They take children who are still in their mother's wombs as brides and turn them into mothers."

"The suitor is a grandfather while the bride is a child eager to continue in school." He paused, then added, "I want both the father and the suitor arrested and prosecuted."

"Who?"

"The girl's father and the suitor. Something should be done to stop the marriage."

"You have to put down your complaint first."

"Can I have a sheet of paper and a pen?"

She laughed. "Does this place look like a stationery store to you? Go find sheet and pen outside if you want to write."

Amadi went out to get paper and pen from one of the kiosks fronting the station, where cops go to let up a bit. He was writing on the counter when a male constable dragged in a boy no older than sixteen by the belt. A girl about the same age followed closely behind. The boy had been fighting the girl, the constable explained. He was panting from dragging the wild-looking boy with a short lock of hair. The girl looked defiant in shredded clothes, with the quick raptorial flair of a hawk. She had left a signature on the boy's forehead, a check mark crafted with a sharp talon.

Iron Lady focused her attention on Amadi, who in a few lines had put down his complaint and was handing the paper over to her, but Amadi was quick to protest when he was asked to provide funds to fuel the vehicle with which to travel to the remote community for the arrest. He was shocked at the request. He spoke so many big English words and only stopped because Iron Lady suddenly lost interest in him and switched her attention to the fighting juveniles.

"I am not even sure I want to go to those herdsmen-infested communities to arrest anyone," she said curtly, and turned to the boy. "So, she refused to sleep with you, and you decided to tear her dress and force your way, eeh." Her voice was grim, her glare falling hard on the boy. "You even had to lock your hair and wear earrings like a girl."

The boy made a protest and got a smack across his mouth. "Ka nnukwa pim. If I hear you talk again, I will cut off that thing dangling between your legs. Are you not ashamed that you chose a girl to fight? How many boys have you fought in your miserable life? I am sure if you have fought any, he must have fed you with sand, but when you see a lady, that's when your thing will stand up. Today you will show all of us here the size of that thing that is so troublesome. Lance Corporal. Oya yipu. Undress him from the waist."

The boy started to protest and fought him off as Lance Corporal Okute reached to carry out Iron Lady's order. Iron Lady was notorious for the way she handled males who thought themselves tough and was rumoured to grab criminals by their balls and squeeze them hard to get the truth out of them.

Amadi hadn't given up. He insisted on talking to the Divisional Police Officer, and he made so much fuss about it the DPO himself came out of his office, summoned by Amadi's voice. When he saw Amadi, he asked Lance Corporal Okute to bring him to his office. If Amadi recognized Lance Corporal Okute, he did a good job of cutting him dead. He was waved into a seat by the plump, smiling, and handsome middle-aged man in bright blue and black uniform.

"What is the problem, gentleman?" The DPO smiled a bright smile.

"I find it shocking that it should be asked of a complainant to fuel the vehicle that will be used for an arrest," Amadi fumed.

The DPO sat in silence and listened to him until he raged himself out. He leaned forwards on his desk and smiled again. "I apologize if in any way my men have said or done anything to offend you. You see, people often misunderstand us when we make these appeals, but the truth is, the imprest we get from the Nigeria Police Force is far from enough to run the affairs of this station. We, the officers in the station, must make personal financial commitments to ensure things are moving smoothly. This is why we ask for a little assistance from well-meaning citizens to help us serve you better."

Amadi wasn't swayed by the DPO's soft-voiced tact.

"But not to worry." The DPO smiled in concession. Amadi looked like trouble. Occasionally he had to deal with people like Amadi who were sticklers for the rules. He always treaded carefully. "By the way, are you having problems with anyone?"

Amadi told him he was after a man who was going to sell his daughter into slavery.

"Really? Slavery in this twenty-first century? Sounds interesting," the DPO said. "You sound very enlightened and fascinating, like you are not from around those remote communities."

Lance Corporal Okute, who stood by waiting for further orders, knew his boss was wondering about Amadi's refined voice and frayed shirt.

"Fascinating maybe, depending on what you mean, but someone not from around there, no," Amadi said. "I am only a concerned man at variance with the way and manner things are being run around me. Maybe I should blame it on the revolving imprest system instead of putting the blame on you and your men."

"You have been most understanding, most cooperative." The DPO shook hands with him and gestured to Lance Corporal Okute. "Make sure he gets the best possible service. I don't want to hear he is not satisfied with your handling of the case. I'd like to see the twenty-first-century slave trader when he arrives."

Lance Corporal Okute saluted and ushered Amadi out of the office. On their way back to the counter, they ran into the boy who beat up a girl as he was being shoved down the dingy cell corridor by the constable. He had been stripped of his clothes and left only in his boxers, unclothed of his male virility by Iron lady, by the unforgiving blue-yellow-green stripes of the penal institution. The inmates seemed to smell the new arrival, their itching hands protruding out of the iron bars of the cell, beckoning. Iron Lady took over again from Lance Corporal Okute, stomped about, and bawled at the junior officers while Amadi waited patiently.

Finally, they left in a Toyota van: Iron Lady, Constable Okpogwu, Lance Corporal Okute, and Amadi. Iron Lady had insisted Lance Corporal Okute be part of the team since he was from that community.

"The marriage ceremony is probably taking place about now." Amadi glanced at his wristwatch. "I should be able to deliver both the suitor and the father of the bride to you with any luck."

"You chose the right time to strike," Iron Lady growled like a beast of prey. "I can't wait to lay my hands on that dirty old man. Would you have the suitor prosecuted?"

"I want the marriage annulled to give the bright little girl a chance to continue in school, that's all I want," he said.

The Power of Money

THE DPO ASKED TO SEE THE OFFENDER WHEN THE team returned, and they took Papa Ekwe straight into his office. The DPO was lost in a note he was writing when Lance Corporal Okute walked the suspect in and saluted. He wrote for another short while.

"Is this the man who wants to sell his daughter into slavery?" The DPO looked up.

Papa Ekwe started to protest.

"Old man. I don't want to waste time. I am not going to ask them to put you in a cell, out of respect for your age. But before we let you go, you are going to sign an undertaking. I understand your daughter is about twelve years old. I also understand she would like to continue with her studies, but because of your greed for a fat bride price you are forcing her to marry a man your age. You will sign an undertaking giving us the power to prosecute you if you insist on forcing your daughter into a marriage of convenience. After signing the undertaking, we will then consider releasing you on bail."

The DPO dismissed Papa Ekwe and Lance Corporal Okute, who walked the offender back to the counter where Amadi waited. Amadi seemed satisfied with the conditions for the bail after Lance Corporal Okute explained them.

Iron Lady did not like the way her boss wanted her to handle the case. She wanted Papa Ekwe to sleep in a cell.

"Agadi. How many wives do you have, old man?" she said in a taunting voice.

"I have three wives." Papa Ekwe said.

"How old is your youngest wife?"

"She's nineteen years of age."

"And how old are you?"

Papa Ekwe scratched his chin. "My father didn't keep birth records. I guess I was born in the year the Burma war ended."

Iron Lady looked around for help from the other police officers. "Would anyone remember when World War II ended?"

Lance Corporal Okute said it ended in 1930, another officer said it was in 1950, and another said 1943. They started to argue. Iron Lady shouted them down, saying they were illiterates who could not answer a question as simple as when World War II ended.

"1930, 1940, 1950," she mimicked. "It's unfortunate the war ended too early. I think it should have lasted longer, as more men should have died in it, men who now subject their wives to domestic violence and sell their daughters into slavery."

"What is it you have against men, Iron Lady?" Lance Corporal Okute said.

"If you want to know the answer to your question, ask this old man." She gestured towards Papa Ekwe. "I am sure he is pushing towards seventy." Her eyes widened. "A close-to-seventy-year-old-man married to a nineteen-year-old."

She rolled her eyes. "Where's your strength, old man? I pity the sexually famished lady in her dungeon of poverty and deprivation called marriage."

Amadi said the war ended in 1945.

Amadi had left the station when the suitor got there. The suitor knew his way around and was familiar to the police officers who hailed him as he charged in. He slapped some currency notes on the counter. "This is for drink." And then he let the officers playfully fight over the gift and turned to speak with Papa Ekwe, who sat behind the counter. They talked for a while.

Iron Lady walked in, and they greeted each other familiarly. She told the suitor she was the investigation police officer handling the case. He asked to see the DPO, whom he was told had taken interest in the case.

"Take him to Oga." Iron Lady gestured towards Lance Corporal Okute.

"Come, let's go, sir." Lance Corporal Okute led the way to the DPO's office, returned alone almost at once, and beckoned to Papa Ekwe. "Follow me, old man. Oga wants to see you."

"What I want is simple," the DPO said to the suitor and nodded routinely again to acknowledge Corporal Okute's salute as he led Papa Ekwe in. "You are going to sign an undertaking to stay away from that little girl to enable her to pursue her schooling dreams. Her father will do the same. When this is done, we shall let you take the old man home."

"But who says I will not sponsor her schooling." The suitor gave him a big smile. "That's exactly what I plan to do after the wedding. I don't have any intention of interfering with the pursuit of her career. And those who claim she's being forced to marry me, they are only my detractors. The man Amadi, who had my would-be father-in-law arrested, is half mad. He lived all his life outside of the community and returned recently empty-handed to foment trouble."

"I am not interested in how long Amadi has lived abroad and what his long absence might have done to his psyche; I am only concerned about the girl's future, which I believe is what Amadi is fighting for."

"We are saying the same thing here." The suitor whipped out a checkbook and a pen, wrote on it, signed the cheque, tore out a leaf, and pushed it across the desk. "I know the importance of education in the life of a young woman."

DPO Ogazi studied the leaf with a startled look. "What is this for?"

"A small gift for you. It's my own little way of supporting the police force."

DPO Ogazi pondered the gift. "Well. Thanks for the money."

"Don't mention it."

"We are just making sure the little girl is not denied her schooling." DPO Ogazi's voice softened. "She could be your child, you know. She could be mine."

"You have my word, DPO. I will make sure she gets a good education. Something her father and the so-called relative cannot give her."

DPO Ogazi shook hands with the suitor. "Thanks again for the contribution." He turned to Lance Corporal Okute. "Tell Inspector Agatha to prepare the old man's bail bond."

▲▲▲▲▲

Papa Ekwe called for another cup of water as he finished narrating his ordeal at the police station to his family and the small crowd of neighbours. He was looking harassed. The compound was littered with the debris of the abandoned marriage ceremony: perplexed pots with half-cooked food stood dejectedly over ashes of dead fires, vultures sidled close to the grill where Papa Ekwe had been making kebabs. The suitor and his entourage had met the compound in these ruins, with Papa Ekwe's disconsolate wives and children and sympathetic neighbours sitting with chins cupped in hands. Mama Ekwe fetched another large cup of water for Papa Ekwe, who finished it in a few mighty gulps and belched. Mama Ekwe genuflected as she took the cup back. She didn't use to curtsy to Papa Ekwe. Ekwe wondered if she did now because he was arrested and released again. Perhaps, wives grew fond of and curtsied to husbands after they were arrested by the police on the day of their daughter's marriage ceremony.

The suitor had driven Papa Ekwe home after bailing him out, when it was already late in the day and most of the guests had left, so the marriage ceremony had to be postponed. Besides, no one knew what Amadi's next move would be, a feeling that left the air tight with apprehension.

Lance Corporal Okute would narrate the details of what happened after Papa Ekwe was released on bail. Over a drink with Papa Ekwe under the neem tree, he apologized to the family for being part of the team that arrested Papa Ekwe. He was only doing his official duty as assigned to him by his superiors. He narrated how Amadi returned to the station to know the progress of the case, how he met Iron Lady at the counter, who was cold and almost hostile, and asked after the detainee, and how strongly he reacted when she told him Papa Ekwe had been released on bail. For answer to his whys and hows, she hissed and told him to find out from the DPO.

"I am sorry, but we couldn't continue to detain a man of that age for such a minor offence," DPO Ogazi said.

"We had an understanding." Amadi narrowed his eyes. "He was supposed to sign an undertaking before his release. Can I see a copy of the document?"

DPO Ogazi shook his head. "I am sorry, but there was no undertaking, no need for one, really."

Amadi was livid. "You can't possibly have released him without his signing an undertaking to protect the poor little girl from any harm."

The DPO switched on his bright smile. "No one is coming to any harm," he said softly. "I spoke with the suitor, and I believe he has some noble plans for her."

"I want this case taken to court," Amadi thundered.

"It's pointless going to court over this," DPO Ogazi said, calmly. "Our hands are tied. You are a learned man. I don't have to remind you there is nowhere in the Nigerian constitution where it is written that a man cannot give out his daughter in marriage until she is of a given age, and even if it's there, you and I know that in this country, the law is only for the poor."

"Nonsense!" barked Amadi. "Not when the girl is being married to a man who is her father's age against her will. I insist I want this case prosecuted."

"How certain are you about that?" DPO Ogazi said. "And how sure are you that you can establish a case of forceful marriage against him? He's the father of the girl, remember, and from what I understand, she is just a child, vulnerable to parental influence. Do you think a girl of that age can testify against her own father in a court of law? Have you thought of that? My good friend, I'd advise you not to waste your time fighting an age-old tradition, a battle you will most certainly lose."

Amadi stormed out.

Jollof Rice

EKWE NEVER WANTED THIS TROUBLE WITH THE POlice, he just wanted to save his sister, and had involved Amadi to accomplish this, but now he hated the man for humiliating Papa Ekwe and willed Amadi to fall from any of the trees he went about planting and break his legs. He wished upon the man a nagging wife and a mother who did not cook rice on Sundays. But he wasn't sure Amadi's mother still lived. She was probably gone. He figured she passed without a daughter-in-law or a grandchild from Amadi.

Ekwe was confused. He didn't know what Amadi or the suitor were planning to do next, he didn't even know what he himself was going to do; everybody was waiting, waiting for the other person to make a wrong move, like the men who played draughts at the motor park, like two crouching animals—one listening with cocked ears, poised to spring to safety, the other waiting for the right time to leap and kill without missing. Someone close to Amadi had told Papa Ekwe that the man had vowed not to stop until he brought down the corrupt police officers who had accepted bribes and perverted justice, until he had sent the suitor to jail for child marriage and abuse.

"That man is a fish bone stuck in my throat," Papa Ekwe had lamented.

One afternoon, as Ekwe was eating lunch with his family, as he was busy shovelling jollof rice into his mouth, a shrill voice pierced the afternoon air. Hands hung over food, mouths paused in their chewing, ears cocked like those of a hare. The voice, long and urgent, repeated the call, urging the villagers to flee for their lives because the militants had stormed the village.

"Oya, follow me now," Mama Ekwe barked at Ekwe and his sister and cousin as she swept up the twins in her arms.

She dashed towards the door. Oyibo and Azuka darted after her, knocking their plates of food over and colliding at the door. Ekwe hesitated, hungry eyes fixed on his plate of rice. People had raised the alarm before and caused everyone to shoot out of their homes like small animals out of their holes only to realize that it was a false warning raised by mischievous village boys. But today, there was something about the voice, an intensity in it that sent panic notes echoing through the village.

Ekwe shovelled two quick spoonfuls of rice into his mouth and dashed out, clenching his plate of food. He saw Mama Ekwe flying towards Papa Ekwe's barn, light as a kite, the twins like wings upon her arms. Oyibo and Azuka ran after her, Ekwe's half-siblings dashed every which way, his big stepmother crashed on her stomach like a muturu. In a moment when Ekwe paused to scoop at least one more spoon of rice into his mouth before fleeing after Mama Ekwe, he caught glimpses of frantic movements in the surrounding shrubbery.

A man loomed up with weapons behind the house.

Ekwe froze.

The plate of food had tumbled down in the dust before Ekwe realized that the man was Papa Ekwe. Papa Ekwe had dashed out with a machete and a bow at the first hint of alarm, not in escape, but to wait in ambush in the banana grove, bow poised to take down any intruder with the intent to harm his family. The militants would have to go through him first to get to his family.

He was furious now as he walked out of hiding. "This nonsense has to stop," he fumed. "The village constitution must be amended to include punishment for mischievous people who raise false alarm in this community." He looked from Ekwe to the fallen plate of rice as he leaned his machete and bow against the neem tree and settled on the bench.

Mama Ekwe and others started to come out of hiding.

"The person who raised that false alarm will never see any good in his life," Ekwe's big stepmother swore as she lumbered back, covered with dust.

"To think my stomach was emptied of the good lunch I was having for nothing." Mama Ekwe hissed with the twins in tow.

Papa Ekwe turned to Ekwe "Have you ever heard of the saying, 'The head falls prey to the belly'?"

Ekwe frowned, feeling angry and stupid.

"It means, That which kills a man lies in his stomach," Papa Ekwe said. "I would have finished you off if I were a militant, all because of your greed."

Ekwe stood scowling at the plate of rice lying face down in the dust.

Acknowledgments

I would like to thank my Fayetteville mentor and the founding director of the Arkansas International Writer-at-Risk Residency Program, the novelist Padma Viswanathan, and her husband, the poet and translator Geoff Brock.

I wrote this book during my fellowship with the Artist Protection Fund/Arkansas International Writer-at-Risk Residency Program and would like to thank Alison Russo and Mary Margret; Audra Johnston, who passed away in 2025; Zelo Safi and all the staff of the Artist Freedom Initiatives for their humanitarian services.

I would also like to thank my friends: David Jackson and Laura Jackson, Bill Spear and Laura Spear, Charles and Sharon, Gabrielle Idlet, Laura and all my friends in Fayetteville. To my professors at the Iowa Writers' Workshop: Lan Samantha Chang, Jamel Brinkley, Tom Drury, Cristobal McKinny, the very kind Sasha Khmelnik, and everyone who has inspired me in the places where I have found and made community and friends since relocating to the United States of America, I say thank you.

And to my friends Robert Lopez and Jeffery Renard Allen, I say thank you for not giving up on me.

Acknowledgments

With gratitude to my agent and the founder of Enliven Endeavors, Annie DeWitt and Mary Alice, for believing in me.

To you I am grateful, Kendall Storey and every member of staff at Catapult whom I have had the privilege to work with.

Thank you all!

© Andrew Kilgore

UCHENNA AWOKE is a writer from Nsukka, Nigeria, and the author of *The Liquid Eye of a Moon*. His short stories have appeared in *Transition*, *Elsewhere*, *Trestle Ties*, *Oyster River Pages*, *Evergreen Review*, *The Arkansas International*, and other publications. He has received fellowships from MacDowell and the Vermont Studio Center. He is an Artist Protection Fund Fellow and the inaugural Arkansas International Writer-at-Risk Residency Fellow, and currently a graduate student at the University of Iowa Writers' Workshop. He was also a 2019 Graywolf Press African Fiction Prize finalist.